SMALL TOWN LAWYER

Defending Innocence

Influencing Justice

Interpreting Guilt

Burning Evidence

Prescribing Doubt

PRESCRIBING DOUBT

KIRKLAND & HALL

BLURB

A murdered millionaire could be the key to a sinister medical conspiracy...

Running his own law firm is harder than Leland Munroe ever imagined, but he's determined to make it work. Judy Reed, accused of killing her wealthy father, is just the kind of high-profile and high-paying client he needs to keep his firm afloat. Yet the deeper he digs, the more complex her case becomes.

Nurse LaDonna Winters's financial situation isn't as ideal. Struggling to make ends meet, she can barely afford legal representation. But her case is compelling—accused of a crime at her hospital she insists she didn't commit, LaDonna is desperate to clear her name.

Juggling these two demanding cases, alongside his responsibilities in Basking Rock, Leland struggles to keep up. The deck is stacked against LaDonna, and Judy's unpredictable behavior makes defending her challenging. As Leland delves deeper, he begins to suspect that their cases are intertwined, and that something deeply disturbing is happening at the local hospital.

Tangled in a web of small-town secrets and deceit, Leland unearths information that points in some very dangerous directions... for himself as well as his clients.

The closer he gets to the truth, the more he fears that solving these cases could be a fatal mistake.

CONTENTS

1

NOVEMBER 30, 2022

A t the defense table, waiting for the jury to come back in, my
client—twenty-one-year-old Chase Richardson—was playing
a video game. He was holding the phone on his lap so Judge
Ambleton wouldn't spot it when she returned from her chambers.
Only lawyers were allowed to have phones in court, but in our small-
town courthouse, security could be a little lax. Especially when it
came to someone like Chase, a tall, athletic kid whose tailored gray
suit might've cost more than the retainer I'd charged his father, the
senator.

The jury had retired to deliberate at about eleven o'clock, so Her
Honor had called an early lunch break. In our war room just outside
the courtroom door, I'd been halfway through a ham sandwich,
watching Chase shadowbox in the corner to let off steam, when the
bailiff knocked and told us a verdict had been reached.

The bailiff's news left Chase looking unsettled. It was the first time
I'd seen his confidence waver but very far from the first time I'd seen
a young man in his position go from wealthy-college-kid confidence
to the sudden awareness that things were getting real.

I always wished their bravado could run out earlier—ideally much earlier, before they did whatever foolish thing landed them with criminal charges in the first place. Unfortunately, poor decision-making was a standard feature of most kids that age.

"What does it mean when the jury makes its mind up that quick?" Chase had asked as he put his suit jacket back on.

I'd shrugged. "Just that they all thought the evidence was clear. It doesn't tell you for sure which way they thought it pointed."

That was true, but it was also true that a short deliberation most often meant a guilty verdict. There was no point telling Chase that now, though. I'd told him up front—many times—that the case against him was strong, but he'd refused to take a plea. He was of a generation that seemed to think walking around with marijuana in your pocket was about on par, in terms of criminality, with taking a sip of beer before you turned twenty-one. Accepting a permanent blemish on his record for something so trivial was offensive to him. The fact that it was still a Schedule I narcotic didn't even register.

Chase was at the screw-up stage of life, which many Southern boys went through. The options for this developmental phase ranged from drug arrests and intoxicated vandalism to catastrophic DUIs. Chase's "growing pains," as his mother had called them the one time I'd talked to her on the phone, consisted of flunking out of Vanderbilt and getting arrested one night on Basking Rock beach with two baggies of pot in his backpack. He and his drunk friends, celebrating the Fourth of July a week early with beer, weed, and bottle rockets, had had the misfortune of catching the attention of a passing cop car with a drug-sniffing K-9 in the back.

And South Carolina was old-fashioned in many ways, including our drug laws. According to the statute books, a person convicted for possession of more than one ounce of marijuana faced up to five years in state prison and a $5,000 fine.

Even after we lost on the motion to suppress the evidence, which I'd told him up front would happen—one of his buddies had filmed their encounter with the police on his phone and uploaded it to his TikTok, inadvertently showing the entire world that the cops had handled the stop-and-search perfectly—Chase had shrugged off my advice. I could not get him to take the case seriously. He was too young and too rich to take anything seriously.

So he was cocky, but he hadn't hurt anybody, and his daddy paid all my bills within three days of getting them. I'd done the best I could with the facts we had. If Chase wanted to drag this dog of a case before a jury and put his fate in their hands, that was his call.

As we waited for the jury, the two of us and the bailiff were the only people in the courtroom. Senator Richardson hadn't come down from DC for the trial. He couldn't go anywhere without media attention, and neither of us wanted that spotlight on his son. Whatever the details, rich Southern fathers did what they could to sweep their kids' mistakes under the rug. In Senator Richardson's case, that included keeping himself, his wife, and their press entourage up in DC.

The trial had lasted a day and a half, and our local media magnate, Dabney Barnes IV, hadn't seen fit to send anybody to cover it. I assumed the senator had influenced that decision.

While I was no fan of drugs, and I sometimes wished opiate dealers could be shipped out to Guantanamo, I did think five years for mere possession of a substance nobody had ever overdosed on was too harsh. But my opinion didn't matter; nobody had asked me what the law ought to be. My only job in cases like this was to reduce the number of people that the State of South Carolina could hit with a sentence that unfair.

The usual way to do that, if you couldn't get the evidence tossed, was a plea deal. In a case like this, any kid whose daddy was not a politician would've begged me to get him one. That's what both of Chase's friends had done—and I'd made sure to let the jury know about their guilty pleas, since Chase's only real defense was that the drugs found in his bag were theirs.

But Chase knew perfectly well no judge in the state would sentence a senator's son to jail time on his first offense for marijuana possession. Since that meant only his record and his bank balance were at stake, he wasn't afraid to roll the dice.

Or so he'd told me at the time. As he sat beside me now, I could feel his nerves. That's why he was playing a video game: it was the only thing he could do to distract himself from what was coming. I'd seen it many times in the cases I handled for the sons of Basking Rock's luminaries. This was the point where the defendant broke out in a sweat, questioning whether he'd made the right call.

I heard the courtroom doors open behind us and gestured to Chase to put his phone away. I knew from the clack of men's shoes on the terrazzo that it wasn't our prosecutor coming up the aisle, but I was still surprised, when I turned around, to see Aaron Ruiz. He'd become solicitor for our judicial circuit a couple of years earlier, and since then I hadn't seen him in court. We were friends, so to avoid any hint of impropriety, he always assigned my cases to one of his assistant solicitors.

I gave him a nod.

"Afternoon, Leland," he said. "I'm just stepping in real quick for Mrs. Barnes. She can't make it back—had a family emergency come up."

"Oh, sorry to hear that."

Although Ginevra Barnes ranked high on my list of least favorite people, I'd had my share of family emergencies and wouldn't wish one on anybody. That said, if the suffering family member was her brother-in-law, who was in the habit of using his media clout to take potshots at me and my clients, my sympathy would dry up pretty fast.

The chambers door opened, and the bailiff called, "All rise."

The clerk stepped out first, but Judge Ambleton overtook her in about two strides and was up on the bench, seated and ready to go, before the clerk even reached her desk. Ambleton had gotten her law degree from Columbia, and I imagined that was why she walked so fast: living up north had gotten her in the habit of moving like New Yorkers did.

Chase, standing next to me, was fidgety. He didn't seem to know what to do with his hands. I gave him a nudge, and when he glanced over, I clasped my hands in front of me. He took the hint and did the same. It was a good posture for a defendant. It made him look respectful and aware of how serious things were.

At the bailiff's next command, we all sat back down. The judge stated for the record that we had a verdict and asked if counsel had any remarks. We didn't. From his silence and her apparent lack of surprise, I figured Ruiz must've stopped by chambers to let the clerk know what he was doing there.

When the jury filed in, the forewoman kept her eyes on the judge. I got the sense she was purposely avoiding looking our way. That wasn't a good sign.

After explaining why a different lawyer was sitting at the prosecutor's table, Judge Ambleton asked the forewoman, "Have you reached a verdict?"

"We have, Your Honor."

"Will the defendant please rise and face the jury?"

The two of us stood back up. Chase clasped his hands in front of him again. The jurors—five Black, seven White, equally split between male and female—were all looking at the judge, not at us.

"On the first charge," Ambleton said, "misdemeanor drug possession, how do you find?"

"Guilty, Your Honor."

Chase froze. Most people did when they heard a jury call them guilty. I didn't let it show on my face, but I was relieved. I knew what that verdict meant. It was good news.

"And on the second charge, felony drug possession, how do you find?"

"Your Honor, we find the defendant not guilty."

Chase exhaled.

Satisfaction hummed through my veins. Chase had been charged with a felony because the cops found more than an ounce of marijuana in his backpack. My argument had been that the drugs were in two separate half-ounce baggies and had obvious differences—the plastic bags weren't even the same brand—and the State hadn't proven that both of them were his.

I'd shown the jury the video of the police encounter, first at normal speed and then in slo-mo, pointing out when one and then another of Chase's friends had stepped out of view. Perhaps, I'd suggested, one of them had tried to save himself by dropping his own baggie into Chase's backpack where it sat on the sand, in the dark, out of view of the camera. Had the State proven otherwise, beyond a reasonable doubt? When the evidence was two completely different baggies and a chaotic TikTok video, was that really enough to convict this fine young man of a felony?

The misdemeanor charge was for possession of less than one ounce. One baggie, in other words. When the forewoman had announced that Chase was guilty on that, I knew they'd found him innocent on the felony.

. . .

Afterward, Ruiz stayed behind to talk with the judge about rescheduling a few things in light of Mrs. Barnes's emergency, and Chase and I went to our war room so I could call Senator Richardson and give him the news. He was a busy guy, and not a fan of chitchat even when he wasn't busy, so I got to the point.

"It's not guilty on the felony," I said.

"Great. The misdemeanor trip him up?"

"Yep, guilty on that."

"Dammit. What sentence are we expecting?"

"Already done. They do the sentencing immediately when it's only one misdemeanor. No jail time, of course. The solicitor wanted a one-year suspended sentence, five hundred hours of community service, and a thousand-dollar fine, but I got it down to one year's probation, four hundred hours, and five hundred bucks."

He chuckled. "Four hundred hours? That'll be a shock to the system. Maybe a wake-up call. Do they have full-time community service?"

"Yep. The probation officer will have a list of places he can work."

"Good. He needs some kind of consequence to make him grow the hell up. Hopefully this'll do it."

"Yeah, it often does. And with the probation, unlike the suspended sentence that the prosecution wanted, if he stays out of trouble for the full year, he can get his record expunged."

"Perfect. Thanks. How's he doing?"

I glanced over at Chase, who was wolfing down the sandwich that he hadn't eaten on our lunch break.

"He was sweating bullets," I said, "but he's okay."

After we hung up and Chase threw his sandwich wrapper away and wiped the mayonnaise off his face, I peeked out the door. Apart from the bailiff standing guard outside the courtroom—Antoine Williams, a tall, older Black man who'd been doing this job for various judges for almost thirty years—there was nobody in the hallway.

I beckoned to Chase and had him follow me around a few corners to the elevator at the back. I only left the courthouse by the front steps when I wanted to talk with the press—which was rarely.

On the ground floor, I took him around another couple of corners to a side door not far from where he'd parked.

"This is where I stop," I said, and held out a hand to shake. "It's more discreet for you if we leave separately."

"Oh. Okay. Uh, cool."

We shook hands.

"So," he said. "Uh, four hundred hours? That's a lot, isn't it?"

I shrugged. "It just means working full time for about two and a half months."

"Full time, as in nine to five? Damn."

I smiled and said, "Welcome to adulthood."

He left, and I headed back up to see if Ruiz was still there. I had about fifteen fires to put out at work—since starting my own law firm earlier that year, I'd found out that being your own boss meant being responsible for every problem that arose, and new ones arose just about every day—but it had been a while since I'd touched base with Ruiz.

8

Upstairs, the bailiff gave me a nod.

"How you doing, Antoine?" I said. "Anything exciting going on?"

He flicked his eyebrows up and down in a way that meant *that depends on what you count as exciting.*

Behind him, through the small, square window in the courtroom door, I saw Ruiz heading toward us. Antoine glanced over his shoulder, probably calculating how long to wait before opening the door for him, and said, "Not too much. Had my grandbabies up from Georgia for the holiday. Work-wise, things been pretty calm since that pole vaulter the other week."

I laughed. An irate defendant had jumped over the defense table and launched himself at a witness on the stand, only to be tackled by Antoine and a police officer who was waiting to testify.

"You ought to get a medal for that," I said.

"Well, thank you." He opened the door with a flourish, and Ruiz came out, dragging his battered rolling briefcase behind him. "Afternoon, Mr. Ruiz, sir."

"Afternoon, Mr. Williams. Hey, Leland. What's up, you forget something?"

"No, I was just congratulating Antoine on his heroics with that jumper."

"Oh! Yeah, he's legendary now." In response to Antoine's *aw, shucks* shrug, he said, "You know I mean that. He could've seriously hurt that woman."

"Yes indeed," I said. "Hey, I'm sorry to hear Mrs. Barnes is, uh—"

"Having problems? Yeah." He held up a hand to say goodbye to Antoine, and we headed toward the main elevator. "It's not a tragedy, nobody died, but you might have to see me in court once or twice until she gets things squared away."

"That's fine. It'll be like the good old days."

"Will it?" He looked at me. "Maybe if you dye that gray out of your hair. Don't take this the wrong way, but you look a little rough."

His tone was friendly, but I had a mirror at home; I knew he was right.

"Let's call it silver," I said. "That sounds better than gray. I guess running your own practice makes a man look more distinguished."

"Yeah," he said with a laugh, "that's not the word I had in mind."

The elevator dinged. Ruiz and I automatically stopped talking until the doors opened and we saw that nobody was inside to overhear.

"Business okay?" he asked, stepping in and hitting the button for his floor. "Solo practice, man, that's something I never wanted to do. Marketing, chasing clients down to pay their bills… too much stress."

I didn't want to get into my problems, so I pivoted to our usual dark humor. "I don't know, having a defendant attempting murder right there in the courtroom seems pretty stressful."

"Well, I got Antoine for that. And the other bailiffs. Who do you have? Terri, I guess?"

She was my private investigator. "Yep, and I hired a paralegal now too."

"Good, good. More power to you."

"Thanks."

Now that he'd mentioned her, I realized I'd hardly seen Terri lately. I emailed assignments to her, but I'd been so focused on building the business that I had no time for anything else.

"Do anything fun for Thanksgiving?" Ruiz asked.

"Yeah, Noah came down from Charleston." My son had graduated from community college and launched himself into adulthood less than a year earlier.

"Oh, that's nice. It's always good having the kids around the table."

"Sure is." The elevator was slowing as we reached Ruiz's floor. "If Mrs. Barnes needs me to move anything around, that's no problem. I know what it's like when things hit the fan."

"Thanks. But she'll be back in the saddle in a week or so."

"Good. I guess she's got to be. Hasn't she got that Reed case coming up?" A local heiress had been charged with murdering her father.

"Yeah, that's in two months. But even if it were tomorrow, you know her and homicides."

The doors opened. He wheeled his rolling briefcase out, looking up and down the hall to check for eavesdroppers before he finished his thought.

"And, I mean," he said, "a patricide? For the inheritance? That's straight-up biblical. Brings out the crusader in her."

I nodded. "I'm sure she's like a dog on a bone with that."

"Oh, she'd try that case from her hospital bed if she had to."

2

DECEMBER 1, 2022

The next morning, I parked in the lot outside my new office a few minutes past eight. My paralegal, Rachel, wasn't there yet; her silver Kia usually rolled in around twenty past, after she'd dropped her kids at school. I headed in to get the coffee started—I'd already had a cup at home, but that was just a starter to get me fit to drive.

My office was in a one-story brick building that also housed an urgent care clinic and an optometrist. In other words, I worked in a strip mall. It lacked the genteel charm of the beachside bungalow that Roy Hearst ran his firm out of, but it was right downtown, four blocks from the courthouse.

After leaving Roy's firm a few months back to go out on my own, I'd worked from home for a couple of weeks, but that couldn't last. No criminal defense attorney wants clients and witnesses coming to his house, and my neighbors didn't like it any more than I did. I was selective about my clients—my goal was to help decent folks who were innocent or who, like Chase Richardson, had been hit with charges more serious than they deserved—but my neighbors didn't know that. All they knew was that some guy they'd seen on the news getting arrested was parked on their street.

Because a lawyer can't land good clients if his office makes him look like a failure, I'd chosen a recently remodeled one. It didn't have the traditional cherry-veneer or old-oak look that you saw in long-established law firms—and there were a lot of those in these parts, firms founded by the granddaddy or great-granddaddy of the current owner —but it suited my purposes. The floors were gray tiles made to look like wood, and most of the furniture was black. The amount of money I had to fork over for the place each month made my blood pressure rise every time I wrote the check.

The romance of running my own business had worn off around the time I signed the lease and started watching most of the money I brought in go flying right back out the door. Rent, utilities, malpractice insurance, my paralegal's salary and benefits, Terri's investigation fees, computer equipment, IT services, office furniture, a Westlaw subscription for my legal research—the list was longer than the Bible and as expensive as a New York City divorce.

I was pouring my third cup of coffee—it was almost nine—when Rachel finally arrived. She rushed in looking like a TV news reporter chasing a scoop: perfect blonde hair, perfect makeup, slightly out of breath. "Leland, I am so sorry," she said. "Brady woke up with pink eye this morning, so I had to drive him out to his grandma's after dropping his sister at school. And by the time I got someplace with good reception, my phone battery had gone and died."

"Oh, it's no problem. It's not like we're at trial." I splashed some milk into my cup.

She set her purse on her desk and said, "I will not let it happen again.

First thing I'm doing this morning is ordering myself a charger for the car."

"Well, that'll be good to have. Hey, I saw that 10 a.m. new-client appointment on my calendar. Who's that for?"

"Let me send it on over. Sorry, you would've had this half an hour ago if my morning hadn't blown up on me." She sat down and logged in to her computer. As she was clicking on things and typing away, she said, "Now, I should tell you up front, this isn't a big-money case. I mean, she's a nurse who's lost her job—how much can she pay? But I do know how you love fighting for the underdog, and from what I've been able to find out, that might be what this is. You heard about that nurse up at the hospital who got fired a couple of months ago for stealing meds? Allegedly. LaDonna Winters?"

"Oh, yeah, I saw that." Our local news website had run an unflattering photo of Ms. Winters alongside a screed on what it called the "epidemic" of nurses stealing opiates and other medications from their workplaces. Nothing in that article had given me any desire to represent her.

"Well, she called on Monday, while you were in court, and I said you might be able to meet later in the week, after the verdict came back."

"Interesting," I said, and took a sip of coffee.

"I thought so too," Rachel said.

She hadn't known me long enough to realize that "interesting" was the word I used when I thought something was nonsense, but I was trying to be polite.

She clicked on something and said, "Okay, the case summary will be in your inbox in a second or two. Anyway, she told me straight up that she didn't do this—"

I raised an eyebrow.

"I know, I know," she said. "If we listened to them, we'd think every prison in America is full of innocent people. But there was… It's hard to describe. Just something in her voice that got to me."

"Huh."

I hadn't known Rachel long enough to gauge how good a judge of character she was. She was a sensible person, though, and she'd spent four years as a paralegal for the local prosecutor's office before quitting to be a stay-at-home mom when her kids were small. She didn't strike me as the type who'd be taken in by a sob story. I figured I might as well give her the benefit of the doubt.

"And then she called back," she said, "when you were still at the courthouse yesterday. She's desperate. Since the verdict was already in, I figured you'd be free today. Oh, she said she was referred by the mother of a client of yours—a lady she used to work with, called Ms. Baker?"

"Oh! Simone Baker's mom?"

"Yeah, she mentioned that name."

Two years earlier, I'd successfully defended a disabled health-and-wellness influencer on murder charges. Her mother was a local nurse. I'd gotten to know both of them pretty well.

"So Ms. Winters said they used to work together?" I asked. "She mention any other connection to Ms. Baker? They're not related, are they?"

"Uh, not that she said."

I could see she thought that was a weird question, but she screwed up her eyebrows like she was trying to remember the full conversation. After a second, she said, "No, they're colleagues. Former colleagues. That was the word she used. Why?"

"Well, if you met Ms. Baker... I don't know how much time you've spent in hospitals, but I've seen some real friendly, warmhearted nurses, and... let's just say, she's not one of them. She's very good at what she does, from what I can tell, but she doesn't seem to like *people* all that much."

Rachel laughed. "Well, my word, I can't blame her for that."

It was my turn to laugh. For that comment alone, my esteem for Rachel went up a notch.

"Oh, I see what you mean," she said. "She's not the type of person who'd be handing your business card out to everybody she knows who's got a problem?"

"Exactly. I mean, nurses meet a whole lot of people, but I haven't gotten so much as a traffic court referral from her since I got her daughter off. So I wonder why she's sending Ms. Winters my way."

A few minutes before ten, Rachel knocked to let me know Ms. Winters had arrived. I went to meet her in the waiting area. She was a slim, well-dressed Black woman—light sweater, pinstripe pants, a coat neatly folded over her arm—who looked about Rachel's age, early thirties or so. When I said hello, a smile flashed and vanished on her face; she was too nervous for it to last. Her hair was cropped strikingly short, and when she stood to shake hands, sweeping a tote bag off the floor and onto her shoulder, I realized she was as tall as me.

We walked back to my office, chatting about the unseasonably cold weather.

"When I saw the temperature this morning," she said, "I thought, Lord, pray for me. I am not made for 45 degrees."

"Oh, me neither."

We moved on to the topics of traffic and where she was from. My first order of business was always putting a person at ease and building rapport. Without that, folks wouldn't confide in you. I had learned pretty quickly that the less folks confided in me, the harder it was to do my job.

As I held my office door for her, I noticed she was wearing sparkly purple clogs. Almost all nurses seemed to choose that type of footwear. As I gestured her to a chair, I wondered if nurses had their own shoe stores that nobody else knew about.

When we were both seated, I said, "So, I understand Ms. Baker sent you my way. You two used to work together?"

"Oh, yes. When I was first up at the hospital, right out of school, I kind of latched onto her. Nursing is such a steep learning curve when you're starting out, and the stakes are—I mean, they can't *be* any higher. People's lives are on the line."

"Of course. So she… took you under her wing, or—?"

"More like I put myself there. And thank goodness, she let me. She'd been around so long, and, you know, she held her own. She was just so *competent*. Nothing fazed her. And she had real good intuition, you know, like if something wasn't right with a patient. Or if the doctor wasn't listening, she knew how to push him without making him mad. So I saw that, and I was like, that's the wing I want to be under."

"Uh-huh." I was nodding. I could see Ms. Baker taking a liking to this woman. There was a warmth to her that anybody would like, but she didn't hold herself in the relaxed, informal way that usually went along with warmth. Like Ms. Baker, she was more orderly. From the way she sat—perfectly straight, everything tucked in—I might've thought she was in the military. I mentally classified her as the type of client who probably kept a nicely organized folder or binder full of information about her case.

"So, how long ago was that?" I asked. "I don't think Ms. Baker still worked at the hospital when I met her."

Ms. Winters flicked her eyebrows like she could tell quite a story about that. "Well—yes. It was, uh, before she chose to leave." She paused; that story wasn't going to be told right now. "Anyway, I've been a nurse for eleven years. Up at the hospital the whole time, until…" Her jaw clenched for a second. "Until the reason I'm here right now."

The way she lifted her chin and looked at me brought to mind a line I'd read somewhere: *bloody, but unbowed*. She was resolute. She had dignity. I liked her.

"So tell me about that," I said.

She took a breath. "You know what I'm charged with, I assume."

Rachel's case file had informed me that LaDonna was facing multiple felony charges for fraudulently obtaining controlled substances, plus three misdemeanor counts for simple possession. Like most cases of healthcare professionals stealing narcotics from hospitals, the case had been charged federally instead of at the state level, with the DEA investigating and the local office of the United States Attorney prosecuting.

The chances of a not-guilty verdict on criminal charges in federal court were less than 1 percent. The feds almost always won their cases. I opted not to tell her that now. I needed more information before I could get a sense of what her chances were.

"I do know the charges," I said.

"Okay. And I did not do any of that." She was looking into my eyes, not blinking, not smiling. I got the sense she was the type of person who'd rather go to the electric chair speaking the truth than get a plea deal for a lie.

I had a highly developed BS meter, and it stayed put at zero. What she was saying, she believed.

"You know what," I said, "I do know the charges, but I'm not that familiar with how hospitals work. So could you tell me in plain English what they're alleging you did?"

"Of course. So—do you know what a dispensing cabinet is?"

I shook my head.

"Okay, it's where I go on the unit to get a patient's meds. Actually, I brought some information that might help." She reached into the bag at her feet and pulled out a Trapper Keeper. I hadn't seen one of those since junior high. She opened it, flipped past the first couple of tabs, and pushed it across the desk.

The page she'd opened to, which was between a red tab and a blue one, looked like a product brochure. The item it displayed was a cabinet. I silently patted myself on the back for knowing that she'd have a binder like this. I liked that. The less chaos a client brought to the table, the easier my job was.

"So it's basically a metal cabinet with a bunch of locked drawers," she said, pointing them out, "and a computer over here. That's a refrigeration unit on the other side, for the meds that need to stay cool." She circled the picture of the computer screen with a ballpoint pen. "The way you get the meds out," she said, "is by logging in on this touchscreen here. Every nurse gets their own user ID and password."

"Oh, I see. So, is that their evidence? That meds were stolen using your ID and password?"

"Yes, and *that* is the point. Thank you. Because the thing is, on my unit, the dispensing cabinet was right in the hallway beside the ladies' room. You punch in your passcode on the screen, and anybody going by can see it."

"Okay. And do you have any idea who, specifically, might've seen yours? And then done this?"

"I mean, I have my thoughts. There's people I don't trust. But I can't point to anyone for sure, because—you've got to understand, I didn't know these thefts were happening. They did an audit in September and told me, oh, on this day back in July or in August this vial was stolen. You know, after the fact. So by that point, I didn't remember who'd been on shift with me on that exact day. And I couldn't say, like, show me the time stamp on that log-in, and I can prove it wasn't me because that's when I was intubating Mrs. So-and-So in room three. I couldn't do anything to defend myself."

She was getting emotional. I pushed a Kleenex box across the desk, and she took one.

My cell phone vibrated. I ignored it.

When she'd pulled herself together, I grabbed a pen, got my legal pad out from under my mouse, and said, "Okay, what we're going to need is testimony from anybody else who worked there—it doesn't have to be a nurse—about how folks passing by could see you logging in." I scribbled a note about that. "And photographs of how things were set up. If I show the jury a picture of that cabinet sitting in the hallway by the ladies' room, they'll see what you mean right away. We all use ATMs at the bank; we know the risk of letting people see over our shoulder. That alone might create reasonable doubt. If you don't have any photos, I might be able to get my PI to slip into the unit and take some."

"PI?"

"Private investigator, sorry."

"Oh, of course." For the first time since I'd greeted her in the waiting area, she smiled. "I'm starting to think Ms. Baker pointed me to the right guy."

"Well, thanks." I hadn't realized I was auditioning for her, but of course I was; this interview was a two-way street. She didn't want any old warm body with a law degree. There was too much at stake. Spending a couple of years in the federal pen was a horrifying prospect for anybody, but for a nurse, the punishment would last the rest of her life. Conviction on any of these charges would mean economic ruin. Even if she escaped a prison sentence, the best-case scenario was that her nursing license would be suspended for a year or two—more than long enough for her to fall behind on mortgage payments and lose her home.

"When they found those drugs missing under my log-ins," she said, "they made me do a drug screen." A microexpression flickered across her face: disgust at the indignity. It was degrading to have to pee in a cup at work.

"And I assume it came back negative?"

"Of course. There is no point in my life when it would've come back positive. That's what I said to my charge nurse, but, I mean, she knew. She apologized for me having to do it."

I wrote that down. "And what's her name?"

"Candace O'Malley. There's more than one charge nurse, for different shifts, but I clicked with Candace right from the start." She sighed. I could tell she missed her.

"Have you and Candace stayed in touch since you left the hospital?"

She winced. "No, it's… I feel like it might get her in trouble if we did. I mean, this is a small town."

"It sure is. It might be a good idea to reach out discreetly, though. See if she's got anything useful or if she knows somebody who might. Did you talk with her about any of this before you left?"

"A little bit. She asked me about my log-ins. Like, in the sense of 'Is there some mistake here?' Because she knew that system wasn't really secure. We all did. I mean, you type in your password right there in the hallway."

"That kind of... would you call it laxness?"

"Yes, I would. That's what it was. It was a problem there."

"Okay. That laxness strikes me as so strange, in this day and age." I shook my head and looked out the window. What was different now, compared to when I was a kid, was that the veil of innocence had been lifted from our eyes. We knew that anybody—priests, doctors, nurses—could do bad things, and in most places we'd put up guardrails against that. "Do you have any sense as to why they set it up that way? Or why they let it persist, once folks started noticing?"

She shook her head. "I mean... we're not the Mayo Clinic. We're a small-town hospital. We're underresourced, and I would say a little understaffed. And it's the CCU. We've got some very medically fragile people. If you don't have what you need to take care of your patients *and* keep that cabinet secure—I mean, if you can only pick one of those things—then you'd choose patient care, right? And maybe the log-ins didn't seem like that big of a risk. We don't have patients walking around—they're too sick for that—and the visiting hours are pretty limited. So it's not going to be patients or visitors who see your log-in. It's the folks we know and basically trust, right?"

"Yeah, I guess."

Out the window, in the parking lot, a police officer walking back to his car with a cup of coffee in his hand stopped to peer with slight suspicion at somebody I couldn't see. I was pretty sure I looked at most people that way. I couldn't imagine trusting a dozen or more coworkers with my log-in.

22

"Well," I said, turning back to LaDonna, "I'm glad you cooperated with the drug screen. A negative test doesn't prove your innocence, but it helps. From what I understand, most of the time, when nurses steal meds, it's because they're drug users in need of a fix."

"Oh, I know. It's happened before."

"At the hospital?"

"Yes. I'm not saying it's common, but it happened on another unit, I want to say last year? And we had a travel nurse on our unit last winter who—according to her, the way we did things was a little lax, like you said. I never worked at any other hospital, so I had nothing to compare it to, but that's what she called it."

As I wrote that down, I said, "Speaking of work, what is it you've been doing since leaving the hospital?"

"Worse work for way less money. And it still took a while to find. Because of this case, I went from thirty-six dollars an hour in the critical care unit to eleven an hour in home care."

"Eleven dollars?"

She heard the shock in my voice. "It's because my license is suspended. I can't serve as a nurse. I'm working as a healthcare aide."

"So, that's... what, helping folks with disabilities get in and out of bed?"

"And brush their teeth, and toileting, and so forth. Yes."

I shook my head in sympathy. "For eleven dollars... I can't believe that's all that pays. Yeah, charges like this really hit your life hard."

"And not just mine, Mr. Munroe. I had to take my baby out of her preschool. She was learning to read already. Now she stays with a neighbor lady while I'm at work. And it's, you know, *clean*, but... that's about all it is."

"How old is your daughter?"

"She just turned four. And I'm all she's got. Her father is not in our lives."

I regarded her across my desk for a second. If Ms. Winters did any prison time, her daughter would go into foster care.

"Well," I said, "if you're willing, I'll take your case. We'll get this figured out."

After she left, I went out to Rachel's desk.

"You were right about her," I said. "Could you whip up an engagement letter and get it out to her to sign?"

"Sure. Which fee arrangement?"

I thought for a second. "Put a $1,000 retainer on there."

She gave me a look. She'd been working for me long enough to know that for a client indicted on felony counts, even a $5,000 retainer was a major discount.

I shrugged. "Like you said, it's not a big-money case."

"I guess not. I mean, at least that'll cover the gas for the trips to Charleston."

I chuckled. We didn't have a federal courthouse in Basking Rock. LaDonna's case would be tried up in the city.

"Yeah, her preliminary hearing's next week," I said. "I'll make a day of it. Have dinner with Noah or something."

"Okay," she said, scribbling a note on her pad. "I'll call the clerk and confirm the schedule. Oh, you got a call when you were in there with her."

"Somebody I know?" I assumed whoever had made my cell phone vibrate during the meeting had called the office next.

"Roy Hearst. He said he was heading out for a game of golf around eleven thirty, but—"

"Oh! I'll go call him now."

I hadn't talked to Roy in about a month, so we shot the breeze for a minute, catching up. He complained about my departure in his usual friendly way: "You know this'll be my first golf game in almost two weeks? I blame you."

I laughed. "Sorry I can't hold the fort for you anymore."

Our arrangement when I'd worked for him had been that I did most of what he called the boring part of lawyering—the legal research and writing, plus the petty criminal hearings for sons of his clients who'd gotten in trouble—while he handled the wheeling and dealing. He had a genius for bringing in business. It seemed like nearly every landlord and entrepreneur in the county relied on him, and he spent most of his time out golfing with them.

"I forgive you," he said, "since I know how you must be suffering from having to be a businessman all of a sudden."

"You're not wrong." I'd worked as a prosecutor for seventeen years, and then as Roy's right-hand man for another four. I'd never had to run a law firm or any other enterprise in my life.

"I know it," he said. "But listen. I got something for you, maybe. I made a referral—whether she reaches out to you, we shall see."

"Oh, thanks. Wait, 'she'? Did one of your clients' *daughters* get herself a DUI?" Roy's referrals had almost universally been rich boys going through the screw-up phase.

"No, no. This is not some penny-ante thing you can handle in a week. She's the daughter of an old friend. She's got a lawyer—Kirk Dickenson, maybe you know him—but last week he got a real bad diagnosis, and she might need somebody else to step in."

"Oh, yeah, I went up against him a couple times back in Charleston. I'm sorry to hear he's ill."

"Yeah, it's tough as hell." Roy sighed. "About Judy, though, she's kind of particular. I'll tell you up front, I wouldn't want to put her in front of a jury."

"Why not?"

"She's... She can be hard to connect with. She doesn't respond to things the way most folks would. I'm giving you a heads-up in case she calls you. It can be a little off-putting, but I've known her since she was a bump in her mama's belly, and she's a good person. If she does call, I'd appreciate it if you could look past the, uh... personality. Help her out, as a favor to me. And bear in mind, I wouldn't ask you this if I didn't know she's got the means to pay."

"Okay, happy to talk with her. Who is it? What are the charges?"

"Judy Reed. I don't suppose I need to tell you she's been charged with killing her daddy."

3

DECEMBER 8, 2022

The morning was clear but brisk as I slammed my car door and headed to Broad Street, a couple of blocks from the Charleston federal courthouse, to get a cup of coffee. LaDonna was about fifteen minutes behind me, bringing Ms. Baker with her for moral support, and we were going to walk to her preliminary hearing together. Security was tight there, like it was at any federal building, and I wanted to be on hand to prevent any hiccups.

Down on Broad, the sun shone on the stucco buildings and the palm trees that lined the avenue. The few regular trees that had been planted alongside the palms were leafless; that was the only sign that it was winter. After LaDonna's hearing I was planning on heading over to the French Quarter to meet Judy Reed, and by then it was supposed to be upward of 55 degrees.

As I walked, I read the emails Terri had sent on the different cases. One was a link to a story on our local news site, where some plastic surgeon, acting as hospital spokesman, commented on LaDonna's case. "Basking Rock Hospital is committed to the highest standards of integrity," blah blah blah, and then he threw my client under the bus.

The next email was Terri's summary of Judy's case. I didn't tend to trust what news accounts said about indictments and trials—it was usually painfully clear that the journalist didn't understand much about the law—so I'd had Terri run a quick investigation to get the story.

Judy, the email said, was the twenty-nine-year-old only child of Conway and Margaret Reed. Conway, the deceased, was a local real estate investor and racehorse owner; his wife had been an accomplished equestrienne in her youth, but she'd been paralyzed about fifteen years earlier in a horse-riding accident.

I scrolled down. I didn't need the social history today. When I saw the word "death," I stopped.

Conway had collapsed at home in June 2021 and been rushed to the hospital with what was initially misdiagnosed as a heart attack. He died later that day of what turned out to be an allergic reaction to a common antibiotic, cephalosporin. He and his entire family were well aware of his allergy; the medication had not been prescribed to him. Judy denied ever using that medication herself, but the evidence showed she'd gotten a prescription for it just days before he died. Her alleged motive was the inheritance, estimated at north of $20 million.

As a prosecutor, I had tried defendants who killed for the contents of the victim's wallet. Twenty million was more than enough for a jury to find motive.

On that cheerful note, I swung into a café.

When I got back to the parking lot, sipping my coffee, LaDonna was holding her passenger door open while Ms. Baker swung her legs out and stood up. They were both wearing their Sunday best.

"Ms. Baker, good morning!" I stepped forward, and we shook hands. "It's been a long time! How's Simone?"

"Oh, she's doing well. Still going strong on the internet, you know."

"Good, good. Yeah, I saw a video she posted the other day about, what was it, vitamin D? She said some eye-opening stuff."

"Yes, she did. I helped her with that one. She wants folks to have all the information they need."

I wasn't a regular visitor to Simone Baker's Instagram, or anybody's Instagram for that matter, but I'd taken a gander at it so I'd have something to chat about with her mother.

As we walked to the courthouse, I said a few things to try and boost LaDonna's morale. We couldn't talk much about her case in front of a third party, so I reminded her of a basic truth that we'd already discussed: The goal today was not to win, since—barring a miracle—the defense never won at a preliminary hearing. The goal was to find out what evidence the prosecution had, to see for ourselves how credible the prosecution witnesses sounded, and, if the opportunity arose, to get a few facts into the record that we might need later. She nodded. I hoped she understood.

Courthouses always seemed designed to be intimidating, and federal courts were at the pinnacle in that regard. Ours loomed tall, with modern architecture on top and traditional stonework on the bottom—the type of stonework, it occurred to me, that you mostly saw on old-fashioned prisons. The building itself was a show of power, and maybe that's why LaDonna shivered as we went in.

As we waited in the security line, I said, "Would you ladies mind getting your cell phones out? They've got cubbies to keep them for you while we're here. Only lawyers are allowed to bring their devices in."

"Oh, my word," LaDonna said.

"Now, don't you worry," Ms. Baker told her. "Everybody's got their rules."

"It just feels wrong. I can't remember the last time I was more than about five feet from my phone."

We watched folks being asked to turn their bags and pockets out before stepping through the metal detector. When our turn came, the guard scrutinized my bar card like he thought it might be counterfeit. The security staff all gave us the sort of thousand-yard stare that made me wonder if their pay got docked any time they smiled. I was glad not to have sent LaDonna and Ms. Baker through on their own.

While Ms. Baker was watching a guard paw through her purse, I asked LaDonna quietly, "Any luck reaching out to that, uh, your charge nurse? Candace?"

She shook her head. "I left her a message. And I left one for another friend there. I don't think they're allowed to talk to me at this point. They're probably afraid for their own jobs, you know?"

As I nodded, Ms. Baker approached, and I escorted the women over to the elevator bank. I let the first two elevators fill up with other visitors and leave so that we could have one to ourselves. As we rode up to our floor, I tried to humanize the place by telling them about the ceremony I'd attended a few years before leaving Charleston, when the courthouse was renamed in honor of a judge who'd spent the decade after World War II making rulings against racial segregation— and dodging death threats as a result.

I was trying to make them feel like this was a place where justice really could be done, but it didn't land right. The point I'd had in mind was that we as a country had evolved to where we honored that judge by naming a building after him. From the pensive look on LaDonna's face, though, and the resigned way Ms. Baker shook her head, I sensed that they didn't agree things had changed all that much.

And I couldn't say they were entirely wrong. I wanted to believe that the American justice system worked for everyone, but we still had a long way to go.

As we entered the courtroom, Ms. Baker whispered, "My goodness." The whole place was framed in polished cherrywood, from the rows of spectator pews to the columns looming on either side of the bench and the massive beams dividing the high ceiling into coffered squares. A chandelier hung from the center of each square, and generations of judges looked down on us from oil paintings on the walls. We were walking on a deep blue carpet decked out with stylized golden stars.

The Basking Rock courtroom in which I'd defended her daughter on murder charges was practically a bus station by comparison.

We were scheduled for 10 a.m., and it looked like about a dozen other folks were too. I directed the ladies to a pew with nobody sitting nearby. I wanted to be able to speak without eavesdroppers.

After we sat down, I said, "So the way this works is, we wait here until our case is called, and at that point, LaDonna, you and I will step up to the defense table there. But Ms. Baker, if you could stay here?"

She nodded. "Of course."

"And at any point, if you hear me clear my throat, that's my way of asking that you just…" I looked for the right word. "Well, stay calm, basically. Don't say anything, don't react. Because, in federal court especially, we've got to maintain decorum. And also, of course, we don't want to give anything away. Okay?"

"Okay."

"Great. So, the first thing that happens—and this could be any minute now—is, the magistrate comes out, and we all stand. Then his clerk will call out which case they're going to hear first. Depending what order things go in, we might be waiting a while."

"So, the magistrate," LaDonna said. "That's the same thing as a judge?"

"Right, they're the lower-level judges. The district judges appoint them to handle pretrial hearings and other routine things. That's the type of judge you would've had at your arraignment." She'd been arraigned the week before Thanksgiving.

LaDonna frowned. After a second, she said, "I don't mean to be disrespectful, but… They let low-level judges make decisions like this? Whether the prosecutor gets to try and put me in *prison* or not? I mean, this isn't routine to me! This is my life. This is everything!"

"Yeah, it is everything. But again, at this point the prosecution just has to show that a reasonable person could believe this happened the way they say it did. It's not the same level of proof as at trial, and it hasn't got the same consequences: No matter what happens at this hearing, when it's over, you're free to go home. So it really is fairly routine." I glanced around at the dozen other people whose fates were hanging in the balance today. If they were all here for preliminary hearings, then unless somebody had a lottery-level stroke of luck, every one of them would be bound over for trial.

The thing was, after the magistrate gave the thumbs-up to the prosecutor at this hearing, pressure would be applied to the defendants. The looming trial date, with its threat of serious prison time, would scare most of them into accepting a plea bargain. That was how the system worked. The government didn't have the resources to give everyone a speedy trial, so without plea bargains, cases would drag on for years.

"That's why, like I said before," I went on, "today we're here to fight, but probably not to win. The point is to find out what the prosecutor's got on you, and to show that we're willing to go to war."

She nodded, but her eyes were closed tight. There was nothing I could say that would make this anything but hard for her.

"All rise," the bailiff called out.

We stood, and Magistrate Jefferson swept onto the bench. He was a tall Black man of about fifty, with a mustache and the high forehead men got from receding hair. I didn't have to look at LaDonna and Ms. Baker to sense their surprise. I hadn't told them he was Black; it made no difference to our case, and in any event, in the twenty-four hours since I'd learned who was presiding over this hearing, I hadn't been able to think of a way to mention it that wasn't awkward.

We obeyed the command to sit back down, and the clerk called the case of a defendant on the other side of the aisle. I was glad to have a chance to see the prosecutor and the magistrate at work before it was our turn. I hardly ever practiced in federal court, and I hadn't been able to tap my friend Garrett Cardozo for any intel on Jefferson or the man at the prosecutor's table. Since Cardozo was a federal prosecutor up here in Charleston, it was his office that was handling LaDonna's case. He obviously wasn't about to give me any tips.

The first defendant was a heavyset young White guy from New Jersey who'd booked a Charleston hotel room to rendezvous with someone he thought was a local dealer. It was actually an undercover cop, and as the detective on the stand explained, "upon executing the search warrant on the defendant's room, he was found to be in possession of 2,438 tablets of fentanyl, which were manufactured in such a way as to appear to be legitimate medication. We also recovered three firearms."

Every one of those tablets could've killed somebody. My own son had flirted with death in high school by taking prescription opioids that a friend of his had stolen from his parents' medicine cabinet. Until he'd managed to drag himself out of what was turning into an addiction, he was exactly the kind of customer dealers targeted with fake meds like the ones this defendant had been caught with. I wanted to throw the guy in jail myself, and although I didn't normally like the fire-and-brimstone type of prosecutor, I would've forgiven it here.

But that's not the tone this prosecutor, Mr. LaRue, took. He kept the focus on the job that law enforcement had done. He painted them as guardians of order, keeping the forces of chaos out of the District of South Carolina. Thanks to them, men like this defendant were stopped before they could destroy what we all held dear.

Magistrate Jefferson was nodding. This resonated with him. That was good to know.

The fentanyl defendant was bound over for trial, and our case was called.

Ms. Baker leaned over to LaDonna and whispered, "I'm praying for you, girl."

I grabbed my briefcase and escorted LaDonna up to the defense table. Jefferson was looking at me, so I said, "Good morning, Your Honor. Leland Munroe, counsel for the defense."

"Morning. I don't believe you've been before me previously, have you?"

"I haven't, Your Honor. I'm based down in Basking Rock."

That was my way of letting him know I normally worked in a small-town state court. I wanted to set his expectations low; it was better for my clients if the judge underestimated me. Even in a city, coming across as a city slicker in a three-thousand-dollar suit tended to undermine the cause.

He nodded. "Okay, Mr. LaRue, are you ready to proceed?"

"I am, Your Honor." LaRue looked at the binder lying open in front of him. "Your Honor, the United States of America has indicted the defendant here, Ms. LaDonna Marie Winters, on five felony counts and three misdemeanors relating to her betrayal of the trust placed in her by, among others, Basking Rock Hospital, where she worked as a nurse; her patients, who trusted her to provide them with the medication they needed to alleviate their pain; and insurers, including the federal Medicare program, which paid for two of the vials of hydromorphone that she stole."

He looked over at LaDonna, shaking his head as if she had disappointed him.

"As I'm sure Your Honor is aware," he said, turning back to Jefferson, "nurses are the backbone of the American healthcare system. The vast majority of them work diligently to provide extraordinary services when we are at our sickest and most vulnerable. And perhaps at one time, Ms. Winters was among the legions of good and hardworking nurses. Maybe so. But not anymore."

That was a great line. When you prosecuted someone who had no priors, someone who'd led a good life up to the time of the alleged crime, you had to acknowledge that; you couldn't paint them as a monster. In a preliminary hearing, what he'd said was just good atmosphere, but at trial, with the jury in the room, it could do damage. He could use it to undermine any witness I might put on to testify that LaDonna was a good nurse. I jotted down a note; I was going to need to prep the witnesses with that in mind.

"Your Honor," LaRue said, "while I don't typically rely on demonstratives at the preliminary hearing stage, I'd like to put one image up, if I may."

Jefferson nodded and looked up at the screen. A second later, a picture of a dispensing cabinet appeared. Unlike the one LaDonna had showed me, it wasn't a page from a brochure; this was a photo taken in what looked like a hospital hallway. While I scribbled myself a note to ask for a copy of the demonstrative, LaRue explained briefly how dispensing cabinets worked.

Then he continued, "Your Honor, this dispensing cabinet sits in the critical care unit of Basking Rock Hospital, where Ms. Winters worked. This past September, an internal audit at the hospital revealed that on three different occasions when Ms. Winters was logged into this cabinet, a total of five vials of hydromorphone were removed. For the record, Your Honor, hydromorphone is an opioid medication that's a vital part of pain management for certain patients, but also, unfortunately, has high abuse potential as well."

Thanks to the microphone up on the bench, I heard Magistrate Jefferson sigh. I was sure he'd heard plenty of cases about illegal opioids.

"Also, Your Honor," LaRue said, "the audit found that on those three occasions, Ms. Winters viewed five patient records without lawful authority, and she then falsified those records, making it appear that the medication had been withdrawn for them. However, other evidence shows that those patients never received it, and indeed, that for two of them, it had never been prescribed. Instead, as part of her scheme to divert these vials of medication to her own benefit, Ms. Winters entered false prescription records into the unit's e-prescribing software to indicate that the hospitalist had prescribed it, when in fact he had not."

He stopped and let that sink in.

"Of course, the hospital immediately suspended Ms. Winters and reported her to the state Board of Nursing. So in short, Your Honor, we believe the evidence will show probable cause to charge Ms. Winters with three counts of obtaining controlled substances by misrepresentation or fraud under 21 United States Code section 843(a)(3), two counts of false statements relating to healthcare programs under 18 United States Code section 1035, and three counts of possession of a controlled substance under 21 United States Code section 844. And that's what we've done, and what we're here today to support."

Jefferson looked at me. "Anything you'd like to say before we proceed, counsel?"

He hadn't talked much himself, so I didn't think he was the type to like prefatory remarks. I reached for the microphone on my table, clicked it on, and said, "No, thank you, Your Honor."

I turned off the mike and looked at Mr. LaRue, waiting for him to call the lead detective. I didn't know if he'd start with the local cop who'd handled the initial investigation, or if we'd get right into the thick of things with the DEA agent that the cop had handed things off to.

He didn't call either of them. He said, "The United States calls Mrs. Candace O'Malley, charge nurse for the critical care unit at Basking Rock Hospital."

4

DECEMBER 8, 2022

LaDonna gasped. I cleared my throat, and she got the signal. Beside me, she took a deep breath, then let it out slowly, like she was doing her best to calm down. I kept my eyes on Nurse O'Malley, who was approaching the stand. O'Malley was a heavyset redhead, around fifty years old, with a face that was tired but not unkind. She'd dressed up for court in slacks and a blazer, but on her feet she wore dark blue hospital clogs.

After she was sworn in, LaRue started the usual questions: name, employment, background. More than once, he had to remind her to speak into the microphone. Her voice was on the quiet side, and she clearly wasn't used to testifying in court.

LaRue laid the groundwork, eliciting the testimony he needed to let His Honor know that O'Malley was experienced and credible. She explained that she'd been a nurse for twenty-three years and that she'd gone into that field after seeing how important their work was when her father had a heart attack. "For almost nine years," she said, "I've been the CCU charge nurse at Basking Rock Hospital. It's some of the hardest work there is, but it gives me such a sense of *meaning,* every single day."

"I'm sure," LaRue said. "And I'm sure all of us here thank you for doing such tough and important work."

I could see what he was doing. "Federal government versus a dedicated nurse with a previously unblemished record" was not a great look for his case. He'd started this hearing by putting O'Malley on the stand, instead of the lead detective, because this way it looked like her honorable profession was on the prosecution's side: "federal government and dedicated nurse versus a traitor to nursing."

He studied his notes for a second. "Mrs. O'Malley, could you explain what your duties are? In other words, what exactly does 'charge nurse' mean?"

She nodded in a way that told me this question was familiar to her. He was allowed to prepare his witnesses, but there wasn't much need to at the preliminary hearing stage, since the prosecution could pretty much win just by showing up. I hoped LaRue was simply the type who overprepared for every case. If he wasn't, then the fact that he'd overprepared for this hearing might mean he had some kind of axe to grind.

"Well, I like to say the charge nurse is the coordinator-in-chief," O'Malley said. Our mission is to make sure that every patient on the unit gets the care they need when they need it. That means we need to match the right people with the right tasks."

LaRue nodded. "Your Honor, if I may, I do have one more demonstrative."

It was allowed, and some type of flowchart appeared on the screen. It was titled "Charge Nurse Orientation." He explained that nursing schools used this to teach what a charge nurse was responsible for.

As he walked O'Malley through it, asking questions that brought out her impressive experience and responsibilities, I jotted down *P over-prepares vs. vendetta?* P meant prosecutor. It was never good to go up against a lawyer who'd made your case his personal mission.

Since getting intel from Cardozo wasn't an option, I'd have to have Terri pull some info on LaRue to get a better sense of what he was like.

"So, to sum up," LaRue said, "can you explain for the court how you coordinate patient care on any given shift?"

O'Malley leaned toward the microphone and said, "Yes. My basic responsibility is to determine which nurse is the best fit for which patients. That means I need to understand every patient's medical needs as of that day, and their other care needs, as well as their personality. I need to know all of that so that I can assign them the nurse whose capabilities are the best fit. Oh, and also the nurse's personality. Ideally, I want to make sure that's a fit too. We've got a two-to-one patient-to-nurse ratio on the CCU, but with the level of care our patients need, I have to balance things so we avoid over-loading the nurses. For that, I need to know how each nurse handles stress, how quickly they do the particular tasks that patient needs, and so forth. So it's very complex." She finished her little speech and sat back, looking relieved.

"And so, Mrs. O'Malley," LaRue said, "would you say you know the nurses you supervise very well?"

"Oh, yes. I couldn't do my job otherwise."

"Uh-huh. And how well did you know the defendant, Ms. Winters?"

O'Malley glanced at LaDonna and then looked down, sighing. She seemed genuinely sad. "I guess the best way to put it is, I *thought* I knew her very well."

"And how long had you known her?"

"Well, she started working on my unit seven years ago. So, that long. It's a lot of time to spend together, especially on a smaller unit."

"How large is your CCU?"

"Twelve beds. So with our ratios, that's six nurses per shift, plus the respiratory therapist that we share with the rest of the floor."

"So would you say you worked closely with Ms. Winters?"

"Oh, yes. Very."

"And did you trust her?"

"Well— You mean before?"

"I'll rephrase. Was there a time when you trusted her?"

"Oh, yes." She was nodding. "I put her with my most medically fragile patients. I've put her with patients who were comatose, and on a couple of occasions, ones who were suffering from aphasia—that's an inability to speak or to understand speech. She just— I would say she was unflappable, and... I apologize if this sounds a little strange, I really do, but this is a word we use: she had an intuition with people. And she was reliable. So yes, I trusted her implicitly."

"And did there come a time when that changed?"

She sighed. After a second, she said, "There did, unfortunately. I didn't want to believe it at first."

When she didn't go on, LaRue said, "Could you explain?"

"Yes. I'm sorry. Well... What happened was, this past July, one of my newer nurses approached me to report that she thought she'd seen Ms. Winters pocketing a vial of medication that she'd taken from the dispensing cabinet. Which I—now I realize I shouldn't have dismissed that. I understand that was wrong, and I've taken ownership of that, but at the time, I thought this newer girl must've misunderstood what she saw. I thought she must've seen LaDonna—that is, Ms. Winters—putting something in her pocket to take to a patient."

Beside me, LaDonna drew in a harsh breath, but she kept quiet.

O'Malley stopped there, so LaRue said, "And is that normal on your unit? To carry patient medications around in your pocket?"

"No. I mean, it's not supposed to be. It's… not strictly correct, is what I'd say, but sometimes there's so much going on, and you might just put something in your pocket because your hands are full. So I realize now that I shouldn't have assumed, but I did assume that that's what had happened."

Her repeated groveling made it pretty clear she'd been reprimanded at work. I made a note to ask LaDonna what she knew about the hospital administration in general and O'Malley's relationships with higher-ups.

"And did there come a point when you changed your assessment of the situation?"

"Yes. In September, we did—or the hospital did—an internal audit. And, um, I was informed afterward that it had uncovered some diversions on my unit, which means some medications went missing and were diverted from their intended use. And, unfortunately, on five occasions where there were diversions, the log-ins on the dispensing cabinet showed that it was LaDonna—I mean, Ms. Winters—who was responsible."

She was looking right at LaDonna. Witnesses testifying against the defendant usually didn't look at the defense table, either because delivering bad news made them uncomfortable, or, in cases involving violent crimes, because they were scared of the guy. The ones who looked right into the defendant's eyes, like O'Malley was doing, were rare. Usually they bore some type of personal grudge and wanted to let the defendant know that retribution had arrived.

This wasn't the place to do it, but I was going to need to ask LaDonna more about this woman. The level of emotion in her face seemed out of proportion.

On my legal pad, I scribbled a note: *Did she know log-ins not secure? People could see screen?*

LaDonna wrote back, *Yes!!! Everyone did.*

LaRue concluded his direct, and I got up for the cross. As I walked up to the podium, I gave O'Malley a quick smile. Whatever grudge she held against LaDonna, I needed her to not hold it against me.

"Good morning, Mrs. O'Malley," I said. "I'm Leland Munroe. Now, before we get into this, I want to say—I'm sure you've seen far too many patients and families to recall mine, but I actually live in Basking Rock, and a couple of years back, my son was in your ICU."

"Oh my. Is he...?" Her eyebrows were tilted up in the middle, full of sympathy. That was good.

"Fully recovered. Y'all did a great job with him. So I thank you folks for the attention you give to patient care. I know it's your number one priority."

"Oh, it certainly is. It's what we're there for."

"Yes, indeed. And I know from personal experience how busy the CCU is. I'm sorry I've got to cut to the chase, but about how many staff, medical and otherwise, would you say are on the unit on any given shift?"

"Oh, let's see. Well, normally we would have six nurses, the RT—" She was counting on her fingers. "That's the respiratory therapist.

And me, although if a nurse called off, I'd have to step in for her, at least until we could get another one in. And janitorial staff come through twice a shift, and then there's kitchen staff at mealtimes, to deliver the trays."

She had all her fingers up.

"So that could be ten or more people at a time?" I said.

"Yes."

"Plus the doctors, I imagine?"

"I'm sorry, yes. They round once a day. Nine a.m. And then whenever there's a medical need for a particular patient."

Remembering how things had worked when Noah was hospitalized, I said, "And you generally get two or three of them rounding together, correct?"

"Yes, that's right."

"And X-ray techs, and so forth? To take patients for scans?"

"We actually have a mobile X-ray machine now. So they come over and do that on the unit. Although we do send out for CT scans and MRIs."

"In which case some kind of tech or aide comes over to get the patient from the unit?"

"That's right. My, you were paying attention," she said with a smile, "weren't you! I mean, when your poor son was with us."

"Well, as they say, it's burned into my memory."

"Oh, I'm sure. It is *very* hard on the families." She was a nurse of the warm and friendly type, that much was clear. Her heartstrings could be pulled.

That was good to know. On the witness stand, a severe or buttoned-up person was much harder to lead. Knowing that about her wasn't much use now—there wasn't a lot I could do with that knowledge at a preliminary hearing—but at trial, with a jury watching, it might come in handy.

I counted a couple of my fingers and said, "So where are we at now, fourteen or fifteen people on the unit? Plus the twelve patients?"

"That sounds about right. We might get an administrator in there once in a while, and, of course, family members."

"So, close to thirty people, plus family?"

"Yes, I guess that's right."

"Okay, thank you. And you had mentioned a newer nurse had approached you and mentioned seeing Ms. Winters doing something, correct?"

"Pocketing the medications, yes."

"One vial of medication?"

"Oh—well, on that occasion it was just one, yes."

"And who was that newer nurse?"

"Her name was Cherylin Martin."

"Was?"

"Well, it still is, probably, but she's not with us anymore. She took a travel-nursing job. I want to say she moved to Texas."

"Oh, okay. Thank you." I flipped through some pages in the binder I'd had Rachel make for me. Then I said, "Actually, if I may, would the clerk be able to show Mr. LaRue's demonstrative again?"

I wanted to get O'Malley on record saying that this was how the dispensing cabinet looked. Preliminary hearings weren't recorded in our local state court, but they were in federal court; this was an opportunity I wasn't going to miss.

I talked through it with LaRue and the clerk, and a minute later, the photograph of the dispensing cabinet reappeared on everyone's screens. Federal courtrooms had flat-screens for everybody: one at the witness stand, one in front of the judge, and three of them facing the empty jury box.

"Now, Mrs. O'Malley, is that the dispensing cabinet on your unit?"

"Yes, it is."

"And that door there, that we can see part of on the right of the photo —am I mistaken in thinking that's a toilet sign on the door?"

"No, you're not. That's the ladies' room."

"Okay, thank you. And just to make clear what the layout is there, am I correct in recalling that once you go through those automatic doors into your unit, it's basically one big hallway with patient rooms on either side?"

"Patient rooms and restrooms and storage, yes."

"But all of that along the one hallway?"

"Yes."

"So this dispensing cabinet is right there in the hallway, correct?"

"Um..." She hesitated. I could tell she knew where I was going with this.

"Whoever designed the unit," I said, "which obviously wasn't you, but whoever it was, that's where they chose to place the dispensing cabinet?"

"I—well, I'm sure the hospital was built long before there was such a thing as dispensing cabinets, but yes."

"So, yes, it's right there in the hallway?"

"Yes."

"Next to the ladies' room, so anybody using the facilities would walk past it? Or next to it?"

"Yes."

"And that computer screen we see on top of it, that's its normal position?"

"I'm sorry, what do you mean by position?"

"Well, it's affixed to the cabinet, correct?"

"Yes."

"And it's facing you as you use the cabinet, correct?"

"Oh, yes, of course."

"So it's facing out toward the hallway, correct?"

"It's— Yes, I suppose."

"And that's a touchscreen, correct? No keyboard?"

"Yes."

"So when you go to dispense a medication, you type your log-in right up there on the screen?"

I was air typing, as if there were a big touchscreen in front of me, but to give the court reporter something she could put down in the record, I added, "Like with your index finger, you tap out the PIN code?"

"Yes. The PIN code, yes."

"And that's a four-digit code, correct?" LaDonna had told me that, but I wanted it on the record.

"Yes. Each person gets their own four-digit code."

"Right. Now, in this photo, there doesn't appear to be anything attached to that screen, does there?"

"Attached?"

"That is, it's just a normal flat, black, rectangular screen, correct?"

"Yes."

"With nothing attached to it—no blinders or shields or any other barriers to viewing it?"

"No, there's nothing attached to it."

"No blinders attached. So, looking at this photograph, is it fair to say the screen is just sitting there in the open?"

She hesitated, then looked at the image. After a second, she said, "I guess that's fair to say, yes."

"Okay, thank you. Mrs. O'Malley, I have nothing further for you today, so I thank you for your time."

I'd gotten what I needed from her—the name of the nurse who'd reported LaDonna, and the facts I needed to show that their log-in system wasn't secure—and it was on record, so she wouldn't be able to deny it or walk it back later without losing credibility. And LaRue was now on notice that any evidence he got on the hospital's lax computer security was highly relevant to my defense and had to be turned over under the *Brady* rule.

I asked for a copy of the demonstrative, and then LaRue called the lead detective. About forty minutes later, as expected, we lost. When

Magistrate Jefferson announced that LaDonna was bound over for trial, she sat perfectly still, not reacting. She knew how to act dignified in a court of law. Only I could see that she'd clamped her left hand onto the arm of her chair so hard that her knuckles had turned white.

As I walked LaDonna and Ms. Baker back to their parked car, I tried to reassure them that we'd done well, even if it didn't feel like it. LaDonna nodded, but I could tell she wasn't convinced.

"We're putting our trust in you, Mr. Munroe," Ms. Baker said as she opened her door. "LaDonna didn't do this, and we need you to prove it."

I simply said, "Yes, ma'am."

I waved as they drove off, then looked at my watch. I was supposed to meet Judy Reed at her home after lunch. I topped up my meter and walked to the French Quarter to grab a sandwich.

After eating, I headed over. At a corner, waiting for traffic to pass, I clicked my briefcase open and got the one-page printout of the map that Judy had sent. I knew my way around the neighborhood, but since I'd never known anybody with enough money to live there, I wasn't real familiar with its residential parts.

I'd glanced at the map the previous day, when Rachel handed it to me, so I already knew it was a little unusual. Now, looking at it closely, I saw individual pen strokes and realized that somebody with striking artistic skills must've drawn it by hand. It showed a slanted 3D view of what appeared to be every building in this part of the French Quarter, with the Ravenel Bridge swooping gracefully in the background. One of the buildings at the bottom of the map was catty-corner from where I was standing. Every detail on its facade, right down to the stamped-tin pattern on the ground floor flower boxes, was included in the drawing.

Typed below the picture—or, I realized, hand printed, but the writing was so clear it looked artificial—was a caption reading "Three-quarter elevation view of the French Quarter," followed by a numbered list of directions from the corner of Broad and Meeting to Judy's house. On the map, a pale blue line snaked its way through the streets, stopping at my destination. That house was the only building on the map that was colored in. Every terra-cotta tile on its roof, and every wooden plank on the rooftop terrace, looked to be hand tinted.

I chuckled, shaking my head, and crossed the street. It would certainly be a new one, I thought, if I ended up defending some sort of female Leonardo da Vinci on murder charges.

It was a sunny day, and as I headed east, the wind picked up a little, carrying the scent of salt and sulfur. The French Quarter was a minute or two south of where the fresh water of the Cooper River met the tidal salt water of the harbor, and the combination gave our city its own peculiar smell, which I'd always loved.

When the grassy expanse of Waterfront Park came into view, I followed the map's pale blue line onto a side street too narrow for a car. The road surface here was red brick, and on either side, a jungle of greenery sprang from big pots or straight from the ground. The cast-iron fence and gate surrounding what I took to be Judy's house were covered in ivy so thick I couldn't see the yard.

This was the oldest part of Charleston, the most beautiful part. I didn't need to check listings to know that anybody living here must've paid upward of $2 million for the privilege.

I checked her map again to confirm the address and noticed the last line she'd written, across the bottom: "This map should suffice. See you Thursday 1 PM. Punctuality matters, lateness not tolerated."

Roy's warning that Judy didn't respond to things the way most folks would came to mind, and I laughed. While I was well aware that Southern graciousness was often theater and not extended to everyone, the fact that Judy Reed hadn't bothered to make an attempt before we'd even met gave me little hope that our interactions would go smoothly.

5

DECEMBER 8, 2022

Judy Reed swung the door open. She was tall, with the horsey look I'd seen before in some old money types, and she was wearing a navy blue pinstripe pantsuit.

"Mr. Munroe?" she asked, without smiling.

"Yes, indeed. Pleased to—"

"Good." She turned and walked away.

I stepped inside, closed the door, and hurried a little to catch up to her. She was halfway across the living room, which was starkly modern, all pale wood and steel. None of the exterior's antiquated charm was visible here.

She reached a hallway and kept going. Over her shoulder, she announced, "I like to sit on my terrace after lunch. Everything's set up there."

"Well, that sounds lovely," I said.

She didn't respond.

I saw a stainless steel bowl on the floor by a couch and tried to make conversation: "Oh, do you have a dog?"

She stopped and turned to me, tilting her head a little. "What? No."

"Oh, okay. I just saw that bowl, and—"

She looked where I was pointing, then back at me. "That's a sculpture," she said. "The artist intended it to be displayed on the floor."

There wasn't a hint of humor on her face. I put a lid on my urge to make a joke. She was still focused on me, and it was getting awkward, so I said, "Sorry, I've got a Yorkshire terrier at home, and I'm always on the lookout for a dog to pet."

"Really?" She turned back around without waiting for me to answer, and we started walking again. "Dogs are certainly useful for security," she said. "At least, the bigger ones are. But I don't know how the owners deal with the hair. If I see it on furniture, I can't even sit down."

"Huh." Yorkies didn't shed much, but I didn't think I was going to win her over on the subject of dogs, so I decided to keep quiet.

After another hallway and two flights of stairs, we stepped out onto the rooftop terrace I'd seen in her drawing. My heart was pounding—I really needed to find time to get back in shape—but the view was stunning. We were in one of the last blocks before Waterfront Park, so we could see the whole panoramic sweep from Drum Island and the bridge, across the Cooper River to the sparkling harbor, and all the way out to the ocean. The tops of a couple of palm trees nestled against the edge of her deck.

"My goodness," I said. "This is incredible."

"Yeah, I do like to face east. Not sure if you're aware, but traditionally, churches face east. It's a human thing. For some reason, we like doing that. As opposed to herds of wild deer and bovines—did you know they tend to face north whenever they eat or rest?"

She sounded like a human trivia machine. I had the disconcerting sense that she was playing a preexisting track, rather than talking to me. What she'd said had nothing to do with me; probably anybody who showed up at her door—a neighbor, a pizza guy—would've been served the same information.

"No, I wasn't aware of that," I said.

She nodded as if she wasn't surprised. She was looking at a point somewhere past my shoulder, as far as I could tell. I resisted the urge to turn around and figure out what had caught her eye.

For lack of anything better to say, I added, "That's interesting, though."

"There's some speculation that they sense the earth's magnetic fields," she said. She was looking higher up than before; I wondered if she was tracking an airplane. "But I'm skeptical. Although I shouldn't really talk. It's not my area of expertise."

"And, uh, what *is* your area of expertise?"

"I'm a geospatial consultant. Or GIS consultant, some people call it."

"Oh," I said. "And, uh, what is that?"

"I work with location-based datasets. I suppose in the common parlance, although it's oversimplified, you could say I 'make maps.'"

Her tone on the last two words was withering, as if only fools called it that. As I followed her over to the seating area in the middle of the terrace, I was thinking that if she got up on the stand and spoke like that in front of a Basking Rock jury, her trial would be over before it even began.

"Have a seat," she said, gesturing to a wicker chair at the umbrella-shaded table. "And help yourself to snacks."

We sat. The only snacks in sight, sitting on a very modern, asymmetrical wooden tray, were a six-pack of spring water, a tall bottle of Macallan scotch, and a box of what were apparently called "Entertainment Crackers."

"So," I said, "did you just come from work?"

"No." She looked baffled by my question. "Why do you ask?"

"Well, it's a weekday, and I noticed you're wearing a suit, so—"

"Oh, this? No, I just find it's easier to wear the same thing every day. I don't understand people who waste their time and energy thinking about clothes. I mean, something so trivial."

"Uh-huh."

I always liked to establish a rapport with folks I met, but I wasn't sure how that was going to happen here. Talking with her felt like reaching out to open a car door and finding it didn't even have a handle.

I tried again. "Can you tell me a little bit about your work? I don't believe I've ever met anybody who does what you do."

"Oh, yes, well, there aren't many of us."

In the silence after that, I pictured a tumbleweed blowing past.

"Uh-huh," I said. "And what is it that y'all do, exactly?"

"Geospatial asset management, mainly. That's my area. Mapping the vulnerabilities of historic properties, for instance."

"Oh, historic properties," I said, grabbing on to one of the few parts of her sentence that I had understood. "Yeah, you must know a heck of a lot about that. That map you drew me of the French Quarter was incredible."

55

"Well, the French Quarter is fascinating. Its architectural assets are exceptional."

"Uh-huh. I would agree with you there. And when you say vulnerabilities—"

"The main ones around here are flooding and hurricanes, so I look at things like topography, historical weather data, construction materials and techniques... In some areas, though, you have to look at subsidence. If a structure was built on top of an abandoned mine, for instance."

"Huh. So your maps are... 3D, I guess?"

"To say the least, yes."

I felt schooled, as if I had just told an art collector that his $50 million Monet was real pretty. I picked up one of the bottles of water, opened it, and took a sip.

"Wouldn't you like some scotch?" she asked.

"No, thank you."

"Really? My daddy always drank that. I think of it as what a man drinks."

"Huh."

"Is there some medical reason you're not drinking? Like a medication you're on that can't mix with alcohol? Or is it a personal issue?"

She was looking me right in the eye, finally, with a stare that was somehow both blank and intrusive. My hackles were up farther than they ought to have been, because my late wife's alcoholism was the reason I didn't drink, and being reminded of that by this stranger's interrogation had not been on my agenda for today.

I looked out at the harbor and took a deep breath. I recalled Roy asking me to please overlook this woman's personality and trust his judgment that she was a good person who deserved help.

As a favor for a friend, I resolved to do that.

I took a sip of my water and said, "Well, anyway, enough about me. Tell me about your case. I understand your trial's starting right around the first of February, but unfortunately Mr. Dickenson is unable to continue?"

"Yes, he has stage four bowel cancer. It's going to be a terrible way to go." Her voice was breezy, devoid of emotion. "I sent him some information about a clinic in Switzerland that does a very peaceful assisted suicide, to avoid the pain, but he wasn't interested."

While I concentrated on keeping my facial expression neutral—I didn't see much point in letting people know when I was appalled—she opened the cracker box and shook a few into a bowl.

"Uh-huh," I said. "Well, I'm very sorry to hear he's going through that. But could you tell me anything about his trial strategy? What were his thoughts on having you testify?"

"He told me I shouldn't," she said, munching a cracker. "But that didn't make sense to me. I would think the first thing an innocent person should do is tell the jury they didn't do it. I mean, you have to get *that* squared away right off the bat."

I leaned back in my seat and looked at her for a second, trying to think how I might explain the American justice system to an alien such as Mr. Spock, or to a highly intelligent but extremely sheltered child. "You don't watch a lot of crime shows, do you?" I asked. "Courtroom shows, that sort of thing?"

"No, there's not much on television that interests me."

"Uh-huh. Well, forgive me if this is a little basic, but are you aware that, strictly speaking, a defendant doesn't have to prove their innocence? The State's got to prove them guilty?"

"Obviously, but why would you not get up there and clear your name? It's a nasty thing to walk around with. Being accused of murdering your own father? People look at you like you're scum."

Despite the words she was saying, her voice still had the same unnerving blankness. It sounded like she was reading a shopping list out loud. "Oh, I know it's hard," I said.

"And I don't see why you wouldn't get up there and say it's not true. I mean, that's the conclusion that the jurors have to reach, so... Without that, you might as well give them a map that doesn't even have New York on it and tell them to use it to get to the Empire State Building."

"I hear your point, and that's an interesting way to look at it. But the thing is, once you're up on the stand, you're there until the prosecutor's done with you. And if you watched a few of those courtroom shows, you'd know how a good cross-examination can twist things. By the time the prosecutor's done, you can end up looking a whole lot worse than you would've if you'd just sat there at the defense table not saying a word."

"That wouldn't apply to me. I imagine some people might get flustered when someone challenges them, even if they're telling the truth, but that's not a problem I have."

"Uh-huh. Yes, well, folks can get a little emotional."

I stopped. I wasn't about to tell her that her lack of emotion itself was the problem. Saying so might offend her or it might not—I wasn't sure she was capable of being offended—but either way, there was no point. You couldn't coach a witness into being somebody other than who they were.

"Still, though," I said, "I have to agree with your lawyer's advice not to testify. His strategies have served you well so far, haven't they? I can tell he did a great job, because we're sitting here talking on your rooftop terrace. Did he explain to you how unusual it is for a South Carolina judge to let a murder defendant out on bail?"

"He did, yes."

"Most folks facing charges like these would've been sitting in the county jail since the day of their arrest. So he did an exceptional job."

"He explained that, and I appreciate it. Although I had to turn in my passport, and this ankle bracelet is obnoxious." She gestured toward her foot. Her pant leg hid the bracelet, but I'd known no lawyer could've persuaded a judge to let her walk free without any monitoring.

I nodded. "I got a client out with one of those on. She was facing murder charges too. Real uncomfortable, had to charge it for hours every day. Made her feel like a dog stuck inside an electric fence. But compared to the Basking County Jail, I mean..." I gestured to the beautiful view. I wasn't about to tell her so, but I might've consented to wear an ankle bracelet myself if it meant I could live in a place like this.

"Yes," she said. "I obviously prefer being at home. I don't know how I could get any work done in jail. Is there even Wi-Fi there?"

I stared at her, then redirected my view back out to the water. It was going to take me more than a minute to understand how her mind worked. "No," I said slowly. "No, there's no Wi-Fi in jail."

She nodded. "That would be a problem."

I didn't respond. Out on the water, a red boat was going past, trailing a white wake. I focused on that. I couldn't tell whether Judy had some mental issue or was just oblivious to how the world worked. But I might never get the answer to that question, and I certainly wasn't getting it today.

I moved on.

"Can I ask, is this a family property? Or is it yours?"

"Oh, it's mine. It was my grandmama's, but when I turned eighteen, she put it in a trust for me."

"Uh-huh. And was that your paternal grandmother or—"

"Yes, my daddy's mother."

"Uh-huh. Okay, so, pardon me for asking, but under the terms of the trust, is this place basically yours for good? Nothing you or your daddy did could change that?"

"That's right, it was all done when I was eighteen. I believe the term for it is an irrevocable trust."

"Okay, thank you." That was good. A jury might be less inclined to think she had a motive for murder if I could help them see that she'd already been rich.

I tucked that thought in my back pocket. "Okay, anyway, as I said, the fact that you're awaiting trial here instead of in jail tells me Mr. Dickenson was doing a great job on your case. So his advice on not testifying may be worth listening to."

"I don't agree. I'm going to get up there and say my piece."

I clenched my teeth to stifle a sigh of irritation. "Well, we can cross that bridge when we come to it," I said. "In the meantime, if you'd like to move forward with me—"

"I would. Roy Hearst said great things about you. I've known him since—well, for about as long as I can remember. How do you know him, again?"

"I used to work for him. You might call him my mentor."

She looked confused. "Was he or wasn't he?"

"Uh… yes, he was. I mean, it wasn't an official title or anything, but that's what he was to me, yes."

"Oh. All right."

I took a sip of my water, wondering if every conversation we ever had would be like this one: awkward and punctuated with odd misunderstandings.

"Anyway," I said, "I'll need Mr. Dickenson's office to send me over the file so I can get up to speed. Two months is not much time to prepare for a case of this nature. Did he have a private investigator looking into anything, do you know?"

"I told him he should, but no, he didn't. I was actually going to hire one myself and see what they could find. One of the things about this case that I think is a little sus is that nobody really looked at my father's mistress. My—"

"He had a mistress?"

"Oh, yes. Alanna Carpenter. Ever since my mother's accident, he— well, maybe before that, too—he started… I guess he might've said 'having fun.' But she was the first girlfriend of his whose name I knew. She wasn't just some side piece; she was really insinuating herself." For the first time, there was emotion in her voice. Indignation, and even a hint of hurt.

"How do you mean, insinuating?"

"Oh, they were not discreet at all. And the amount of money he had to be spending on her…" She shook her head in disapproval.

I had a long catalog of crimes in my head—seventeen years as a prosecutor and nearly four in criminal defense would do that—but I'd never heard of a mistress murdering the man who was showering her with money. "So... what is it that leads you to suspect this Ms. Carpenter had something to do with your father's death?"

"Well, for one thing, the way she looked at my mother. She—"

"You—wait, you saw her, or ran into her, with your mother?"

"Yes, the day before the Kentucky Derby. We went down to the stables with Mother's aide—"

"By 'we,' you mean you and your mother?"

"Yes, and they were there. Alanna and my father. It was super upsetting to my mother, and the way Alanna looked at her was... angry? She was pretty salty, and I couldn't understand why, since my mother hadn't done anything wrong, but... Anyway, they left, and then one of the stable hands told us they were flying to Louisville to see the race."

"The Derby? This Ms. Carpenter and your father?"

"Yes. Which ruined it for my mother—she couldn't watch the race. That was literally the only time in my entire life that she missed watching the Kentucky Derby."

"And this was, what, a little over a month before your father passed?"

"Yes. I'll never forget it."

Watching Judy describe this incident was like watching a car crash in slow motion. If Mrs. Barnes got into this topic with her on the stand, it would not go well. I could see the prosecution's theory already: out of rage at her father—rage for stepping out on her tragically injured mother—and fear that he would marry this harlot and change his will in her favor, Judy committed murder. In the hands of a mediocre prosecutor it might be a soap opera, but Mrs. Barnes would, as Ruiz had said, make it biblical.

Either way, it was a story any juror could understand.

And the story would practically tell itself if Judy got up on the stand and Ginevra asked her about her dead father's mistress.

"Okay, and so… What was it you were hoping to find by investigating Ms. Carpenter?"

"A motive," she said, and bit off half of another cracker. "Or maybe even proof of an accident. We all knew about his allergy—we never had cephalosporin in the house, to make sure there was no risk of contamination. Emma Jean—my mother's aide—didn't even take it at her own home. But did *she* know? Do people talk about their medical backgrounds when they're having extramarital affairs? I have no idea."

Alanna as an accidental source at least sounded halfway plausible. Although if the police hadn't investigated it at the time, it'd be hard to do a good job of it now, a year and a half later.

"Okay, well, I have an excellent private investigator," I said. "Terri Washington. She works on all my cases, and she is a wizard. So I'll talk to her about the mistress and see what we can find."

"Good plan," she said. "Maybe she can get someone to spill the tea."

"Can I just ask, so I'm clear," I said, "what evidence did the police have in regard to the cephalosporin? Did they recover a bottle at the scene, or—?"

"No. They never found a bottle. What they said is that I went and got a prescription for it a couple of days before he died. Which is ridiculous. I've never gotten a prescription for that in my life."

"Do you happen to recall— I assume you had a preliminary hearing?"

"Yes."

"And do you recall what evidence they put in of this prescription you supposedly had?"

"Yeah. This urgent care doctor I saw testified."

"Oh, so you had seen a doctor shortly before your father passed?"

"Yeah, I had a urinary tract infection. It was getting pretty painful, so I went to urgent care down there instead of waiting to see my normal doctor in Charleston."

She spoke with complete frankness and no trace of embarrassment. She might as well have been talking about rotating the tires on her car. For about the third time since arriving at her home, I recalibrated my expectations about how our conversation was going to unfold.

"Uh, okay," I said. "So the doctor who treated you testified at the hearing. And they said they'd written a prescription for some type of cephalosporin?"

"That's what he said. He read it out from hospital records. It wasn't true, but I didn't get to say that at the hearing."

"Huh." I didn't see how I could put her up on the stand to insist she'd never been prescribed the drugs that hospital records and her treating physician said she had. There was no formal rule against it, but my own personal rules included not doing anything stupid. Grasping at straws, I asked, "Was there any evidence of you actually picking the prescription up? A pharmacist on the stand, or security camera footage, or…?"

"They didn't get into that at the hearing, but I did pick up my prescription, of course. Have you ever had a UTI yourself?"

It took some effort to keep from showing how inappropriate I thought her question was. "No, I don't believe I have."

"Yeah, they're not common in men. They're no joke: if you leave it untreated, it can damage your kidneys. So the fact that I picked the meds up isn't the point. The point is, I would've insisted on a different drug."

She ate the last cracker out of her bowl and then gazed meditatively at the bottle of scotch.

"It hits weird," she said finally, "that he's dead. Although everybody has to die at some point. Nobody's special." She looked at me with her wide, blank eyes and said, in a tone like she was asking where I'd parked, "Did you ever have somebody close to you die, Mr. Munroe?" I gritted my teeth and looked out at the water again. As I was doing my deep breathing, she said, "I guess that's a silly question. At your age, you must have."

I almost laughed. I didn't even want to think about what ridiculous things this woman might say if I put her on the stand.

After a second, she said, "Oh, I forgot to ask about fees. Mr. Dickenson needed a $75,000 retainer. Is yours about the same?"

"Mine's a little higher," I said, watching another boat sail past. I figured I'd need something to compensate for the headaches she was going to give me, not to mention the dental work I'd need after spending the next two months gritting my teeth. "It's $100,000."

6

DECEMBER 14, 2022

O n the golf course, with the sun on my back, I watched Roy
poised over the ball, making light practice swings. I'd called
to ask a question about Judy Reed, who Terri and I were meeting up
with the next day, and he'd invited me to join him out at his club,
because the guy he'd planned to go with had canceled. I'd never
played golf this close to Christmas, but then I hardly ever played it
at all.

"The normal etiquette," he said, "just so you know, is, you stand
out of my line of sight so you don't distract me. But I am determined to improve your swing, so stay right there where you can
see. First thing is, you've got to loosen your grip." He stood up
straight and showed me how much play his club had in his
hands.

"Yeah, okay," I said, trying to hold my rented seven iron the
same way.

"The reason that last one went flying off to California, or wherever it
ended up, was you were holding on too tight. That screws up your
angle."

"But then how do you control it? I mean, you've still got to hit it hard."

"Right, but it's a golf ball, not a punching bag. There's some nuance to it. Like this." He swung his club back in a smooth arc, then forward as if he and gravity were in perfect alignment, and whacked the ball farther than I could see.

It took me three shots to get my ball as far down the fairway as his had gone.

"You've got to loosen up," he repeated as we headed to his ball. "A golf course isn't the place to be on high alert. You look like you're half expecting gunfire to break out."

"Well, bear in mind I practice criminal law."

He laughed. "Fair point." With a crack, he sent his ball flying again. I shielded my eyes with one hand to watch it land on the putting green.

We walked on.

"You know what," he said, "I'm sure glad I picked the line of work I did. Any type of criminal law, prosecution or defense, sounds like hell to me. Some folks think business law is on the dull side, but I'll tell you one thing, I don't lie awake at night sweating bullets about a franchise agreement or the lease on a business park."

I smiled. "Yeah, sleeping well and playing a good golf game... I don't know much about either of those."

"I'm sure. Her case keeping you up?" I knew he meant Judy. There was nobody within five hundred yards of us, no possible eavesdroppers, but we had a long habit of having whole conversations without saying anybody's name.

"Well, let's say I keep thinking about switching to a different type of practice."

"You mean business law?" He sounded skeptical.

"No, I've pretty much accepted that that's not my thing. But it's tricky to run a criminal defense practice when you don't want to defend any actual bad guys."

He laughed. "See, again, you're making me glad I do what I do. That's another thing that would keep me up at night: wondering if my hard work put a killer back on the streets."

I shuddered. "Yeah, exactly. I sometimes think I ought to get a job at some nonprofit working to get innocent folks out of jail."

"Oh, the DNA stuff? Or like that thing you did last year?"

Back while I was still working for him, I'd helped a woman who'd been wrongly convicted of murder prove her innocence. That case hadn't involved DNA, but like most lawyers, we'd both heard about plenty of people who'd been exonerated after decades in jail when genetic evidence proved that they were not the perpetrator.

"Yeah. Lately, when I'm not liking my job, that's what calls to me."

Roy stopped to pull a club from his bag and tap a torn-up chunk of grass and dirt back into place. Evidently another bad golfer had been down this fairway before me. "I guess I can see the appeal of that kind of thing," he said. "It's... clean. No moral ambiguity."

"Exactly."

He slid the club back into his bag, and we started walking again. "You know what the problem is, though," he said.

"The pay?"

"I was going to say the burnout. Although, not to rehash my joke about nonprofit lawyers, but—"

I smiled. "They're lawyers who don't make a profit. Okay, that one's true."

"I don't know all that many of them, but almost every nonprofit lawyer I've ever met, either they're married to somebody who's bringing in the real money, or they're the kind of people who think being poor is a good thing. Something that makes them morally superior."

I winced. I'd met both those types myself. And I was well aware that if I were poor, I wouldn't be strolling across a golf course in the sunshine on a weekday morning. I'd be working in a factory, or maybe a restaurant—or both, like my mother had done when I was little; she'd needed two jobs for us to get by.

"I don't know," I said. "The pay for those innocence-lawyer things doesn't look *that* bad. It's not great, but it's survivable, especially now that Noah's grown up and got himself a job."

"You really want to tighten your belt for the rest of your life?"

He had me there. "Not really."

"I didn't think so. And I tell you what," he said. "Most folks think the great thing about having money is that it means you can pretty much do what you want. Buy that car, take that vacation, and so forth."

"Isn't that a good thing?"

"Oh, hell yes! Didn't I just get back from the Virgin Islands? I'm the last person who's going to knock that." He chuckled. "But the other thing—although folks don't talk about this anywhere near as much—is that if you've got plenty of money in the bank, then whenever you see an injustice or a problem, you can just write a check. Won't cure all of them, but it takes care of a lot."

I looked at him in surprise. I'd never pegged him as a do-gooder.

69

But then I thought about when I'd first been working for him after losing my prosecutor job. The car I drove then was a half-dead beater held together with duct tape. I couldn't even afford to repair it, much less get anything better. And Roy had leased a new car for me, putting it down as a business expense, because, he explained, it made the firm look better to have me in a decent car. I'd driven that car for two years for nothing more than the cost of the gas.

"You know," I said, "that's a really good point. You can solve a lot of problems for a lot of people."

"Yep," he said. "I know. Money's a damn good tool, long as you control it and not the other way around. Also, get yourself rich enough and you can afford to take any case you want, for free, if you really believe in it."

"Uh-huh." From that perspective, Judy's case looked perfect: taking it would keep my firm afloat for six months all by itself. It meant I could work on LaDonna's case without worrying about how I was going to keep the lights on. "By the way," I said, "thank you much for referring that client to me."

He smiled. "Of course. She needs what you've got, and vice versa. I thought it'd be a good fit. And it's before Judge Davenport. You could do a lot worse."

"Yeah, trials always run smoother with a smart judge."

"Yep. But back to that client. Tell me, how do you find her? You two get along?" There was a little extra music in his voice. I could tell he was amused.

"Well, you know. Like you said, she's real particular. And she'll be a tough one to put in front of a jury. Hard to get them to warm to her."

"Yeah, I don't envy you that," he said, as we arrived at my ball. "You want your pitching wedge for this one," he said, tapping one of the clubs in his bag to show me what it looked like.

He took a ball out of his pocket, dropped it on the ground, and demonstrated what I should do. I hacked at the earth a few times and finally got my ball up on the putting green.

He pulled out a club and used it to push the bit of turf I'd damaged back into place.

"Sorry, let me get that," I said. I patted it down, hoping it would survive.

As we walked up to the putting green, he asked, "You bringing Terri over to meet with your new client?"

"Yeah. I want to get her take." Terri was an uncanny judge of character, and she had a knack for getting people talking.

"Uh-huh," he said. "She's a good woman." That was as close to a nudge as I was likely to get from him. He wasn't the type to ask me directly about my personal life, but I knew what he meant.

"Yes, she is."

"Something to think about," he said. He got into position, lined up his putt, and tapped his ball. It rolled right into the hole.

"Well, these days," I said, "folks think it's weird if you ask somebody who works for you on a date."

"Oh, everything's weird these days, isn't it?" he said, sliding his club back into the bag. "Life's too short to worry about that."

"Yeah, fair point." I didn't want to keep talking about Terri with him, so I asked, "You got any tips for handling this client?"

"Oof. About all you can do is get used to her. She is how she is."

"Uh-huh."

I had plenty of questions I would've liked to ask, but sometimes questions revealed too much, and I couldn't talk with him in any detail about Judy's case. Since we weren't part of the same firm anymore, sharing confidential information wasn't allowed, and I drew the boundaries of secrecy a little farther out than they needed to be in order to keep myself from making a mistake.

But I could ask him his opinion. There weren't any rules against that.

As I prepared for my first putt—I assumed there would be several more—I said, "You know her a lot better than I do. And I'm sure you've seen on the news what the prosecutor thinks her motive and means were."

"Oh, yep."

"So why is it you don't buy that? Is it just knowing her all her life, or..."

"You mean, why don't I think she did it?" He seemed surprised that I would ask.

"Yeah." I tapped the ball, and it rolled about four feet. The hole was another six feet away. I looked over at him, puzzled by the fact that he wasn't chuckling and shaking his head at my bad shot.

He wasn't watching my game at all. He was looking out at the ocean. After a second, he said, "I mean, obviously I've been on this earth long enough to know that some folks are *real* different behind closed doors. People you'd never expect it from can do some horrifying things."

A gust of wind rustled the nearby palm trees. When he didn't go on, I said, "But?"

"But… Well, look, you've spent more than twenty years practicing criminal law. You've seen some real lowlifes up close. So you tell me if you think I'm wrong, but I've always thought it takes passion to kill a person that you know. It's not the same thing as killing a stranger."

"I don't know." I went over to my ball. "Passion's kind of a funny word."

"Oh, you can call it jealousy, or anger, or greed—as far as I'm concerned, it all amounts to the same thing. I think murdering your own father takes something on that level. Which she just doesn't have."

"Huh." I putted again and watched the ball curve around the hole like some force field was keeping it out. "Yeah, there is something of the automaton about her. That was my first impression, anyway."

"That's been my impression since she was a toddler rattling off lists of dinosaur names. That was all she talked about until she was five or six. I mean, she's obviously real smart, in her own way. It doesn't take more than one conversation with her to know that. And she's got her interests, and she cares about her mom…" He shrugged. "She's loyal, the way a robot would be loyal if you programmed it to be. But even as a little kid, she was so levelheaded that it was almost creepy. She's got no passion about anything at all. Or none that I've ever seen."

"Huh. You might be on to something there. Although I saw my share of psychopathic killers back when I was a prosecutor, and I can't say it was passion that drove them."

"Oh, sure," he said. "But the psychopaths are different. Hell, I see enough of them in business law—the functional ones, anyway. Aren't they usually pretty charming?"

"Yeah, no, you're right. They can come across as warm. They know how to connect and draw people in."

In a deadpan tone, Roy said, "I can't say that entirely describes her."

I laughed. "If she ever had any Southern charm, it must've been surgically removed." I lined up my shot and hit the ball a yard past the hole.

Roy chuckled. "Good thing your business doesn't depend on taking clients golfing."

"Yeah, it's not really top of mind as a thing my clients want to do while they're awaiting trial. Plus, I can't see some fancy club like this being happy to see me show up with whoever just got indicted for murder."

"You're right there. I don't run into that problem. Thibodeau fits right in."

"Oh, the hospital guy?"

"Yeah."

His friend, or client, who'd canceled today was the CEO of our local hospital. I made a mental note of that. On the one hand, I'd need to make sure—even more sure than usual—that I didn't mention anything about LaDonna's case to Roy. On the other hand, he might have some useful perspectives on the hospital, if there was anything he was able to share.

"You trying to land the hospital as a client?" I asked. "I don't really think of you as a healthcare guy."

"Oh, no. They've got people for that stuff. Compliance, med mal, I stay well clear of all that. I've done some of their contracts, and a few times, when they've got a crisis-management issue, they'll have me look at what their PR team put together before it goes out."

"To make sure the marketing guys don't say something that screws up a case?"

"Exactly."

Two strokes later, my putt made it in. As we walked to the next hole, I said, "You know her last lawyer? From what I've seen in his files, he was doing a damn good job."

"I guess he earned his reputation." He sighed. "It's a damn shame, what he's going through now."

"Uh-huh." I didn't tell him how breezily, almost callously, Judy had spoken of Dickenson's illness and possible death.

Roy teed up. When we first went golfing together, he'd explained to me that whoever had the lowest score on the previous hole teed up first. At no point in any game we'd played since then had that been me.

He sent his ball down the fairway and said, as I bent down to place my tee, "You're meeting with both of them tomorrow, right? The client and her mother?"

"Uh-huh. It's going to be a little strange. I can't say I've met with a murder defendant and the victim's widow at the same time before."

"I wouldn't worry. Her mother's got zero doubt about her innocence, and on top of that, she's very personable. There's no awkwardness in her at all. She's a real nice gal, especially considering what she's been through."

"And what exactly was that, again?"

"Here, focus on your ball. Give it a whack, and then we can talk. And remember, loosen your grip."

I did as instructed. To my surprise, the ball flew a hundred-plus yards straight ahead.

"There you go," he said. "You stop trying to force it—just trust it'll work—and it does."

"I guess so." Trust and relaxation weren't really in my repertoire, but I thought I might try to make an exception when it came to golf.

My phone buzzed with a text, and I looked at it.

"Oh, damn," I said. "The client wants to postpone by a few days. Her mother's come down with the flu."

"That's a shame. Yeah, her health can be a little delicate."

As we walked, Roy looked around to confirm we were still nowhere near any other human beings, and then he said, "You know she was a competitive horseback rider, right?"

"The mother?"

He nodded.

"You mean before her marriage?"

"Oh, way before. She was barely in high school when I met her—she was good friends with my little sister—and she was already doing it then. Racking up some championships at the junior level, I seem to recall."

"I didn't know you went that far back."

"Doesn't everybody, in this town? Or that town, I guess." He gestured in a southerly direction. We were about forty minutes north of Basking Rock.

"Yeah, we mostly do," I said. "For good or ill."

"I didn't know her that well, then," he said. "We only overlapped for a year before I headed off to college. But when I came back, after law school, she was married, and her husband was one of my first clients."

"Oh? Was he still, when he passed?"

"No, within a few years he got some business partner who didn't like me, and that was that. But you know me, I stay friends with everyone."

"Uh-huh. I always thought that was a good policy."

"It's the only policy, if you want to have a good life in a small town."

"Oof," I said. "So much for my prospects."

I was thinking of Ludlow, the former circuit solicitor whose career I had more or less destroyed, and his friend Dabney Barnes IV, who hated me for what I'd done to Ludlow and probably for several other reasons too.

Roy laughed. He knew all about the enemies I'd made. "Well, you can at least start making up for it," he said. "Get on the good side of this family, and that'll go a long way."

"I'll do my best."

We got to my ball, and I gave it another relaxed whack. It made it a decent way farther.

"As I was saying," Roy continued, "she was a competitive rider, but then her daddy ran into some trouble and lost everything, so she had to stop. I don't know the details—I wasn't here at the time, and I was too young to care anyway."

"But she ended up marrying a rich guy."

"Yeah, so she did fine. And she started riding again, with her daughter, once the kid was old enough. I guess it was a bonding thing for them, until the accident."

I shook my head in sympathy. "What happened there?"

"The same thing that's cursed riders ever since God first put a man on a horse. It reared, or it shied, or something—I don't know the exact details—and she fell. I don't know if she broke her neck or her back, but whichever it was, she can still breathe on her own. And she's still got some movement in her arms."

"But she can't walk at all?"

"Not since that day."

"That's awful. How old was…?"

"Her daughter? I want to say she was about fourteen."

"God, what a shame."

"Yeah, terrible shock for the whole family."

"How have they managed since?"

"Well, money helps. And she's tried to make something good out of it. Started a nonprofit for folks with spinal injuries. Gave her something to do with herself."

"Wow. She's got some grit, I guess."

"That she does. Took her a few years to get there, but that's understandable." We walked in silence until we got to Roy's ball. He sent it easily up onto the green.

"How'd the father react to the accident?" I asked.

Roy gave me a look as if to say I didn't want to know. "On the surface, things looked okay," he said. "I mean, he didn't divorce her. But let's just say he wasn't a man of strong character."

I nodded. Conway had stepped out on his wife pretty quickly, it sounded like. That fact might help neutralize any argument from the prosecutor that Judy had killed her father out of anger at his infidelity.

But I knew that if I were the prosecutor, I wouldn't try the case on that theory—not unless Judy got up on the stand and made it easy for me.

If she didn't testify, a $20 million inheritance was a motive any juror could understand. And all I had to neutralize that was the fact that she didn't need the money as much as most folks did.

That had seemed like a decent argument when I was looking at the bay from her rooftop patio. But on reflection, it amounted to saying that a wealthy person wasn't capable of greed.

I doubted there was a juror alive who'd believe that.

7

DECEMBER 18, 2022

Margaret Reed's home was, as Judy had put it, "an equestrian property" on sixty-odd acres outside of town. It was about three o'clock when I arrived. I pulled up beside the tall cast-iron front gates, facing one of the moss-covered stone pillars framing the driveway, and waited for Terri to catch up. When her green Subaru appeared over a nearby hill, I texted Judy to let her know we were there. A few seconds later, the black gates parted, and we headed up the winding drive, shadowed by giant pin oaks, for two hundred yards or so until we reached the house. It was a stately, sprawling yellow Victorian with a deep porch along the whole front and down both sides.

I parked near a black Tesla, which I took to be Judy's, and Terri parked on the far side of me. I knew her well enough to guess what she was thinking: she didn't want to get any closer to an $80,000 car than she had to. Things happened sometimes—one door could bump another, or a kicked-up pebble might ding the paint—and you never knew how the type of folks who owned those things would react.

We got out of our cars and said our hellos.

"It's been a while," I said. I couldn't remember offhand the last time I'd seen her in person. She still had her hair in locs, but they were longer now. She looked great.

"It sure has," she said. "I don't remember you ever being this busy."

"Which is a good thing, I guess."

"Mm-hmm."

We turned and headed up the wide porch steps, putting our smiles away and getting back to business. It wasn't right to look cheerful when you showed up at the home of a widow to discuss her husband's death.

As I was reaching for the doorbell, an ornate brass thing with a mother-of-pearl button, somebody appeared in the hallway inside. Through the beveled glass, I couldn't tell if it was Judy, but when the door swung open, I saw it wasn't. Apparently, Mrs. Reed had staff; a pale woman in her forties gestured us inside, saying, "Good afternoon. I'm Mrs. Reed's aide. She's very glad y'all are here."

The foyer was large, with a sweeping staircase that split in two halfway up and rose to opposite sides of a second-floor mezzanine. "My goodness," Terri said, stopping to admire it. To the woman we were following, she said, "What a gorgeous place this must be to work in."

"Oh, it is. I can tell you, I never worked anywhere that came close to this."

"Well, I sure haven't either," Terri said with a smile. "It must be nice."

"Yes indeed," the woman said, smiling back at her. "Mrs. Reed and her daughter are right in here."

She'd stopped at the wide doorway of a parlor on the left. Judy was standing by a grand piano a few feet away from Mrs. Reed, a well-dressed fiftysomething lady in an electric wheelchair.

Mrs. Reed smiled warmly. "Mr. Munroe, Ms. Washington, thank you so much for coming by."

"Of course," I said. "I hope we can be of help."

Mrs. Reed set a pen and the envelope she'd been writing on down on the piano and said, "What can we offer y'all to drink? We've got sweet tea, of course, and also hot coffee, sparkling or still water, and about any soft drink or spirits you might care to name."

"Oh, don't go to the trouble," Terri and I said in near unison.

"It is no trouble at all. You just let us know what you'd like, and Emma Jean will take care of it."

The woman who'd let us in, who was still standing in the doorway to the foyer, gave a nod and said, "Happy to."

We sent her off with our drink requests and followed Mrs. Reed's instruction to "make yourselves at home" on the couch. We chatted about how our drive out to their place had been, and Mrs. Reed asked some friendly questions that revealed our total ignorance about all things equestrian.

Judy asked, "Really? You don't ride at all? Does that mean both of y'all grew up poor?"

"Oh, darling," Mrs. Reed said, rolling her eyes. "Bless your heart. You stop that."

"Mama, I only—"

"Hush now."

Judy sat down on the piano bench, looking chastened and truly confused. I got the sense that she couldn't understand why a straight-forward question would bother anyone.

"Well, everybody's got different backgrounds," Terri said with a gentle smile. "Everybody's different. And that's okay."

I saw a flash of gratitude in Mrs. Reed's eyes when she smiled back at her. An unspoken connection had been made. "Are you a mother, Ms. Washington?" Mrs. Reed asked.

"No, ma'am. I have not had that privilege."

"Well. I'm sure you'd be a good one."

"Thank you."

I considered myself pretty good at putting people at ease, but Terri's ability to connect put me to shame. Mrs. Reed had clearly heard something important when Terri said it was okay for everyone to be different. She'd heard acceptance and forgiveness for her socially awkward daughter.

Judy seemed to have missed it entirely. She was turning the pages of some sheet music, looking engrossed, as if she'd forgotten we were there.

"Does your daughter play?" I asked Mrs. Reed.

"Yes, and I should hope so," she said, smiling, "after nearly ten years of lessons."

"I didn't know her," Terri said, "but I'm told Mr. Munroe's late wife played the piano very well."

Mrs. Reed looked at me with sympathy. I knew that was why Terri had mentioned it. "Oh my. I didn't realize you'd lost your wife. You know what it's like, then."

I nodded. "I wouldn't wish it on anybody."

"No. Especially not the first year, my goodness." She turned to Judy and said, "Darling, play something nice for our guests."

Judy didn't respond. She continued looking through the sheet music.

With a faint rattle of crystal, Emma Jean brought in our beverages on a tray.

"Thank you, sweetheart," Mrs. Reed said. "And if you could just put that in the mailbox?" She gestured toward the envelope on the piano.

"Of course."

After Emma Jean left, Mrs. Reed began the ritual of polite chitchat about whether our drinks were sufficient or did we need anything else. Then a pause came that felt like an opportunity to take the conversation in a more pertinent direction.

"You know, Mrs. Reed," I said, "if I may, I was hoping we could touch on some questions I had about your late husband and what happened to him."

"Yes, of course."

"We are so sorry about your loss," Terri said.

As Mrs. Reed thanked her, Judy suddenly began to play the piano. The hairs on the back of my neck stood up. She'd chosen a melancholy classical piece called "Für Elise," meaning "For Elise," which was my wife's name. The first time I'd ever heard it was when Elise played it for me while we were dating.

I searched my memory, but I had no recollection of telling Judy my wife's name.

I chalked it up to coincidence—the piece was very well-known—and refocused on Mrs. Reed. She was saying, "It was kind of a one-two punch, really. First we lost him, and then..."

She gestured to Judy and shook her head. Her pleasant-hostess mask slipped, and for a second, she looked exhausted.

Judy continued playing.

"Mrs. Reed, I cannot imagine," Terri said. "You've been through so much."

"We have. Yes, we really have. Thank you. I mean... These accusations against my daughter are positively ludicrous, and to be hit with them at a time like that... it was such a shock. At first I thought someone was just trying to scare us off our lawsuit, but it's still going. I keep hoping to wake up from it all, like a bad dream."

Terri was nodding sympathetically. She tipped her head with faint curiosity and asked, "Your lawsuit?"

I'd seen a brief mention of a legal dispute in the files Dickenson's office had sent over, but no details, and Rachel hadn't found anything in the local court records.

"Oh, yes," Mrs. Reed said in a tired voice. "Against the hospital. It wasn't exactly a lawsuit—our lawyer never got so far as to file anything with the court. It was just some back-and-forth with their lawyers, until we realized we were wrong."

"That sounds so hard. What did you realize you were wrong about?"

I appreciated Terri for a lot of reasons. Her ability to elicit information gently was one of them.

"Well, when Conway was taken to the hospital—I should say, right from when the paramedics arrived—the assumption was it was a heart attack. Because a man his age who... collapses... that's the assumption."

"Of course," Terri said. "He was sixty-three, wasn't he?"

"Yes, that's right. And in, you know, normal shape for a man his age. You can see there."

She pointed at a framed picture on the wall. Conway Reed was standing in a field, wearing a pair of chinos, a button-down shirt, and a blazer. He was a broad-shouldered, strapping man, though he looked forty or fifty pounds overweight.

A nostalgic smile lit her face. "He was the last person you'd see at a marathon or a triathlon or whatever folks do these days. He didn't own a bicycle or even a pair of sneakers. He was a little too old-school for that."

She gazed at the photo for a second longer. My line of work had made me well aware that the surviving spouse of a murder victim was a potential suspect, but her affection and grief struck me as genuine.

"Can I ask," I said, "was he old-school about his phone, too? Like, not texting much, and—"

"Oh, yes. He was not a big texter. I mean, he must've been close to forty by the time he got his first cell phone, so…"

"Never developed the habit," I said, nodding. That explained why the cell phone records I'd found in the files were of near-zero interest. I'd worked on plenty of cases where a murder victim's phone contained crucial information, but this wasn't one of them.

I took a sip of sweet tea and then asked, "So the legal back-and-forth with the hospital, was that a concern on your part that they'd misdiag-nosed him? Or delayed the care that he needed?"

"Yes. You know," Mrs. Reed waved one hand as if to say it was very sad, but it was water under the bridge, "at the time we thought that if they'd realized what was really going on with him, they could've started the proper treatment sooner, and he might've been saved. And they ought to have figured it out, I thought. A few years back, he was in the hospital for a couple of days, and when I visited him, I saw the allergy pop up in a red box right at the top of the computer screen when the nurse pulled up his records."

"Mm." Terri shook her head. "That must've been *so* frustrating, thinking that they missed it."

"Oh, at the time, yes."

"But you came to realize it wasn't their fault?" I asked.

"A few months in, yes. Our lawyer had an outside expert look at everything, all the medical records, and he told us that there was some overlap in symptoms, so we really couldn't blame them for thinking it was a heart attack. When you go into anaphylaxis, it can affect your heart too. So, given his condition and the time it naturally took to get an ambulance out here, it wouldn't have made a difference."

I did a little mental math. This home was on the outskirts of town to the north, and the hospital was on the outskirts to the south. Even at the best of times, it would probably take more than twenty minutes to get to the ER from here.

"I apologize for my ignorance," Terri said, "and for making you go through this again, but was it not something that an EpiPen could've helped with?"

"It might have," Mrs. Reed said. "But it didn't cross my mind to suggest Judy use one. I hadn't seen him have an allergic reaction since, I don't know, thirty years ago? When we were first dating. It was terrifying, and after that, to avoid accidents, we made sure to never have any cephalosporin on hand."

"Nobody in the house ever used it?" I asked.

"Never. We told all our doctors, including Judy's pediatrician when she was little, that we wouldn't have it in the house, so they'd need to prescribe something else."

"But there was something y'all felt the paramedics ought to have noticed?"

"After the fact, yes. Once we saw the medical records. At the time, I couldn't even see him that well—he collapsed down at the bottom of the porch steps, beside his car. I couldn't get down there in my chair —the wheelchair ramp comes off the back deck, clear over on the other side of the house. So I just yelled for Judy and called 911." She paused, biting her lip, and looked out the window like she was trying to collect herself.

Judy finished the piece and said, in the nonchalant tone that I was getting used to, "It's hard for her to talk about this. He was out cold at the bottom of the steps, and the way he looked—"

"You were here at the time?" I asked.

"Yes. I come down almost every weekend, and sometimes during the week, to ride and take care of Mercator—"

"Mercator's her horse," Mrs. Reed said.

"Oh, did I not tell y'all that? Yes. Anyway, so Daddy was lying there unconscious when the ambulance got here, and I asked them to give me everything he had in his pockets. I didn't want his property to get lost at the hospital. They were busy working on him—his lips were blue, he looked real bad—so I kind of reached around them to get his wallet and his phone. Then they loaded him up and took him away."

"Uh-huh," I said. I envisioned Ginevra Barnes calling a paramedic to the stand to testify that the victim's emotionless daughter was ransacking her father's body while he lay dying on the ground. I always found it useful to play out in my mind how a trial might go.

Since taking this case, every scenario I'd come up with made Judy look bad.

"I still think we ought to have sued them," Judy said. "They didn't even try to treat the anaphylaxis until more than an hour after he keeled over—"

"Honey, please," her mother said.

"All I'm saying is, I was not impressed with that cardiologist." Judy started noodling around on the keyboard. "If Dr. Kassel is the best they've got, it's a sad situation. What a nothing little hospital."

"I'm sorry, could you spell the cardiologist's name?" I had my pen ready. I was going to need to talk to Conway's doctor, if he was willing.

Judy spelled it and then went back to her rant. "I even looked at the autopsy photos," she said, over a bright major chord. "He was covered with these purple blotches—how do you look at that and think heart attack? It's malpractice, and it makes me wonder how many other folks they've killed. We should've sued them. You know money's the only thing some folks listen to."

Mrs. Reed closed her eyes for a second, and her jaw tightened like she was clenching her teeth. I recognized the universal Southern body language that meant "Lord, give me strength." If Judy's personality tried even her own mother's patience, I was not going to be able to get a jury to warm to her.

And I was not happy to see that she kept on talking after her mother asked her to stop. Signaling to a witness to let them know to put a lid on it could be important at trial, but it only worked if the witness listened.

"Honey, would you mind going to the kitchen for another pitcher of

89

tea?" Mrs. Reed said. "Emma Jean's gone to the laundry room, and I don't want our guests getting thirsty."

My normal response to that would be to protest that the host shouldn't go to any such trouble, but I sensed that Mrs. Reed was trying to get a moment alone with us. Terri must've read it the same way. We stayed quiet.

As soon as Judy left the room, Mrs. Reed touched the joystick of her wheelchair to move closer to us and murmured, "I am terrified for her. I know what the evidence is—they've got her medical records, and it's all right there in black and white. I don't understand why she can't just say that she *did* pick up those antibiotics, but she didn't realize what they were, and it was all a terrible mistake."

"You think she could've done that?" I asked. "Not realized what they were?"

"Well, sure! Aren't there all sorts of different brand names for those things?"

"For different antibiotics, you mean? Yes, I suppose so." I was not well-versed in pharmaceuticals, but I'd looked a few things up when I took the case.

"Yes indeed. Now, I don't have any type of medical background, but I sure did have to learn a few things because of my husband's allergy. And I know you're not going to see a bottle with 'cephalosporin' printed on it in big letters. It might not even have 'ceph' anywhere in the name."

"You're right. That's definitely something to consider." I couldn't say much about her daughter's case without breaking attorney-client privilege, but she had a point. And she clearly was desperate to help, so I said, "I apologize for having to remind you of all this, but were you the executor of your husband's estate, or did you work with whoever was?"

"Oh, no. I let the named executor handle every bit of that. I suppose I could've helped, since I learned a lot about estate planning and so forth for my charity—we get a lot of bequests; it's a pretty significant part of our fundraising. But I was in no shape for that after Conway died. I had movers bring everything from his work back to the house, and anything that looked financial, I sent to the executor."

"I understand. And what was there that you didn't send?"

"Oh, you know. Family photos, books, his laptop."

"His laptop? Did you ever take a look at what was on there?"

"No, no. It was too much for me at that point. And in any case, he had passwords on everything, so—" Before she could finish, Judy came back in with a full pitcher on a tray. Mrs. Reed smiled up at her. "Oh, thank you, honey. Just set that down right over here."

I tucked away the question Mrs. Reed had asked about the meds. I was going to need to find out from Judy why she was so certain she hadn't accidentally brought a cephalosporin into the home, but I didn't want to ask right now, because I didn't want her to guess what her mother had told us.

As Judy poured her some more tea, Mrs. Reed said, "My husband had all our estate planning done by an attorney here in town, and that's who he named as the executor."

"Okay. And do you happen to know if an estate tax return was filed?" I figured one had been, since, as Roy had explained to me, they were required on any estate worth more than about $12 million.

"I don't," she said. "I think they filed something called... maybe an inventory? Would that be helpful?"

"Not so much, unfortunately. That's just a list of his probate assets. What we want is a complete list, or at least fairly complete, of every-body who benefited financially from his death."

"Wouldn't his will give you that?" she asked.

"Well, the thing is, a will only lists the heirs who receive the things that pass through his probate estate. A lot of assets don't go through probate—like anything that was put in a trust, or life insurance, or his 401(k), things like that."

"That doesn't seem right," Judy said in a tone of moral certainty. "A will ought to include everything. It seems dishonest otherwise. The more you say about how the law works, the less sense it makes."

I looked at her, at a loss for how to respond. Her pronouncements on the American legal system were of zero utility to me in figuring out how to win her case.

Terri saw the problem. She pointed at a photo on the wall of Judy on horseback and asked, with great interest, "Judy, is that Mercator?"

"Yes, that's him."

Terri got up and walked over to the photo. Judy followed, and I breathed a sigh of relief. If anyone could keep Judy talking, it was Terri. I returned to my conversation with Mrs. Reed. "Anyway, that tax return—"

"Yes. Should I reach out and get a copy?"

"If you could ask, it'd be helpful. Do you have a good relationship with that attorney?"

"Oh, good enough, why?"

"Well, he's not required to give you the return."

"My goodness. Well, I'll see what I can do." She smiled in a way that told me she'd understood her mission: Turn up the wattage on her Southern charm and get those papers.

I smiled back and said, "I'm sure you'll do just fine."

"You know what, Mama," Judy said—she'd turned away from the photo of her horse to look back at us—"I think they ought to see the stable. I'll take them down."

"Oh, that'll be nice," Mrs. Reed said.

We said our farewells, and then Judy led the two of us on a hike across the back pasture. Over a hill, out of sight from the house, we reached a paddock near a fancy barn. Judy pointed out her own horse, a reddish-brown one with a black mane, as well as her father's gray one and four others that they boarded for friends.

"We used to have more," she said. "My father had two racehorses. But we sold those after he passed." She leaned on the top rail of the white fence surrounding the paddock. I stood between her and Terri, a step back from the fence; three horses were running around inside, and I didn't want to get too close.

"Who's that there?" I asked. A young man had gotten the gray horse out of the paddock and tethered it to a stand by the barn to brush it.

"That's Paul. He's our groom."

I doubted I was ever going to get used to families that had staff. "He know your father?"

"Not well. He's one of Emma Jean's nephews. She's the best aide my mother's ever had, so when we were looking for a groom, we asked if she knew anybody. But my daddy didn't ride much in recent years, and he had trainers for the racehorses. I got in the habit of riding Argent as well as Mercator, to keep him exercised. Daddy mostly liked to watch the races."

"Uh-huh. So, is this the stable you were talking about when you said he brought his mistress out before the Kentucky Derby?"

"Yes. They parked right down there." She pointed to a small parking area.

"Do you happen to know when they got together? How long before his passing?"

Judy laughed darkly. "No, I didn't make a habit of keeping a calendar of my father's adulteries."

"Did you say he brought a mistress to… your *home*?" Terri asked. She sounded shocked, although I knew the tone was for Judy's benefit. Terri had seen far worse.

"Yes! It was outrageous," Judy said. "So disrespectful." It was strange how this topic, unlike any other we'd discussed, put some emotion into her voice.

"Mm-hmm," Terri said. "That must have been hard. How did your mother respond?"

Judy didn't reply right away. I glanced at her. She was squinting at something in the middle distance. Thinking, maybe. It was hard to tell with her.

"You know," she finally said, still staring off toward the barn, "a lot of folks seem to think my mother broke more than her back in the accident."

She didn't say anything else for a few seconds, so I asked, "How do you mean?"

"They see her in a wheelchair, and they act like she can't think right anymore. But she can, of course. The wheelchair's for her legs, not her brain!"

"I hear you on that," Terri said. "I've seen how folks in wheelchairs get treated."

"It's like she's not a person anymore," Judy said. "Or not an adult. When we go to restaurants, the waiters ask *me* for her order. Even at doctor's appointments, if I go in with her, they talk to me instead. And

94

the things some folks said about my father... as if she'd understand that he had to satisfy his needs elsewhere. Like she should be fine with that. But she wasn't."

"No, of course not," Terri said. She brushed against my arm, and I glanced at her. She was giving me a look.

That look meant *uh-oh*.

8

DECEMBER 22, 2022

On Thursday morning, as I was heading out of the office to drive to Charleston, Rachel stopped me. "Since I'll be out from tomorrow," she said, "I did the accounts and made sure this month's bills were paid."

"Thank you." Nothing urgent was happening over the holidays—no trials or hearings—so I'd given her the rest of the month off to be with her family.

"Oh, of course," she said. "Since we ran through LaDonna's retainer already, I drafted a letter asking her to top it back up. If you're in a hurry, you just head out now and you can sign and send it when you get back—but I wanted to remind you, since I won't be here." She put the letter up on the counter that ran along the front of her desk.

"Thanks again for doing the accounts and typing that up," I said, "but let's not send that. Let her and her kid enjoy Christmas. We're doing fine."

"Oh, okay. I'm sorry. I just thought, especially with Terri's bill probably coming in by the end of the month—"

Terri had been doing what she did, digging up intel to try and help both LaDonna and Judy. She was a hell of a PI, and accordingly, she was not cheap.

"Not a problem, nothing to apologize for," I said. "You're trying to keep this place afloat, and I appreciate that. But we'll be okay without this."

In Charleston, I had an appointment with the federal prosecutor after lunch, but first I was meeting Noah at the Starbucks on the ground floor of his office building to treat him to a sandwich and coffee. I threw my jacket on a chair to claim a table, and I was still waiting in line when he walked in. It did something to me to see Noah wearing suit pants and a button-down shirt, like the young professional he was.

He came over, and I gave him a quick hug. "Man, you look like a grown-up now. When did that happen?"

He shrugged, smiling. "I don't know why this job requires dressing up." He worked for a private detective firm. "I suppose my first paycheck helped make up for the annoyance."

"Yeah, that's a good feeling." We took our drinks and sandwiches to the table and talked about Christmas plans and his job for a little bit. Twenty minutes later, he had to go. "You on a stakeout?" I asked.

"I wish."

I kept my relief to myself. I didn't think I was ever going to get past the conflict between my relief that he'd found a career path he was interested in and my concern that the one he'd chosen had a dangerous side. "You don't get enough of those?"

"No, I get all the jobs the other guys don't want. Lots of paper pushing."

"The guys with more seniority?"

He nodded and started gathering his napkins and other trash.

"You find yourself a mentor yet?"

"I don't know, kind of."

"Well, you find one that's more than 'kind of.' Somebody you can look up to, who respects you and gives you interesting work. And if you can't find one where you are, stick it out for a year and then start looking for something else."

"I know, I know." I had given him the same advice before. Apparently he'd heard it enough.

He came back from ditching his trash, I stood up, and we shook hands to say goodbye. As he turned to walk away, I said, "You stay safe, now."

"Yeah, yeah." He waved one hand dismissively.

He might be an adult, I thought, but not enough of one to have lost his belief in his own immortality. I mentally thanked his higher-ups for sticking him with the paper-pushing jobs and hoped he didn't lose his youthful confidence the hard way.

As I walked back to my car, I checked my phone on the off chance I'd heard back from Dr. Kassel. I'd left him a message two days earlier asking if we could have a short meeting about the Conway Reed case.

He hadn't responded. Like most folks in his economic bracket, he knew his rights—or he'd paid a lawyer to tell him what they were. Getting folks to talk to me was usually easier when they had less money and less education. They often seemed a little intimidated when I said I was an attorney, like they were afraid they'd get in trouble if they didn't cooperate. That was not a problem Dr. Kassel had.

I drove over to the French Quarter and parked a few blocks from the United States Attorney's Office. As I walked to Meeting Street, for once I didn't miss living in Charleston. The day was overcast, and the lack of sunlight drained the city of some of its charm. As I came around the last corner, the view got worse. The blank office building that housed the USAO would've been soulless even if the sun were out.

I went through security and took the stairs up, patting myself on the back for making the healthy choice. Back when I lived in the city, I'd visited Cardozo at work often enough to know my way around. On the second floor, I popped the door open, swung into the hallway, and nearly collided with, of all people, LaRue. Not a good way to kick off our meeting.

I apologized. He was polite, but I could see a hint of suspicion in him. "Let me take you over to the waiting room," he said, with what I thought of as a business smile: appropriate, impersonal, nothing genuine in it. "It's around the corner here. Were you lost?" In other words, what the hell was I doing back there?

"No, I took the stairs. I like to get a little exercise."

"Uh-huh. Well, so you know, as a rule, we prefer visitors to use the elevator."

"Sorry. I used to be an assistant solicitor here in town, and I was friends with a couple of guys over here, so I got to know the building—"

"Oh, yes," he said, as we reached the waiting room. "I'm aware of your past." His smile had a little bite to it; he was putting me in my place. "Anyway," he said, "I'll be with you momentarily." He left me there, then came back and got me one minute before our appointed meeting time.

99

He showed me into his office, where a single manila folder lay all by itself on the spotless desk. Nothing cluttered his floor, none of the shoes, briefcase, junk mail, and discarded take-out bags that infested my office. It was clear that he and I were two different species.

After the standard chitchat, he asked, "So, what are your client's thoughts about the offer?" He'd proposed a plea deal under which LaDonna would plead guilty to one count of simple possession and one of false statements relating to healthcare, and he'd recommend eighteen months in federal prison, instead of the five to ten years she was looking at otherwise.

"Well, she certainly appreciates that you've got some flexibility," I said. "But let me share where she's coming from. First off, there's her nursing license. We feel a plea on the false statements charge would leave her, if anything, even more unemployable in healthcare than simple possession would. But the main issue is, she's a single mother of a four-year-old girl, and the father's not in the picture, so anything that carries jail time means that child goes into foster care—"

"I hear you," he said with a shrug that said it was out of his hands. "I hear that sort of thing a lot. It's the unfortunate consequence of a parent choosing, for whatever reason, to violate the law."

"Sure," I agreed. "Actions have consequences. And if we were talking about that guy who came down from New Jersey with two thousand some-odd doses of fentanyl to poison our local drug users with, I'd—"

"I'm sorry, who?" He looked like that wasn't ringing any bells. I recalled what my caseload had been like when I was a prosecutor; in a job like his, there was no way to keep all the details top of mind.

"The one whose preliminary hearing was right before my client's. Rented a motel room and tried to sell to some undercover officers?"

"Oh! Him. Yeah." He shook his head, flicking his eyebrows up and down in a way that told me he found that particular defendant even stupider than most.

"Right. If this were about him," I said, "I would not be here having this conversation. A guy like that, selling instant death on the streets of Charleston—nobody ought to be arguing to ease up on his consequences. But the charges against my client are not remotely in that league."

"Well, and neither are the penalties. Look, maybe drug crimes aren't your specialty, but fortunately or unfortunately for me, that is my focus. I'm glad that the nurses who steal narcotics don't usually end up causing anybody's death, at least not directly, but it's still an absolute betrayal of the public's trust."

He was on a roll—this was clearly something he cared about. I wanted to find out what made him tick, so I said, "Oh, when it happens, yes, it absolutely is. Are you seeing a lot of that type of crime?"

"I've got six of them at various stages right now. It's a scourge. One of them's going to trial next month. And last year I handled two from that same hospital alone, if that gives you an idea."

"Basking Rock Hospital?"

He nodded.

"My goodness," I said. "Yeah, I haven't had one of these before, and I certainly don't mean to minimize what you're dealing with."

"Well, good."

I filed away the fact that my small, local hospital had had two cases of this recently, plus LaDonna's charges. That seemed high to me, but now was not the time to get into that.

"Anyway, I think the main point here for me," I said, "is that we've got a hospital that's obviously got some issues with their drug storage, in terms of computer security. Everybody enters their password on that big screen right out in the hallway, like we saw in that photo you showed. Jurors know what can happen if you let folks see you enter your ATM password, for instance, and that's essentially what's happening there."

He shrugged like we were going to have to agree to disagree.

"And then on top of that," I said, "this is a woman with no priors, negative drug screen, no history of abuse—"

"In my experience, those tend to be the cases where she's selling it on the side. Or procuring on behalf of someone else."

"Or she's not procuring it at all, and she's got nothing to do with what happened, because somebody else stole medications under her log-in. Yeah, those three options would be the possibilities."

"Look, Mr. Munroe, if there were evidence that anybody else on that unit was involved, I would've charged accordingly."

Something in the way he said that gave me the sense that there was something he wasn't telling me. What got my attention was the hint of emphasis he put on *that unit*.

"Is there somebody you're looking at who's *not* on that unit?" I asked.

He regarded me for a moment without speaking.

I kept my expression calm, looking at him like I was prepared to wait all day. Meanwhile, I was ransacking my brain for the name of the seventy-year-old Supreme Court case that I thought might be relevant here. I didn't normally practice in federal court, and my mental library of South Carolina criminal case law was of no use here.

It came to me. "Even if you don't feel that information needs to come out with your *Brady* disclosures, assuming you've got some," I said, "there's also *Roviaro v. United States* to contend with. Among others."

The *Roviaro* case expanded a defendant's right to know informants' identities. I couldn't think of any other precedent, but I threw in "among others" on the assumption that there had to be some.

LaRue shrugged and leaned back in his chair. "Well," he said, "you'll get it sooner or later, I suppose. What I'll tell you for now is, her boyfriend might be of interest to you. If we proceed the way I'm expecting to, you'll get more details when the time comes for those disclosures."

I nodded like I knew what he was talking about.

I didn't.

I'd asked LaDonna for the names of everybody she could think of who might be able to speak to anything remotely relevant—her work habits, her character, everything. As part of my process for jogging a client's memory, one of my first questions was always about spouses or partners—casual or otherwise. When I'd asked if she had a boyfriend, she'd said no.

We talked a little longer. LaRue didn't budge. I turned down the plea deal.

9

DECEMBER 22, 2022

After leaving LaRue's office, I walked over to Waterfront Park to meet Terri. She was up in town on some other job—I was not the only person, or for that matter the only lawyer, that she worked for—and I'd thought it'd be more fun to meet her here to catch up on what she'd learned than in our usual hometown haunts.

I was a little early, so I stopped by a café to get each of us a coffee. When I got to the park, I saw her on the far side of the fancy three-tiered Pineapple Fountain, talking on her phone. The sun had come out from behind the clouds, so the water was sparkling as it fell. She was laughing, and then she saw me, waved, and got off the phone.

I rounded the fountain and said, "Hey! Got you a cappuccino." I knew her coffee order, and which local café chain she liked.

"Like my brain needs to move even faster right now." She smiled and took it. "Thank you."

We started walking. A big cruise ship was docked at the pier just north of us, so rather than spend the whole walk staring at it, we turned south when we got close to the river. I took a sip of my coffee and asked, "You got a lot going on?"

"Oh, nothing special. A little industrial espionage, a little adultery. People being sordid, as usual." She shrugged and tried to laugh, but I could see she was tired. If she hadn't been, I might've made a joke about how people doing bad things was the reason we had jobs.

"You ever take a vacation?" I asked. "I hear they're good for the soul."

That made her laugh. "I know you're not speaking from experience."

"No, but I've heard lying on the beach is a thing some folks do."

"I can't remember the last time I did that." She sighed. "Yeah, I guess I could call it a day after this."

"You do that," I said.

"Maybe I will. So, what do you want first, the heiress or the nurse?"

"Let's go with the nurse. That's who my meeting was about just now. Apparently her boyfriend, who I didn't even know existed, might be relevant somehow. You got anything about him?"

"You mean her ex-boyfriend?"

"Maybe," I said.

"Yeah, I dug into what little social media she's got and followed up on her connections. It looks like she was seeing a guy, but it was over by September. Maybe late August."

"Huh. Right after the meds were stolen. I wonder if they broke up before or after she was accused."

"Something to ask her, for sure. Especially since he does have a couple of drug arrests and one conviction. Just for possession, the lowest possible misdemeanor. None of it was recent, though."

"Street or pharma?"

"The conviction was weed, but the arrest was fake pharma. You know the drill: it looks like a legit pain reliever, but it's fentanyl."

"Damn, that stuff is everywhere. How'd he get off?"

"That's not in the record, but it was a vehicle stop. Him and some friends."

"Oh. Probably claimed it wasn't his and ratted out his friends."

"Yeah, probably. And I don't know if there's a connection, but the new girlfriend on his social media works at the same place your client does. Another nurse."

"Huh. Speaking of her place of work," I said, "the prosecutor let slip that there've been two other cases along the same lines there in the past year or so."

"Same type of accusations, you mean?" We turned onto the public pier and looked out at the water.

"Stolen meds, yeah. You didn't come across anything about those?"

"No, but I'll see what I can find."

Seagulls squawked. In the distance, the white cables on the suspension bridge blurred together, making them look like two white triangles or the sails of a giant boat. I had to squint to see them correctly. I wondered if the illusion was intentional. It must've been; an architect wouldn't just happen to do that by accident.

A thought came to me. Somehow shifting focus back and forth while looking at the bridge had triggered it. "That article you sent over this morning," I said. "Why'd they have that cardiac guy talking about her case?"

"Oh, Dr. Kassel? Instead of the hospital CEO, you mean? Or somebody like that?"

"Yeah."

"Don't you know he's some kind of local hero? He's big on serving the underserved, all the Medicaid and Medicare patients who don't normally get good care at all—his thing is giving them the same care he gives the old rich guys. He does a lot of public speaking for the hospital. And, I mean, did you see the photo?"

If I had, I didn't remember it. "I guess I must have, but I was in a hurry. Why?"

"The guy looks like Superman. Square jaw, dark hair, broad shoulders. Everybody loves him."

I rolled my eyes.

"Except you," she added, teasing.

I laughed. "Well, what do you want? I mean, helping the poor is great, I've got to grant him that. But a guy who must earn at least half a million a year, and he's quoted respectfully in the news, and on top of that, he looks like Superman? Yeah, I hate him already."

With a smile, she said, "I hope you manage to keep that to yourself whenever you interview him."

"*If* ever. I've left a couple messages. He hasn't called back."

"The solicitor probably gave him a helpful reminder that he wasn't obligated to talk to the defense."

"Somebody did. Guy who earns half a million a year probably has his own lawyer to talk to." We left the pier and continued down the gravel path.

Terri scanned the horizon and said, "Try the bias thing. Leave him a message that says you want to make sure he's not biased against the defense."

"That could backfire."

"And? Backfiring just means he doesn't talk to you. Which is where you are right now."

"True."

"He's got a bunch of videos online. All professional stuff about the hospital, heart health and that type of thing. Watch a couple of them, get a sense of his personality. Then figure out exactly what message to leave. I'm sure you'll find the right tone."

"Not a bad idea."

A seagull squawked and gave me a sudden flashback to walking along this same path, years ago, with Elise. It was a punch in the gut. I put it out of my mind.

"Anyway," I said, "I know you're swamped, so let's run through what you've got on the heiress so I can let you go."

A couple walking in the opposite direction was getting close. I assumed that's why Terri shifted to a light, faintly bored voice when she said, "I know you were wondering how she still has her job."

"Oh, yeah." I'd mentioned my surprise at that. In my experience, being charged with murder tended to scare off employers.

"So I did my usual deep dive, and I found an LLC she registered that's just called—"

She stopped herself before saying it.

"It's named like a person," she said. "It's her first name and her mother's maiden name, plus the LLC."

"Huh."

"Yeah, so I ran a search on that. And it looks like that's how she operates. She doesn't go by her real name in business. She's got a LinkedIn page under that name."

"Wait, her LinkedIn profile shows a fake name?"

"I mean, it's not technically fake. It's the real name of her business. But yeah, if I saw a page like that, I'd assume that was her name and she just decided to run her business through an LLC."

"So would I. I guess that would explain why she's still working. Even if folks saw her case in the news, they wouldn't necessarily connect it to her."

"Mm-hmm. I'm sure if they were local, they'd know. But she's got testimonials from all over the place. I doubt some company in, like, Seattle is paying attention to South Carolina crime news."

"And even if they are, Fourth is keeping things pretty well under wraps." Dabney Barnes IV tended to underpublicize criminal cases involving the local elite. I shook my head. "I do not like this. If she were a married woman working under her maiden name, that'd be fine. But using a name that's not hers at all?" I glanced around. We were now at least a hundred feet from the couple, and even farther from anybody else. Still, I said quietly, "It's not going to be hard for the prosecutor to make her look… sneaky, you know? Deceptive."

"Yeah, you don't want that."

In theory, juries were only supposed to examine the facts in evidence, but in practice, as I'd heard many times in post-verdict questioning, they had a hard time convicting unless they could convince themselves that the defendant was the type of person who would commit the crime charged.

"I mean, this is a poisoning," I said.

"Mm-hmm. Which is a sneaky kind of crime."

I stopped walking. "Dammit," I said. "I think Roy's wrong."

"Roy? What'd he say?"

I started walking again. "Oh, he has this idea that murdering someone you know, somebody close to you, is pretty much always a crime of passion. That there's lots of emotion behind it. Like, after years of jealousy or resentment or whatever, you finally snap."

"I mean, that's fair. Usually."

"Right, but poisoning? That's calculated. It's cold. And I don't think the prosecutor's going to have any problem convincing the jury that this client is cold."

"Mm, you know, about that. I was thinking. Have you asked her if she's neurodivergent? Like, has she been diagnosed?"

"*Oh.*" I felt like kicking myself. I'd been so irritated by Judy's personality that I hadn't even tried to think of a more charitable interpretation.

"I take it that's a no?"

"Yeah, I can't believe that didn't even occur to me." I thought about it. "We'd need a medical expert. A psychologist, probably."

"To explain that to the jury? Mm-hmm."

"Yeah. That could make all the difference."

I could finally picture a positive moment at Judy's trial: the expert up on the stand, walking the jury through the reasons they shouldn't judge her on her personality or her odd reactions to events. She wasn't an emotionless killer who focused on her father's assets while he was dying; she was just neurodivergent. Hyperlogical.

If that was the explanation, anyway. I hoped it was true.

"Okay, I do have to get going pretty soon," Terri said, "and I think we're far enough from that couple that I can get to the big stuff now."

"There's bigger stuff?"

"Maybe. I leaned on some friends of mine who are still on the force, and they told me something about that mistress."

"Oh, what's that?"

"She got questioned after he died. Standard procedure—you know how they do things when the victim is rich."

I laughed. "Oh yeah, they can be real thorough."

"Mm-hmm. So, she told them a few things."

"Such as?"

"First off, she said the victim had made an appointment to change his will."

"Change it in her favor, I suppose? Okay."

"He had an appointment to meet with his lawyer three days after he died, she said."

"Okay, that's not great, but even assuming that was true, why would his lawyer appointments be something my client would've known about?"

"Well, first off, the guy I talked with was pretty sure it was true. He hadn't reached out to the lawyer himself, but he thought somebody had. I figured you could get the lawyer's name from the widow and confirm that."

"Yeah, I will." I pulled a miniature notebook out of my shirt pocket and jotted that down as we walked.

Terri smiled. "Don't you have a to-do list on your phone?"

"I don't trust those things," I said. "If I want it on my phone, I'll take a picture of this and text it to myself."

"Sometimes you act about twenty years older than you are."

"I'm mature. Seasoned."

I saw her laugh, but a gust of wind drowned out the sound. I buttoned my jacket. What little winter we ever had here was in that wind.

"Anyway," Terri said, zipping up her fleece, "as for how your client would know her daddy was seeing his lawyer, get this: the mistress says *she* told her. The week before he died."

I stopped walking and looked at her. "Wait, the mistress told the daughter—what, that the will was going to be changed? Oh, come on!"

"Mm-hmm, it's unusual." From her tone, she didn't buy it either.

"To say the least! What mistress has ever been stupid enough to tell her rich guy's family—in advance, for God's sake!—that she was about to take their money?"

"Right? She's not stupid, and she's thirty years old, not some impulsive teenager. And she knows her way around money."

I realized I knew nothing about Alanna Carpenter. "What is it that she does?"

"It's all in the dossier I emailed you about two hours ago. She has an accounting degree from Vanderbilt. She's some type of financial consultant."

"Okay, I'm sorry; there is no way this woman told my client that the will was about to be changed."

"Nope."

"If she was going to tell her at all—and I don't know why the heck she would, except maybe to rub their noses in it—at least wait until after the deed is done, right?"

"You would think."

"But telling that to the cops is sure a good way to sic them on my client."

"Yes, it is. She wrapped up a nice big motive like a Christmas present."

"Why would the cops have *believed* her story, though? They would've put a real solid detective on a case like this, right off the bat. Not somebody green."

"Oh, she's got extra cred. She's from a police family. Father and brother."

"What, here in town?"

"No, up in Columbia. Her dad's retired."

I gave a disgusted sigh. If Alanna wanted to throw Judy under the bus, she had a very clear shot. The only obstacle, the only reason Judy wasn't already roadkill, was money. With that, she'd been able to hire Dickenson and now me.

I stepped over to the side of the pathway and kicked a little gravel into the water. I was going to need to talk to this Alanna Carpenter and get a sense of her personality—maybe she regularly did irrational things? —but it was hard to imagine what possible reason an older man's mistress would have to warn his family that he was about to write her into his will.

"You know, sometimes," I said, looking out at the water, "folks make up a story to sic the cops on somebody because they truly believe that person did it. And they want to make sure the cops get him, or in this case, her."

"Sometimes," Terri said. Her tone was skeptical.

"Other times, they know what really happened, and they want to throw the cops off the scent."

"Yep."

No skepticism there.

10

DECEMBER 24, 2022

Terri's dossier was thorough, as usual. It appeared that being a financial consultant with a side gig as a rich man's mistress paid well: Alanna Carpenter lived in a home she'd had custom built on the North Side, the most expensive part of town, and she drove a red Jaguar. Not bad for a thirty-year-old.

I had my own house now, about one-third the value of hers, and I was sitting in my home office looking at a photo of her on my bulletin board. When I'd moved into this place, I'd put corkboard up on all the walls of one of the bedrooms so I'd have plenty of room to pin up maps, photos, and whatever else seemed useful for a case. It was where I came to think.

I liked to run pieces of string from a person's photo to all the other people and places they were connected with. Seeing how people fit together sometimes helped me figure things out. Judy and her parents had strings connecting them to each other and more connecting them to Roy and a few other lawyers and friends. Conway also had a couple of business partners. Strings ran between the Reeds and a photo of the hospital—Conway because he'd died there, Judy because the doctor who'd testified about prescribing her cephalosporin worked there, Mrs. Reed because she'd gotten into a dispute with them that almost turned into a lawsuit.

Terri had dug up some dirt, so Conway also had strings linking him to two women he'd had flings with. They were both in the blow-up doll vein: busty, blonde, marginally employed. A stripper, and a waitress at a place off the highway called Knockers. I needed to talk to people who knew Conway in ways that his family did not, so Terri was investigating what shifts these women worked. Her take was that the stripper might be the best bet for a conversation. We could pay for a private dance, and once we got into the room with her, she'd probably be relieved to find out that all we wanted to do was talk.

From the photos Terri had provided, Conway seemed to have a type, but Alanna was different. Attractive, but brunette, professionally styled, with an actual career.

I still didn't know how they'd gotten together or where they'd met. I'd called her at the number Terri had found, but when I introduced myself, she excused herself and hung up the phone.

And now it was Christmas Eve. I'd just finished breakfast, and according to the text from Terri that I'd read over my second cup of coffee, the red Jaguar had left Alanna's house the night before and hadn't returned. It looked like she'd gone out of town for the holidays.

I drained my coffee and looked at the corkboard again. What struck me about Alanna's photo, besides the fact that she looked so different from Conway's flings, was the lack of connections. Apart from Conway, only two strings linked her to anyone else: one to a Post-it on which I'd written "Cop Brother" and the other to one that said "Retired Cop Dad." Terri hadn't been able to find any other confirmed relatives. Locating family could be hard when the last name was common, and the local grapevine was no use, because Alanna wasn't from this part of the state.

The strange thing, though, was that Terri also hadn't flushed out any exes, friends, or old bosses. No lawsuits, no criminal record, not even any traffic stops. She'd tracked Alanna from her Vanderbilt graduation to a job at some big consulting firm in Atlanta, but after that job —which had lasted three years—there was nothing. Alanna wasn't on social media under any name Terri had been able to find, and although her financial consulting website looked very professional, it didn't have any testimonials or client lists. There was nothing to follow up on, and we couldn't figure out what had brought her to Basking Rock.

I heard yapping from the yard below and went down to bring Squatter inside. I still had a little more work to cram in before the holiday began; Terri was coming over soon. She'd managed to get one of the nurses LaDonna had worked with to agree to talk to us.

Now that I had a fenced backyard, Squatter could roam, although he was too old to care much about roaming anymore. Usually I found him curled up napping in the shade of my crab apple tree, but he was up and barking now, because a squirrel was chittering at him from a branch of the neighbor's magnolia.

"Sorry, buddy," I said, picking him up. "You've got to come guard the house now. I'm going out for a little while. Noah's coming over later, though. He'll be here by dinnertime." Noah was driving down from Charleston to spend Christmas with me, or maybe with Squatter. I was pretty sure he missed the dog more.

Back inside, as I was pouring a fresh bowl of kibble, Terri texted to say she was out front. I went out and got into her green Subaru, and she took off while I was still buckling in.

"Sorry I'm a little late," she said. "Lot of last-minute stuff to do before I leave."

"No problem. You going to see your sister for the holidays?"

"Just Christmas. Noah's coming in to see you, right?"

"Yeah, he's driving down this afternoon."

"Oh, that's nice. Tell him I said hi."

"I will."

I waited a second, in case she wanted to tell me her New Year's plans, but her attention was on the traffic. She did a little zigzag to get around somebody's restored antique car, which was going at an antique speed.

"Thanks for getting that GPS thing," I said. "It'll be some help."

She'd pulled LaDonna's phone records and found that LaDonna, or at least her phone, had not been at the hospital on one of the three occasions when a theft she was accused of had occurred. "Good. You tell her yet?"

"Yeah. She was pretty excited. I let her stay that way—figured I'd let her enjoy her holiday, and we can get into the complexities after the new year. Although I did make sure she understood that this wasn't going to win the whole case for us."

She nodded. "Good call."

LaDonna had been overjoyed by the GPS evidence, which she saw as proof of her innocence. Terri and I both knew that it wasn't—evidence that someone's phone was not at a crime scene didn't prove that the person herself wasn't—but it would play well to a jury, and that was good news.

At a stop sign, Terri did a rolling stop, took off again, and asked, "You told her to keep the GPS thing to herself, right?"

"Always do."

The last thing we wanted was for a witness to get wind of our evidence and change their testimony in response. Some cards had to be kept close to the chest until it was time to play them at trial.

"So where's this lady we're talking to live?" I asked.

"Oh, we're not going to her house. We're meeting at her plot down at the community garden, over on the west side. She didn't want her neighbors seeing us."

"Okay. But aren't we at least as visible there? Out in the open?"

"It's pretty overgrown. And nobody gardens on Christmas Eve. They're too busy cooking. That's what she said, anyway."

"Makes sense, I guess."

The light up at the intersection turned yellow. Terri sighed and swerved down a side street.

"You taking a shortcut?"

"Christmas Eve traffic is not my thing." She downshifted, and we shot up a hill.

"I think you're the only person I know who still drives a standard transmission."

"Better control," she said, smiling at the road ahead. "And extra protection. Car thieves these days don't know how to drive a stick."

I laughed. "Yeah, there's a lot of things this generation doesn't know."

"For real. Anyway, this woman we're seeing, she's who LaDonna's boyfriend moved on to after they broke up."

I'd called LaDonna two days earlier to see if a little prodding would get her to revise her previous statement that she hadn't had any recent boyfriends. It did. His name was Desmond Brown, and he was the head of janitorial services at the hospital. She'd also told me which coworker of hers he'd dated next.

"They still together?" I asked.

"No. And their thing didn't end well."

"Oh, okay. LaDonna wasn't sure."

Terri peeled around a corner and down another side street, then asked, "Did you get into why she hadn't mentioned him before?"

"Not really. I don't judge her for it. People talk when they're ready."

"Mm-hmm. That is the truth."

"I actually got the sense she was a little ashamed of the whole thing. She did say it never got serious enough for her to introduce him to her daughter."

"Oh, okay. Well, good for her. I like the way she handles things."

"For sure." I was thinking of a couple of child-abuse cases I'd prosecuted where a single mom was not as careful about the men she brought around. I figured Terri had similar things in mind.

We finally got to a larger intersection, just as the light turned red. Terri stopped, closed her eyes, and did a moment of deep breathing.

A red car crossing the intersection made me think of Alanna's Jaguar. "About Alanna," I said. "She seems to be doing great on her own, financially. So what I can't get square in my head is, why would she be dating a man more than twice her age?" I looked over and saw her nodding thoughtfully.

"I mean, there are women who like older guys," she said.

"You don't sound that convinced."

She shrugged and accelerated as the light turned green. "I've been thinking about things," she said, "going over this case in my head, and I'm not convinced of much of *anything*. Especially about her. I don't know if she's got something to hide or if she's just a privacy freak. I did what I could—"

"Considering what a low profile she keeps, you did pretty damn good."

"Thank you," she said, "but *why*? Why am I investigating her, apart from the fact that Judy's a little obsessed with her, and we want the basic background on everybody who was close to the victim?"

"Yeah, she is… focused."

"Because it's her daddy's mistress. Okay, I get that. But when I put my cop hat on… would I have investigated her if I were the detective on this case? I'm really not sure." Terri had been a cop for a little over eight years, and even though she'd left the force more than a decade earlier, she still had a good handle on the mindset.

As she cruised around a bend, she added, "I know she said something a little weird to the police, kind of sicced them on Judy, but folks do that. Nobody reacts well when they get the news of a sudden death, and especially not when there's cops on their doorstep asking them questions about it."

The traffic ahead slowed to a crawl. Terri matched it, then glanced at me with a smile and said, "I mean, if you want to keep on paying me to dig up what I can on her, be my guest. But…"

I chuckled. "Yeah, well, I'm sure Judy would be happy to fund that. But put your police hat back on for a minute. If your job was just to solve the crime, what would you do?"

"Okay, well, step one, figure out if it *was* a crime. As opposed to he took it by accident somehow. And I know the police and the coroner determined that here, but, just me personally, I want to read what they had to say first. I'm not starting from that assumption."

"I hear you. I read the coroner's report, and it's... I mean, he had no doubts. Oh, and I'm talking with Dr. Kassel after the holidays, so I'll get his take on it."

"Oh, did you try the bias thing?"

"Yes, indeed. He called back and left a message saying that on the advice of hospital lawyers, he was willing to meet."

She smiled. I could see she was proud of herself.

"You know I always take your advice," I said.

"Mm-hmm."

"So I'll get his take, but it's only going to be one man's opinion. Doctors don't always agree. I'm driving down to Savannah next week to meet up with the medical expert Dickenson hired, see if there's any other reasonable theory."

"Good."

"You want to come with? Two brains are better than one. Especially when the extra brain is yours."

"I would, it's just, I'm not back until after the new year."

"Really? Man, I can't remember the last time you were gone so long."

"Here, hold tight." She launched us off the main drag down another side street. When we'd recovered from the g-forces, she continued— with the work topic, not the personal one. "Okay," she said. "Starting from the idea that it was a crime, obviously the next question is, who had a reason to do it? Right? Because this wasn't some crime of passion. This was cold."

"Right, right. So who would end up better off if he was dead?"

"You mean besides Judy?" She flashed me a *let's get real* look, then turned back to the road. "Not to mention her mother."

I was annoyed with myself. Normally, I would've already put my prosecutor hat on and looked hard at the potential guilt of everyone involved. You had to. Failing to see things from the prosecutor's point of view was a rookie mistake.

I'd only looked at Mrs. Reed for about ten seconds, and not hard. I was off my game. The fact that Roy liked Mrs. Reed and Judy—the fact that my friend and mentor of twenty-plus years had vouched for them both—had softened me up.

As Terri hit the gas, I said, "But the coroner's theory is that somebody put a cephalosporin capsule into his pill bottle. Could she open one of those child safety caps?"

Conway took daily meds for his high blood pressure, and his capsules were almost the same shade of blue as several of the most common cephalosporin capsules, including the brand Judy had been prescribed.

"Mrs. Reed?" Terri said. "Yeah, her hands work fine. Didn't you see her writing on that envelope when we got there?"

"Dammit," I said, shaking my head.

"I'm not saying I think she did it," she said. "Just, we need to know who would've gotten some benefit out of him being dead, and make sure we look at those people."

"Yep. That's where I was going when I asked Mrs. Reed about his estate, but—"

"But we got distracted. Mm-hmm. I think we need to reach out to her again. We need to know where his money went. Or where it's going—didn't she say the estate's still open?"

"Yeah."

"Okay, so how about you do that, and I'll dig harder on Alanna."

I agreed.

A minute later, watching the trees go by, I said, "I still think there's something a little off about her."

"Yeah. You've got to work hard to keep a profile as low as hers. I have to wonder why she wants it that way."

I didn't get over to the west side of town much anymore, but I'd lived nearby as a kid and remembered this area as a jungle. At some point it had been turned into community gardens where the folks in the neighborhood could supplement their food budgets by growing vegetables. The fencing and the plantings were a little ways uphill; the plots, which were decently sized, were separated by chicken wire fencing. Since it was wintertime, the plantings and surrounding grasses were at their least overgrown stage, but the place was still a thicket of green.

We pulled up beside a battered Toyota, the only other car in the dirt lot, and I saw a square of rough wood attached with wire to the chain-link gate. It was a handmade sign. Somebody had painted leaves and flowers across the top, and then, in capital letters, "West Side Community Gardens—We're All Neighbors Here."

I followed Terri along the fence at the back, and pretty soon we saw a thirtysomething Black woman working her plot of earth with a long-handled tool. She stopped and waved at us.

"Hey there, Keisha," Terri said. "Merry Christmas."

"Merry Christmas."

"This is Leland Munroe, LaDonna's lawyer."

As we said our hellos, Keisha wiped her palm on her pants to get the dirt off and reached out to shake hands.

"Those are some good-looking collard greens," I said, pointing at the cracked white laundry basket she'd put her harvest in.

"Yeah, they grow real nice up here," she said, sounding a little surprised that I knew what the plant was. In my blazer and button-down shirt, I probably didn't look the type.

"Leland was raised here on the west side," Terri said.

"Yeah, over on Apollo Drive." I'd had several other addresses as a kid, but they were mostly in the same general area, and the details weren't important. "My mama grew all our greens. I used to help her out in the garden."

"Oh, okay. Yeah, well, I got those, and now I'm working on my broccoli here. It'll be ready in a few weeks."

"That'll be good."

"Mm-hmm," Terri said. "So, I know you got a meal to cook once you finish up here. We don't want to take up too much of your time. But is there something you can tell us about Desmond?"

Keisha rolled her eyes. "That man. I can tell you plenty about him. He goes through women one after the other. Lots of us up there at the hospital. I didn't realize that when we first got together. I only knew about LaDonna."

"Because you two worked on the same unit?"

"Uh-huh."

I kept my mouth shut and listened. One of the reasons Terri and I made such a good team was that, between us, we could cover a lot of different demographics. When we needed to interview a good ol' boy, I took the lead. But in this situation, she'd be a lot better than I would at gathering information.

"And was that why you stopped seeing him, he wanted to move on?"

"No. I mean, I'm sure that would've happened before too long, but…" Keisha looked around. Seeing that nobody but the plants was there to overhear, she turned back and said, "No, it was something else. And I'd heard it before—I should've listened—but I didn't believe it until he tried to do it on me."

"Mm-hmm," Terri said with a sympathetic nod.

I had no clue what this man had done. I wasn't sure Terri knew yet, either, but she had a knack for getting people to let down their walls and confide in her.

"So, what you'd heard," she began, "was that from LaDonna?"

"Yeah," Keisha said. "But I just thought she was jealous, you know?"

"Mm-hmm."

"Because that was fresh for her. They'd only stopped seeing each other in, I want to say, August."

"Right. And what'd she tell you?"

"That he was a thief. That I better not leave no money or nothing lying around my house."

"Okay."

"And that he'd taken meds off of a patient's tray. But I didn't believe her. I thought she just wanted to break us up or get him in trouble. Or both." She sighed. "I'm tired of learning the hard way. Sisters before misters from now on."

Terri *mm-hmm*ed again. "Before all this trouble, you and LaDonna helped each other out, didn't you? Traded shifts sometimes?"

"Yeah, if it worked better for us, or her childcare fell through, or…"

"Do you remember if you traded shifts at all in July?"

"Oh, probably. We did it a lot. But then she got jealous, so that stopped."

"Right. So you thought she was saying things because she was jealous. When did you start thinking maybe she—"

"Wasn't lying?" Keisha laughed. "Right about when fifty dollars went missing from my bedside drawer."

"Mm," Terri said. Something in her posture made me think it might be okay for me to join the conversation, so I gave it a shot.

"He sounds like bad news," I said. "If he stole from you, do you think he might've taken the meds from the patient's tray, too, like LaDonna said?"

Keisha looked wary. "I mean... I can't speak to something I didn't see. But she told me two things about him, and I know one of them was no lie. And part of his job is to clear trays, if the patient doesn't finish their meal until after the kitchen staff has come and gone. So it wouldn't be strange for him to be taking a look at a tray, or handling it."

"Yeah, that makes sense." Remembering when Noah had been hospitalized, I added, "Although, doesn't the nurse stand right there while the patient takes their meds?"

"Well, normally," she said. "But it's the CCU. Things happen. If somebody codes, or chokes..."

I nodded. "You run and help?"

"If it's not being handled, yeah. Or if the nurse who's with the patient needs help. Things can turn real fast." She bent down and started pulling weeds.

When she didn't continue, Terri asked, "Is that what LaDonna said happened?"

Keisha sighed, stood up, and turned to toss the weeds onto a small compost pile. When she turned back, she said, "Look, stealing patient meds is a lot different than stealing fifty bucks. I may have dumped his sorry ass, but I'm not ratting Desmond out for something I didn't even see."

"Yeah, no, I hear you," I said.

She had a point about the difference. Stealing prescription opioids from a hospital—even a single tablet—was a federal felony. But something in the way she'd said it made me think that although she didn't want to narc on her ex-boyfriend, that type of theft wasn't shocking to her.

I tried a different angle. "Don't tell me anybody's name, unless you want to, but how often does that happen up there? Folks stealing patients' meds?"

"At the hospital? Oh..." She looked off to the side, like she was tallying the incidents up. "I mean, I don't know what it is officially. But it does happen. Off a tray, or a cart."

"Or out of the dispensing cabinet?"

"Yeah." She didn't go on.

"As far as *officially*..." I said, "you mean in terms of how it gets reported?"

"Right. There's reporting to the hospital," she said, "so, to the charge nurse, and on up the chain. And then there's some type of reporting to the state, but I don't know who handles that or how it works exactly. Or what triggers it, like, when do you have to escalate."

"Uh-huh. So, you mean, you don't know when it's just reported internally, versus to the state?"

"Right."

DEA regulations required hospitals to report any theft of controlled substances within one business day. There shouldn't have been any that were only reported internally.

Maybe Keisha didn't know that. Compliance rules probably weren't in her wheelhouse.

Still, I wondered why she had the impression that that was how the hospital handled things. I remembered LaDonna saying the traveling nurse had told her that the unit's procedures were lax.

"So is Desmond still working there?" Terri asked.

"Oh yeah. He likes it there. Likes being in charge of folks. And they been having a hard time recruiting ever since the pandemic. You got to make an effort to get yourself let go."

"Uh-huh." I nodded. "But some folks do get let go, right?"

"For stealing meds? Yeah. Ask LaDonna!"

I gave her a rueful nod.

"Who was it that stole meds and didn't get let go?" Terri asked.

I knew why she'd phrased it that way—as if the thing had happened and the only question was who. Sometimes people told you more if you phrased things in a way that made it sound like you knew more than you were saying.

Not Keisha. She said, with a hint of anger, "I told you, I can't speak to what I didn't see myself." She picked up her hoe and banged it on the ground, examining it between blows to see if the dirt had fallen off the blade.

"Sorry," I said. "We just want to get a sense of how things work there. Without naming any names, you're saying getting caught stealing meds doesn't always get a person fired, is that right?"

She shrugged.

"Do you have any sense of what might make the difference?" When that didn't get an answer, I tried, "Is it maybe the internal reporting, versus having to tell the feds?" There was no difference—or there shouldn't be. A hospital that was following the rules should report all thefts.

Another shrug, but she said, "Yeah, that sounds about right."

11

DECEMBER 29, 2022

I was getting ready to drive down to Savannah for a 10 a.m. meeting with Judy Reed's medical expert—and running a little late—when Mrs. Reed called. I tossed pens and a legal pad into my briefcase while she went through the leisurely inquiry into my well-being that traditionally preceded the meat of any conversation here in the South. She asked about my holidays, sympathizing when I told her that Noah hadn't been able to visit after all. As the most junior private investigator at his firm, he'd been stuck with a last-minute surveillance job. His Christmas meal had been a thermos of coffee and a few protein bars eaten in his car. Squatter and I had shared the turkey dinner I'd ordered from the local diner before falling asleep on the couch.

She moved on to the topics of my health and the weather. Hunting through a few pairs of pants in search of my car keys, I responded in kind. Spending my entire life in South Carolina had granted me the ability to engage in small talk without having to actually think about what either of us was saying.

I tuned back in fast when she mentioned her husband's estate tax return. "So he sent it to me, and when I looked through it, which I have to tell you took forever, that woman's name was right there on the list."

She had to mean Alanna Carpenter. I could tell from the indignation in her voice.

"The— You're referring to the woman who—"

"Who was… familiar with my husband, yes."

"My goodness. I am so sorry. And what did it say?"

I heard pages rustling.

While she looked, I checked another pair of pants and found my keys.

"Well, it's got the name of a bank," she said. "Not our bank. It's not even in South Carolina. And then her name, and beside that it says 'pod.'"

"Pod? Oh, you mean P-O-D?"

"Yes, that's how it's spelled."

I felt like I'd won a prize. Alanna Carpenter now had a motive. I could hardly wait to tell Terri.

"Mrs. Reed," I said, excited, "that stands for 'payable on death.' Which means whatever's in that bank account went straight to her when he—"

"Oh my—"

She must've covered the phone, because the rest of what she said was too muffled to understand. The angry tone, however, came through loud and clear.

I grabbed my briefcase and went outside to my car. As I opened the door, she came back on and apologized. "What I ought to be doing," she said, "is celebrating, right? Because surely this has got to help Judy. So, now, should we take this tax return down to the police?"

Absolutely not. But it was rude for a man to speak so bluntly to a middle-aged Southern lady. I tossed my briefcase onto the passenger seat and said, "Well, actually, the police aren't really—"

"Oh, would it be better to bring it directly to the solicitor?"

I imagined sitting in my office in Charleston, back when I'd been an assistant solicitor prosecuting cases there, and having a murder defendant's mother come in waving a tax return.

That was not how these things worked.

"You know what, Mrs. Reed," I said, getting in the car, "that's a thought, but let's hold off on that for now."

She gave a slightly exasperated sigh. "Mr. Munroe, I am not going to go charging in there insisting that this proves my daughter is innocent and he needs to drop this case right now. If that's what you were thinking, then we've had a miscommunication, for which I apologize."

I had been schooled. As a deep-rooted Southerner herself, she knew what my noncommittal words were trying to hide. Her apology was a polite gesture to spare my pride.

"Of course not, Mrs. Reed."

"I am simply trying to get an idea of what the next steps are."

"That's very understandable."

A few next steps came to mind. Terri could call the bank and pretend to be Alanna, to find out whatever she could—although that probably wouldn't work, since her investigation hadn't turned up enough information about Alanna to get through the security questions. I might hire an accountant, on Judy's dime, to pore over that tax return and tell me if he noticed anything else of interest. But Mrs. Reed was not my client, so I couldn't talk about any of that.

I could ask for her help, though. As I drove down my street, I said, "Well, the first thing is, would you mind sending a copy of that return on over to me?"

"Not at all. I can have Emma Jean drop it off this morning."

"Would she be able to stop by later? I'm in Savannah until about two o'clock."

"Oh, I'm sorry, she's got a family thing she's going to. Could she bring it by sometime in the next few days?"

"Sure. Just let me know when she's coming. I'll meet her at my office."

"I'll do that. Oh, before I forget, I'd like to ask you a question. I know I haven't read any of the files, and Judy's not real forthcoming about all this, so there might be something simple that I'm missing. But truly, I don't understand why my daughter got charged at all, because from where I'm sitting, all I see is circumstantial evidence."

The light ahead was yellow, but I stopped for it so I could have a second to think before answering. "Well, of course, Mrs. Reed, you understand I can't share anything confidential—"

"Oh, I figured that. I watch those legal shows sometimes."

"Uh-huh. But without saying anything specific to Judy's case, I can tell you that a lot of folks think circumstantial evidence doesn't count, and that's just not true. All that circumstantial means is that... Well, for example, if a witness says 'I saw Mr. Smith shoot Mr. Jones,' that's direct evidence we can use to convict Mr. Smith. But if he says 'I heard a gunshot from over by Mr. Smith's house, and when I looked out the window, I saw Mr. Jones lying dead in Mr. Smith's yard,' that's circumstantial. Because it doesn't straight-up *prove* that Mr. Smith killed him, right? But—"

"Oh, I see what you mean. It may not prove it, but it sure does narrow things down, doesn't it."

"Exactly. If we've got that circumstantial evidence, we're going to need another puzzle piece or two before a jury will vote to convict Mr. Smith. For instance, maybe we'll also put in some evidence that he was at home that day, and that he had some kind of feud going with Mr. Jones. But we're already partway there."

A horn honked behind me. The light was green. I drove on.

Mrs. Reed sighed. "I guess that does make sense, unfortunately."

As I cruised around a curve in the road, I recalled a question I'd forgotten to ask. "Oh, about that POD bank account. Does it say on the return what the balance on that account was?"

I didn't know what information would be included, because I'd never seen an estate tax return myself. Dead men's wealth was not my field of expertise.

"Yes, it does. It says $32,428."

"Huh. Okay, thank you."

The prize I'd thought I won now looked small and chintzy. People had committed murder for far less than that, of course, but to a woman in Alanna Carpenter's financial position, it wasn't much. Not nearly enough to risk life in prison for.

In Savannah, I drove down Bay Street under a canopy of live oaks, heading for the riverfront hotel where Dr. Hargroves and his wife were staying. The medical expert Judy's previous lawyer had hired was a professor emeritus at Emory School of Medicine, in Atlanta, but he was celebrating New Year's in Savannah and had suggested I come by.

"I'm old-school," he'd said on the phone. "Can't stand all this online nonsense. I like to meet a man face-to-face."

His hotel was a converted Victorian warehouse with intricate brick-work all along the front and large awnings over the entrance and the café terrace to provide refuge from the sun. Inside was all polished wood and ironwork, with ceiling fans twirling above and large windows overlooking the river. I saw the hotel bar off to the left and headed for it.

Dr. Hargroves saw me coming—at 10 a.m., the bar wasn't busy—and raised his arm in greeting. He was wearing a pale blue linen suit. With his mess of white hair and large old-fashioned mustache, he looked like he might have owned this warehouse in its heyday. Only the smartwatch on his wrist proved that he wasn't a time traveler making a pit stop in the twenty-first century.

We shook hands, and I took a seat on the leather-topped stool beside him.

"Order up," he told me, signaling the barman. "They've got some very fine bourbon. This right here was bottled in 1996." He tapped his half-empty glass.

"I wish I could." I trotted out my standard excuse. "Unfortunately, I'm taking some medication right now that doesn't mix with it."

"That is a damn shame," he said. "So you know, there's a few medica-tions where that can cause real problems real fast, but for the most part, that advice is overcautious horseshit. But I know you'll be back on the road pretty soon, so a little caution isn't bad."

"Yep."

I ordered tonic water with a slice of lime and enjoyed his bombastic small talk for a minute. The bar wasn't an appropriate venue for us to discuss the case, so when he finished his drink, I asked if there was someplace more private where we could talk.

"Yeah, why don't we head up to my suite. My wife's over at the spa until lunchtime. She's probably neck-deep in green mud right now."

I settled my bill, grimly amused that I—or Judy, since this was all billable—had just paid six dollars for a glass of water, and we left. We skipped the elevator and headed for the staircase. Dr. Hargroves, expounding on the need for regular exercise, took the steps two at a time.

His suite was the size of the entire ground floor of my house, with French doors at the far end opening onto a balcony overlooking the river. I didn't want to talk about anything confidential on the balcony, since I assumed every other room on this side of the hotel had its own balcony and doors that could carry our conversation to any number of ears. Instead, we sat down on the two leather love seats framing what appeared to be a real fireplace, and the doctor called room service for refreshments.

As he spoke on the phone, I felt my heart lurch and flop like a beached fish inside my chest. It was unnerving. I looked out at the trees on the other side of the river, breathing slowly to settle things down. Maybe my body was rebelling because I'd matched Dr. Hargroves's pace on the stairs. A delayed reaction to acting a little more athletic than I ought to. By the time he hung up, everything was back to normal.

He leaned back, stuck his hands behind his head with his elbows out, and said, "So, between you and me, what you've got here is a real stinker of a case. I already told your client and her old lawyer that. I mean, cause of death, as described. This Mr. Reed had an allergy so severe I'm surprised he made it to sixty-three. Cephalosporins are all over the place—not just in a bunch of different medications. I mean, I've seen studies finding that stuff in rural tap water. And you've got his only daughter, who I assume was one of his heirs, picking up a prescription for the stuff, what, three days before he died?"

"Two."

"Two. Not a good look, after a lifetime of avoiding it like the plague." He laughed. "Going down to urgent care and getting a prescription for it in your own name, that's not exactly what I'd call a perfect crime."

"No. And the thing is, she's an intelligent woman."

"Yeah, what is it she does? Satellites? Topographical, I don't know, databases and whatnot? I don't know the first thing about that, but it does take smarts. I've met her—she and her old lawyer flew down to Atlanta five or six months ago—and she's a weird one."

"That's fair to say."

"Weird doesn't mean stupid, though."

"Nope. Definitely not."

"The other thing," he said, leaning forward, setting his elbows on his knees, "is his heart. I'm not a cardiologist, but it's right there in the records. I don't have the lab tests in front of me, obviously, but my recollection is, his troponin levels were where you'd see them—"

"His what?"

"Troponin. It's a protein that gets in the bloodstream when the heart muscle's damaged. But that being said, anaphylaxis is a hell of a stressor on the system, and sometimes it'll trigger a heart attack or cardiac arrest all by itself. Which, I guess that's probably why they dropped their lawsuit against the hospital, right? I mean, you can't blame a doctor for diagnosing a heart attack as a heart attack, even if it was an allergy that caused it."

"Wouldn't their star cardiologist know that could be the cause, though? With his allergy being right there in the records?"

"Oh, yeah, he's a big shot, isn't he. I forgot about that guy. He the one who looks like Superman?"

I laughed. "Yep."

"Yeah, so, even Superman makes mistakes." He shrugged. "I've been in enough courtrooms to know you can't win a medical malpractice suit without getting some doctor like me on the stand to say the guy you're suing did something no reasonable doctor ought to have done. And I can't see getting up there and saying that failing to figure out the unusual cause of a man's heart attack within a one- or two-hour window is that kind of mistake."

I nodded. That made sense.

A knock came at the door, and Dr. Hargroves bellowed, "Come on in!"

A young man in a white jacket opened the door and wheeled a silver cart over to us. As he served us—pitcher of coffee, pastries, bread basket, charcuterie board—I figured, based on my six-dollar glass of water, that this spread probably cost at least a hundred bucks. I knew the doctor would bill it to Judy, since we were meeting about her case.

Of course, she was effortlessly paying his fees, which were five hundred an hour. She wouldn't care about this hundred-buck snack any more than I'd care about a quarter falling out of my pocket.

I poured my fourth cup of coffee of the day, and once we were alone again, we got back to business.

"So you've got no doubt," I said, "that the cephalosporin is what did it?"

"I can't be absolutely sure it's what caused the heart attack, though it'd be a hell of a coincidence if he just happened to have a minor heart attack the same day he took that drug. But caused his death, yes. The inflammatory markers, the pulmonary edema, the serum tryptase levels—my recollection from reading the coroner's report is that all the signs pointed that way."

"Pointed to an allergic reaction, you mean?"

"Yeah, and the worst kind: anaphylactic shock. Without that, I don't think he would've died. A minor heart attack that got seen in the hospital that quick shouldn't have been it for him."

I sighed. "Would it be helpful to run any more tests? Do you need me to subpoena more samples from the coroner's office?"

"No, the first lawyer did that. I ran a couple of tests for him, which you saw. And I've still got a serum sample left, on the off chance there's more we need to do. But you've got a good coroner up there. He did everything right. Took blood samples twice, at three and twenty-four hours after death, and kept them frozen at twenty below. Ran FEIAs, fluorescent enzyme immunoassays, on both samples to check his IgE for cephalosporins and a bunch of other stuff. It was textbook. There is no doubt in his mind or mine that Reed went into anaphylactic shock from a cephalosporin. And what was the other thing Reed had…"

He squinted out the window, trying to recall.

"Oh, yeah. Maculopapular rash. That's a typical reaction you see in somebody who was allergic to cephalosporins and got exposed. So, yeah. I can do all the testing or retesting that you want, but from a medical perspective, I didn't see anything in the coroner's report that made me think, hmm, I wonder what I'd find if I did this other test. That report was thorough, and it was solid."

I nodded. What he was saying was disappointing but no surprise. The coroner would make sure to do his best work when the deceased was a wealthy pillar of the community.

"Okay," I said, tossing a few olives from the crystal dish they'd been served in onto a saucer. "I'll relay that to Judy. It's her money, and I guess if she wants to spend it, I'll get you more samples. But the other thing I wanted to get clear on is the timeline—oh, and the dose. The coroner was vague about the timing, but from the family and the paramedic reports, we know Mr. Reed collapsed right around 11 a.m. Does that tell you anything about when he must've taken the drug?"

Dr. Hargroves shook his head. "Nope. Could be minutes, could be hours. Reason the coroner was vague is that there's too many factors that go into it. For instance—" He set his coffee down and started counting on his fingers. "Number one, what was the dose? Number two, what was the dosage form? Tablet, capsule, extended release?"

"Didn't the report say they found some gelatin capsule in his stomach?"

"Yeah, but that could've been his blood pressure meds. Number three, did he take one pill or two?"

"You can't tell that?" As I hacked off a piece of cheese, I recalled a detail from Dickenson's files. "I thought his prescription was to take his blood pressure meds once a day, in the morning."

"Sure, but some patients take two if their BP is higher than usual. I've even seen them double up because they forgot to take it the previous day, although that doesn't help at all."

"Can you tell from his blood levels? I mean of the cephalosporin."

He shrugged. "In theory, sure, but there's a lot of factors that go into that. Did he take the drug with food? If not, how long after eating? We've got no way of knowing that. His blood levels are consistent with a whole bunch of variables that we just don't know." He popped a slice of salami into his mouth.

"Didn't the coroner say there was... I forget the exact words, but basically, the remains of breakfast in his stomach?"

"Sure, but his wife didn't know what time he ate breakfast, did she."

I shook my head. It occurred to me that I'd never sat around having snacks while discussing the contents of a dead man's stomach before. I decided to finish my cheese before continuing.

I swallowed the last bite, took a sip of coffee, and said, "She told me she always got up later than him, since she can't just jump out of bed. She's got to wait for her aide to get there, and then... I don't know the details, but apparently there's a whole routine."

"Right, so we don't know. But even if we had a time-stamped photo of him sitting there eating his oatmeal at nine a.m., we don't know if he took the pill—or pills—before, during, or after, right? I don't even know with scientific certainty whether he took an extended-release cephalosporin or not. I know the girl's prescription was for the regular kind, which hits the bloodstream faster, but the scrap of gelatin they found in his stomach wasn't enough to be sure which kind he took."

"You can't tell from the color?"

"Both are blue. Different shades, but not different enough to tell them apart after it's been sitting in stomach acid."

"Dammit."

"I share that sentiment. Like I said, it's a stinker of a case."

I set my coffee down, sat back, and thought things through. In a homicide case, a timeline was practically the Holy Grail. In a lot of cases, if you could prove what happened when, you were halfway to proving innocence or guilt.

"If you don't want to put me on the stand," the doctor said, "I completely understand."

I nodded, mulling that over. Dr. Hargroves had been an expert witness in more than a hundred cases, and he knew how it worked. If he couldn't poke holes in the State's case, there was no point in having him testify. The last thing I wanted was the prosecutor forcing my own witness to admit, in front of the jury, that the coroner was absolutely right.

12

JANUARY 3, 2023

It was late Tuesday morning, and Terri and I were kicking back in my office, eating donuts and updating each other on the case. We were going to drive up toward the islands and get lunch at the strip club so we could talk to the stripper that Conway had had his fling with. Terri had already reached out to his other fling, but she didn't want to talk.

Terri, sitting on my side of the desk with her laptop open, was scrolling through the stripper's Instagram page. Her name, at least on social media, was Tawny Lee.

"And here's what she looks like now," Terri said.

In the photo, Tawny had a turned-up nose, higher cheekbones, and fuller lips than she had in the photo on my corkboard. In a few posts back around Thanksgiving, she'd shared images from a plastic surgeon's office: a selfie with Sharpie lines drawn around her nose to show the doctor where to cut, and a photo of her lying on a gurney waving to the camera as she was wheeled away.

This new face was the result.

"Yeah, I would not have recognized her," I said.

"Me neither. Oh, do you have the cash?"

"Right here." I unlocked my desk drawer and pulled out a roll of twenties. Terri had said we should bring five hundred bucks to the strip club, plus some fives and ones to throw onstage.

"Why don't we each hold about half of that, and whoever's doing the most talking can flash it and pay."

"Sounds good. Although I still don't know how the heck I'm going to describe this on my invoice."

"You can't just put 'stripper cash' under expenses?" She laughed. "Judy approved it, though, right?"

"In general terms, yes. 'Spend whatever it takes' was how she put it."

On the highway, I lowered my window—it was a sunny 70 degrees—and asked, "So do you think we've got a better shot at getting this woman to talk? I mean, compared to the waitress?"

"Yeah, there's two things in favor. For one, it's a lot easier to talk to a stripper in a private room than it is to talk to a server while they're working."

"I love that you *know* that," I said.

She shot me a look. "That's just obvious. She knows nobody's watching, and you're paying for her time." After a second, she said, "Wait, have you never gotten a private dance at a strip club?"

"No, those places aren't really my thing. I went a couple times for bachelor parties, but... I don't know, they're a little depressing. And then the *expense*, I mean..."

145

She laughed. "Oh, I should've known. The guy who always gets a brewed coffee if I drag him to Starbucks, because paying four dollars for a cup of coffee is—"

"It's ridiculous! I can make it myself for less than fifty cents!"

"Yeah, I should've known that wasn't your style."

"Okay, so anyway," I said, chuckling, "we can stop talking about me and strip clubs now. What's the other reason you think we have a shot?"

"Well, we've got to try even if we don't. But I think Tawny might be amenable, because from her social media, she's one of those people who... *overshares*."

"How so?"

"Well, like the plastic surgery. Most people probably wouldn't mention that they'd gotten it at all, but she posted the blow-by-blow. Including some pretty gruesome photos—it's a good thing I'm okay with seeing blood and everything. And all these memes she made about her recovery, and exactly what substances she's in recovery from, and—"

"Boundaries not her thing?"

"Exactly. Which is great for us. She lets it all hang out on her Insta. She lists where she works right in her profile and posts pictures from work. I suppose that's a good way to bring in customers."

"What, pictures of the men? Or her, uh... coworkers?"

"It looked like a little bit of both."

"Really? Huh. I don't want to see myself up on her page."

"Maybe you should've brought a fake mustache." We both laughed at that, and we spent a minute debating what kind of mustache would give me the best camouflage.

After we'd fallen quiet, enjoying the distant view of the blue water over the salt marsh, I asked, "You and your sister have a good time over Christmas?"

"Oh, yeah. I just wish she lived closer."

"Yeah, that'd be great. You spend the whole week there?"

"No, I saw friends too. So I guess I had more fun than you did. I'm sorry Noah couldn't make it. How's he doing?"

I told her, sharing his latest funny story about the occasional indignities of being a PI. This one involved getting his shoe peed on by somebody's dog while he was holding real still, trying to record a nearby conversation.

While half of me told her that story, the other half was mulling something over. I couldn't help but notice how quick she'd changed the subject to my holiday when I'd asked about hers.

I didn't want that thought stuck in my craw. As she laughed at Noah's anecdote, I hit the gas and pulled out to pass the irritatingly slow guy in front of us, telling myself that what she did in her free time was not my business.

The strip club was busier than I'd expected it would be in the middle of the day. As we made our way through the windowless gloom, heading for a table, Terri said over the pulsing music that, according to online reviews, this place served a good lunch. I wasn't sure that was the reason for the crowd, but the waitresses were busy. There were four of them, all wearing red short shorts and blue bikini tops with white stars on them. The one whose feet I could see had on white cowboy boots.

147

On the stage, where flashing spotlights lit up what looked like dry ice smoke in different colors, the woman dangling upside down from the stripper pole was about three sequins short of naked.

We took a seat and used our phone lights to look at the menu. When the bikinied cowgirl responsible for our table came over, we both ordered burgers, with baskets of fries and onion rings to share. Since I was the one driving, Terri also got a bottle of beer.

Our plan was to wait until Tawny finished her set, then ask for a private dance. A few curtained rooms were located to one side of the stage for that purpose.

I felt awkward being in a place like this with Terri, although it didn't seem to bother her. I tried not to watch the show, but after a few attempts, I realized the alternatives—staring into Terri's eyes, gazing at passing waitresses' cleavage, or accidentally making eye contact with some drunk guy at a table with his friends—were worse.

The waitress delivered Terri's beer and my lemonade. Up on stage, the dancer—who was still upside down—did the splits in midair and somehow whirled around the pole.

"That is some incredible upper-body strength," I said. "You wouldn't guess it, with her skinny little arms."

Terri laughed. "You know some women do pole dancing as exercise, right?"

"Really? No, I did *not* know that. I guess I'm not your go-to person for fitness trends."

"Yeah, that tracks."

"Excuse me?" I pretended to be indignant. "I resent that. If you think I need to get in shape, just point me to the nearest pole dancing class, and I will sign right up."

She slapped a hand over her mouth to avoid spitting out her beer. After managing to swallow, she said, "Don't make promises you don't intend to keep. That would be amazing."

"On second thought," I said, "I doubt it would do a lot for my reputation as a lawyer."

"Oh, yeah. Old Fourth would slap a photo of you pole dancing right up on his home page."

"In a heartbeat."

In addition to the other ways he tried to undermine my work, Dabney Barnes IV seemed to take great pleasure in illustrating stories about my courtroom appearances with some of the worst photos of me that had ever been taken. Thanks to him, close-ups of my nostrils had appeared on computer screens all over South Carolina.

Terri and I kept on bantering after our food arrived, contributed our small share to the storm of dollar bills that flurried toward the dancer as she finished her set, and gave each other a look when we heard the announcer say that Tawny Lee was next.

Tawny was a bigger girl, round in all the right places, and once she hoisted herself up on the pole, I kept my eyes mostly on my food. The point of our visit was to talk with this woman, and I'd feel real awkward trying to strike up a conversation with her moments after having seen her various assets exposed at strange and alarming angles. I snagged a couple of onion rings from Terri's side of the table and dipped them in ketchup.

The picture of Alanna Carpenter that was tacked up on my office corkboard came to mind. She was a reasonably attractive young woman, but compared to Tawny Lee, she looked like a senator. Conway Reed wouldn't have started an affair with her out of simple lust. Looking at it from Judy's perspective, I could see why Alanna might've seemed like an existential threat. Unlike Tawny, Alanna was someone that Conway might plausibly marry and have more children with, thereby diverting the family fortune her way.

I mentally added a question to the list I had prepared for Tawny: Had she spoken to the prosecutor or gotten a call from their office? I still hadn't talked to Ginevra Barnes—her family emergency had apparently lasted longer than anticipated—but from a prosecution perspective, the case against Judy practically wrote itself. Not because your father having a serious girlfriend was evidence of murder, but because it was a story that a jury could believe. And stories were how juries made sense of the evidence in front of them.

When dollar bills started flying toward Tawny, Terri made her way over to a bouncer by the side of the stage to ask about a private dance. A moment later, she signaled to me, and I wolfed down the last of my burger and headed her way.

I followed Terri into the private room, and the bouncer let the curtain fall closed behind us, muffling the music a bit. The lighting in there was sensual—the lamps and track lights were mostly red, plus a few that cast a glow the color of candle flames—but nothing else was. The floor looked like bathroom tile, and the chairs were plastic. For ease of cleanup, I supposed.

Terri turned around, and I almost bumped into her. In this light, she looked absolutely beautiful. I tried to think of something funny to say, but I couldn't. While my mental wheels were still spinning in search of words, the music got louder for a second, and Terri looked past me to say hello.

I turned around. Tawny Lee, in lingerie and platform heels, had just come through the curtain. She licked her lips and said, "Ooh, honey, do you *both* want a dance?"

Terri gave her a big smile. "You know what," she said, "you are *so* pretty, Ms. Lee, but is it okay if we all just talk for now? We do understand that the price is the same either way."

"Oh, of course." Tawny blinked, her fake lashes brushing her cheeks like tiny wings. "Would y'all like something to drink? I can have Gabe bring us anything you want."

"Well, he's a little bit of a lightweight," Terri said with a glance at me, "but I wouldn't mind a shot of Johnnie Walker Blue."

"Oh, very nice," Tawny said. She poked her head out the curtain and said something to the bouncer. Based on the amount of clothing she was wearing, it was clear she couldn't possibly be carrying a phone. My concerns over being photographed receded somewhat.

Tawny sashayed back. She fussed over us like a good Southern hostess and got us all situated in a little circle of three chairs. When the bouncer waved his hand through the gap in the curtain to let us know he had returned, she went over and brought back Terri's drink.

"Is this how you like it, sweetheart?"

Terri took a sip and said, "Yes, it sure is."

Tawny perched on the edge of her chair with her knees held demurely together, put her hands on her ample thighs—I didn't recall ever seeing fingernails quite that long—and leaned forward. "What is it y'all want to talk about?"

"Well, so— You know what," Terri said, looking toward the curtain, "that song just ended, didn't it? Here." She pulled out her roll of cash, peeled off a twenty, and held it out.

The next song started with a deep bass throb.

Tawny batted her lashes at me and said, "Honey, would you mind bringing that table over where your lady friend can reach it? She needs someplace to put that."

While I was getting the small table she'd pointed to, Terri said, "I'm not real sure how we do this, but is it okay to pay you by the song?"

"Oh, yes. That's a real good way to do it."

I could feel the music through the soles of my shoes. I set the table down between their two chairs, and Terri put the twenty on top of it.

Tawny leaned forward again, providing an even fuller view of her cleavage, and said, "Now, what is it y'all want to talk about?"

Terri's face took on a hint of sadness. "Well, so, we have a problem," she said. "It's a big problem. We know a woman who, last year, her daddy died—"

"Oh my goodness," Tawny said, with sympathy that might've been real.

"Mm-hmm, and it's been so hard for her. We're trying to help her." Terri took another sip of her scotch and said, "I'm going to be square with you. We're kind of at our wit's end, and we came here because I believe you actually knew him for a little while. Her daddy, I mean. He liked you. And we thought there might be some things you knew about him that she can't find out any other way."

Tawny's sympathetic expression had frozen into a pretty mask. The same song was still playing, but Terri peeled off another twenty and laid it on the table.

Tawny's eyes flicked over to it, then back to Terri. With a flash of white teeth and an innocent shrug, she said, "Well, I know a lot of people. And maybe this is bad, but I don't always remember them all. Who was her daddy, now?"

"His name was Conway Reed."

Tawny laughed, one hand flying up to girlishly cover her mouth. "Oh my," she said. "Well, yes, my goodness." She blinked at Terri, leaving her eyes wide at the end. "Now, is that the poor gentleman that was in the news?"

"Yes, the story was in the news," Terri said. "He died at the hospital, and his poor daughter's been charged with murder."

"Oh my," Tawny repeated, nodding, maintaining her wide-eyed expression. "Now, you know what, a couple of things are coming back to me. I never did meet his daughter, that's for sure. And if y'all looked at his text messages, y'all would know that he and I wrapped things up between us at least a couple of months before what happened to him."

"Oh, absolutely, Ms. Lee," Terri said, mirroring Tawny's nod. "We know. That's not in any doubt."

"He and I weren't even together all that long. It was just a little fun, and for him, I guess, a way to try and make his girlfriend jealous." She tossed her long blonde hair over her shoulder. Something about the way she did it made me think that making another woman jealous was a point of pride.

"Oh my goodness," Terri said. "Look at you! That girlfriend had *no* chance."

Tawny laughed.

The song faded out, and another started. Terri set another twenty on the table.

"You know what," Tawny said, "he came in here just like y'all did. Paid for a private dance, but all he wanted to do was talk. At first."

"Oh, did he? I can see that," Terri said. "You're easy to talk to. You seem like a very caring person."

A flash of sorrow crossed Tawny's face. It looked real, which surprised me. "Well, I try to be," she said. "I do what I can. Because, you know, everybody's lonely, aren't they."

Terri and I both nodded. Tawny looked at me, so I said, "It's a damn shame."

"It *is*! And there's so much of it! I've had men crying on me in here. Some of them just want to tell somebody what's weighing them down. I've heard about every story there is." She gave a sad smile.

"Aw, that's real sweet that you can help them," Terri said. "Was Conway that kind of man?"

"Oh, at first, yeah. With what happened to his poor wife, can you blame him? And then, I guess, he was moving on, and he was real serious about this woman, but it turned out she was two-timing him. I've heard that kind of thing so many times. Just… betrayal. People treat each other so bad."

"Mm-hmm," Terri said. "Ain't that the truth."

I kept the sympathetic expression on my face, but my brain was in overdrive, trying to telepathically urge Terri to ask questions about Alanna and whoever she'd been cheating on Conway with. I took a deep breath to keep myself calm and realized she was just reading the tides. This sad mood had to flow out a little more before Tawny would be ready to say more.

The song hit its bridge, which was more uplifting than what came before, and Tawny said, "Anyway, what are you gonna do? Right?"

"Right," Terri said.

"I just try to make life a little more fun, is all."

"That's a real kindness, isn't it. I wish more folks would do that."

"Yeah, that would be nice. It really would."

We all appreciated that sentiment for a minute, and then Terri said, like it was an afterthought, "Did Conway know much about that other man? The one his girlfriend was two-timing him with?"

"Oh, yeah, they knew each other. Or knew *of* each other, anyway."

"Who was he?"

"Some doctor up at the local hospital." She laughed like a funny memory had just come to her. "Conway always said he looked like Superman."

13

JANUARY 3, 2023

We were sitting in my office on a video call with Dr. Hargroves, which I'd called him to arrange while we were driving back from the strip club. He was in sailing whites, sitting in a deck chair on a boat; he and his wife were on a day trip out from Savannah. After dealing with some technical issues—he put on noise-canceling headphones, both so we could hear each other and so the wind would stop whipping his wild white hair into his eyes—I thanked him profusely for making time for the call and gave him the upshot of what Tawny had told us.

"Now, stop me," I said, "if you think I've lost my mind. I know this is going to sound kind of paranoid. But here's what I'm picturing, and I want your take on it: Conway collapses at home with a minor heart attack and gets taken to the hospital. The treating physician is the guy who's sleeping with Conway's girlfriend, and—"

"Are you *sure*?" Dr. Hargroves said. Behind him, beyond the teak frame of his deck chair, the blue horizon shifted up and down. "I know that's what that woman told you, but really, what are the chances that's true? That the one cardiologist they happen to bring in is the guy who..."

He trailed off, baffled by the scale of the coincidence, and Terri said, "This isn't Atlanta, Dr. Hargroves. Basking Rock is a real small town."

"We've only got the one hospital," I said. "And Conway had his heart attack right before lunch, middle of the day shift. That's when their star cardiologist is there. I doubt that guy ever works nights."

Hargroves sat back, arms crossed, and looked off at the sky. "So what you're thinking," he said, sounding skeptical, "is that as soon as your guy's medical record pops up on the screen, that cardiologist sees the warning about a severe cephalosporin allergy, and... gives him some?"

"I told you it was going to sound paranoid."

"Yeah, and it does." His bushy white eyebrows went up, and he thought about it for a second, shaking his head. "Okay, as a doctor, that's a real tough thing to contemplate, a doctor killing his own patient. But I guess even if something is ten million to one, some-body's got to be the one."

"Mm-hmm," Terri said. "And from an investigative standpoint, we just need to know if this is something that could've happened, so we can figure out what evidence we should be digging for."

"Well, if what you're asking is just whether that scenario is physically possible, yeah, obviously it is. Although your missing link there is, where'd your cardiologist get the drug? It's not as if we walk around with pockets full of pill bottles or we can just grab what we want off a shelf. Apart from what's in a crash cart—and there's not going to be any cephalosporins in there—everything, not just the opiates and controlled substances and whatnot, is locked up in one of those dispensing cabinets, and nobody's getting it out without a doctor's order."

Thinking of LaDonna, I said, "Sure, but there's holes in that system, right? I mean, thefts do happen."

"Right, but that's usually nurses. Not to cast aspersions on nurses—I just mean that normally they're the ones who retrieve the meds. We doctors issue the orders, but the nurses physically go get what was ordered. Maybe a resident might, but this isn't a teaching hospital, is it?"

"Oh, no. It's—don't get me wrong, we're glad to have it, but it's real small."

"Okay. Myself, I don't think I've ever used a dispensing cabinet in my life. So if you can fill in that missing link, meaning how'd he get his hands on cephalosporin—which, I don't know why that drug would be in the ER or the cardiology unit at all—then, yes, it's physically possible."

"Damn. That's really something."

Hargroves held up his index finger in a cautionary way and added, "Or, I should say, if you can explain how he got his hands on it, *and* how he got a man in the middle of a heart attack to swallow it, then it's physically possible."

"Could it have been in an IV?" Terri asked.

Hargroves made a skeptical noise. "IV cephalosporins exist, but it wouldn't be quick or discreet. You'd have to get the IV bag and a pole, have a nurse or a tech run an IV—as I recall from the file, he already had one for heparin, so you'd have to swap that out for the cephalosporin or run a new line. Either way, that's something the rest of the medical team would notice. Whereas with a pill, if you can get the patient to swallow it, that's done in maybe ten seconds."

"So, how'd he get it in the first place," I said, "and how'd he do it without the order showing up in Conway's file, and then how'd he get it into him?"

"Yeah, those are the questions."

"Uh-huh. Well, any light you can shed on that, based on your hospital experience or anything else, I would appreciate."

He nodded and said, "I'll give it a think. You might need to pull some more hospital records, if I can give you a few ideas of where to look."

"Thanks much. And meanwhile, I'll try and figure out how to get this into evidence."

The doctor laughed. "Yeah, this is one of the ways that your job is harder than mine."

Courtrooms, we both knew, were the opposite of a free-for-all. Judges would shoot down wild theories and out-there evidence before the jury was even picked. What Tawny had told us about Conway's unfortunate love triangle raised some interesting questions, but every bit of it was hearsay. If I wanted to so much as hint at that scenario in front of the jurors hearing Judy's case, I was going to need proof.

After we ended the call, Terri pulled out her laptop and started looking into Dr. Kassel. I leaned back in my chair, closed my eyes, and thought through how to get any of this admitted at trial.

Kassel and Alanna wouldn't divulge their affair voluntarily. If I could get solid evidence, and then ask the court to sequester all the witnesses so they couldn't hear each other testify, maybe I could spring the evidence on them, and maybe they'd give different explanations. Then the jury would think one or both of them were dishonest, which might plant some seeds of doubt regarding the case against Judy.

To do that, I'd have to subpoena Alanna. While Ginevra Barnes and I hadn't exchanged witness lists yet, I knew Kassel would be on her list, since he'd been Conway's treating physician on the day he died. But I doubted she'd call Alanna.

Of course, the two of them would lawyer up and come to trial prepared as hell. They'd probably coordinate with each other to make sure their stories matched.

I sighed, disgusted with the results of my mental game of chess. Subpoenaing Alanna was not a good idea. On top of the fact that Terri and I had been able to learn almost nothing about her, which meant I'd be in the dark as far as figuring out what questions to ask, issuing a subpoena to a hostile witness was the kind of thing that usually only worked on TV. As a kid, I'd watched *Batman* reruns where in almost every episode, the superhero caught the criminal mastermind and got a spectacular confession out of him in the nick of time. Most TV legal shows pulled that same move in the courtroom. But that was not how things worked in real life.

My desk phone rang. It was Rachel, who was twenty feet down the hallway at her desk.

"Yes?"

"A Mrs. Emma Jean Johnson is here to see you. She called earlier, and I let her know when y'all were going to be back."

"Oh! Tell her I'll be right out."

"That must be our copy of Conway's estate tax return," I told Terri.

We both went out. Emma Jean was standing by Rachel's desk. Her mousy hair was back in a ponytail, and she had on a plum-colored velour sweat suit.

She gave a quick smile as we approached. Pointing to a manila envelope on the counter in front of Rachel, she said, "Mrs. Reed wanted me to bring this by. I'm sorry, I hope it's not a bad time."

"Oh, not at all," I said. "Thanks."

"Good to see you again!" Terri said. "Did you have a nice Christmas?"

Emma Jean looked surprised to be asked, and almost pitifully pleased. I figured that, as a healthcare aide, she was normally more or less part of the furniture. "It *was* nice, yes," she said. "And... did you?"

"Oh, yeah. You know, seeing family and friends is always good."

Emma Jean's face twitched with the faintest hint of disagreement. Terri must've seen it, too, because she gave a self-deprecating laugh and added, "Although I guess that depends on the family. Anyway, I'm getting some coffee—would you like a cup?" She gestured to the new coffee-pod machine I'd set up in my waiting area, which Rachel had insisted, correctly, that clients would appreciate.

"Oh! Are you sure?"

"Of course," Terri said. "There's a few different flavors. Come on over and see what you like."

They chatted as they made their drinks. Rachel joined them and pointed out the various flavors of creamer.

I slid the tax return out of the envelope. It was half an inch thick, printed in a font so small it looked like there were about a thousand words and numbers on every page.

I was not a tax return guy. I slid it back into its envelope and announced to the room, although nobody was listening, that I'd be right back.

In my office, I wrote a quick email to Roy asking if he knew a tax guy who could take a look at this thing and let me know if there was anything worth digging into.

A thought came to me before I hit send. Anybody Roy knew would probably be here in town, or farther afield but still part of the circle of local rich men. I wanted somebody who had no link to Conway or his connections at all.

I replaced Roy's name with Cardozo's and mentioned I might be looking for an expert witness with an accounting background. He probably knew some.

By the time I got back to the reception area five minutes later, Terri and Emma Jean were best friends. They stood there chatting away, coffees in hand, before Emma Jean said goodbye to all of us and went out the door.

"She seems real nice," Rachel said. Terri agreed.

I got a coffee started for myself and then went over to Rachel's desk to sign the invoices that she had ready for me. One of them was for LaDonna. I told her to hold off on that one.

As Terri and I walked back to my office, I asked, "You find out anything from Emma Jean?"

"Not much. She went up to Charleston with Mrs. Reed to visit Judy for Christmas."

"I guess that would've been easier to arrange than Judy getting leave to travel with her ankle bracelet."

"Mm-hmm."

As I followed her into my office and we sat back down, I said, "Did Emma Jean spend her whole Christmas with them? Does she not have family?"

"Besides that nephew at the stables? Yeah, she's got some, I guess."

"Y'all didn't get into that much?"

She shrugged. "She mostly talked about the Reeds. I asked if she liked working there, and she said it's the best job she's ever had." She finished her coffee, tossed the cup in the trash, and leaned back in her chair, eyes shut. I couldn't remember the last time I'd seen her look so bone-tired.

"You okay?" I asked.

"Yeah. It's just... a lot. I spent yesterday interviewing witnesses in another case, and then Tawny and Emma Jean today..." She looked off someplace past my shoulder, trying to find the right words.

"You bring a *whole* lot of energy to those conversations," I said. "The way you talk to folks, the way you connect, is amazing."

"Thank you."

"But it's got to take a lot out of you sometimes."

"Exactly. I mean, I'm not faking anything—I really do think there's nothing more interesting than other people. But at the same time, there's nothing worse than other people. People are capable of the most incredible courage and generosity and... and *everything*, but..."

"Right, but also—"

"Yeah, also the worst things."

She shook her head. We didn't need to say anything more about that. Thanks to our work, each of us had a mental catalog of horrors.

Finally, she said, "And the thing is, some folks do the best things and some do the worst, and you don't know for sure which ones are which. So, I mean, I'm *friendly*, but... I'm still watching them. I've got a little surveillance unit in my brain looking at *everyone*."

I nodded. After a second, I had an idea. "You know what, screw this case. Screw work entirely. I promised Squatter I'd take him for a beach run yesterday morning, and I still haven't done it. You want to come with? Take advantage of the weather? I'll buy you a—I don't know—a piña colada or something, whatever you want, and we can watch our dogs run around. They know how to enjoy themselves; maybe we can learn something from them."

She perked up a little bit. "You know what, yeah. I don't need another drink today, but…" She checked the time on her phone. "Yeah. I'll go get Buster. Meet you there in half an hour?"

A few minutes before the appointed time, I pulled up and got Squatter, in his carrier, out of the passenger seat. It was unseasonably warm, one of our rare January beach days. Through the bag's mesh window, I saw him sniff the sea air and start wagging his tail. Terri and Buster were already down by the waterline, and when I got to the sand, I set the case down and let Squatter out. He yipped with excitement at the sight of his friend.

We strolled down to them together—he was going as fast as he could, but these days that wasn't very fast—and I waved. Terri waved back with a big smile. She'd changed into cropped pants in some light fabric that fluttered in the breeze, and I had just noticed her gold sandals when they disappeared beneath a rush of frothy water. As I jumped out of the way—my shoes weren't as beach-worthy—she laughed.

We walked along the shore, watching our dogs playing a few yards ahead. They hopped around, enjoying themselves, and we talked about all kinds of things—funny memes, random thoughts, nothing at all to do with the cases we were working on. It felt like being on vacation, and I hadn't realized how much I needed one of those.

Our dogs were making spectacles of themselves—her huge rottweiler and my tiny Yorkie, with their heads low and their butts in the air, slapping their paws on the sand in sheer excitement at each other's company.

"This was a great idea," Terri said. "They've really missed each other."

"They sure have."

I looked at her beside me. The sun was close to setting now, and it put a coppery glow on her hair and her skin. Ahead of us, the sand glinted golden. The thought came to me that, apart from Noah, she was the best thing in my life.

"Terri, can I tell you something?"

"Of course."

I stopped walking and turned to face her. I heard our dogs' tags jingling as they romped ahead. "Maybe I should've said this a long time ago, but you matter a hell of a lot to me. As a person, as a woman—walking on the beach with you like this is about the happiest I ever am."

I had a lot more to say, but I could see in her face that it wasn't landing right.

I made my voice light and said, "If this is weird, I'm sorry. I know we work together, and that's not something I want to mess up at all, so—"

"No, Leland," she said, looking up at me. Her eyes were wide and sad, and her voice had a plaintive tone I'd never heard from her. "It's not that we work together. It's that I'm seeing someone. That's where I was after Christmas—we went to Miami together for New Year's Eve."

"Oh, okay," I said, trying to sound casual. "Of course. No worries at all." I lurched past her, down the beach, after my dog. When I got up close to him, I couldn't remember why I was there. I couldn't quite remember how to breathe. I crouched down and scratched his ears.

"Leland, I'm sorry—" Terri called.

"No, no, nothing to be sorry about. I was out of line."

Squatter toddled off toward Buster, and I stood back up. Behind me, over the sound of the waves, I heard Terri approaching me on the sand.

"Are you happy with him?" I asked, without looking at her.

After a tiny pause, she said, "Yeah. I am."

14

JANUARY 6, 2023

At seven Friday morning, I was at the hospital, sitting in the gray-and-white office of Dr. Mike Perez. His office wasn't exactly in the basement, but it was below grade, with one small window too high up on the wall to see out of. That told me where he stood in the hospital hierarchy. Seven was not a time that I liked being out of bed, much less in a meeting across town, but there hadn't been much of a choice. Dr. Perez, who already looked frazzled although the day had just begun, had explained that he was booked solid, seeing patients back-to-back for his whole twelve-hour shift.

"Listen," he said, "candidly, I don't remember your client at all. As the saying goes, I couldn't pick her out of a lineup. When I'm over in urgent care, I see thirty-plus patients a day, and that was one appointment eighteen months ago. I don't even know why they want me on the stand—it seems a little redundant, since all I can do is read out what the records say."

"That's why they subpoenaed you," I told him. "They can't just toss the jury a printout of the hospital records. The printout's not in evidence until somebody gets up there and testifies that it is what the solicitor says it is."

"The solicitor?"

"That's what we call the prosecutor down here. Or the DA, as they say in some states."

He nodded.

"So she'll ask you what the records are and what they say, and I'll probably confirm you don't remember my client and ask one or two other questions, and that'll be it."

He perked up a little bit. "Doesn't sound like it should take too long."

"No, you'll be back here seeing patients every fifteen minutes before you know it."

I smiled. He smiled back, shaking his head. I could see he was not a man who was energized by his job.

"So, I'll let you get back to your day in a quick minute," I said, "but before I head out, would you mind showing me what you see on the screen when you pull up those records?"

"Uh, well, because of HIPAA, I—"

"Oh, I brought the form." I flipped my briefcase open and pulled out the piece of paper. "I called the records department, and they told me what to have Ms. Reed sign and notarize."

I set it on his desk. He glanced at it, sighed, and swiveled his chair to face the computer sitting on the cart beside him. He typed and clicked through a few screens, then said, "There you go." Judy's full name, birth date, and a few dozen lines of other information filled the screen.

"And is that how it would've looked when she came in for that appointment?" I asked. "Or have y'all done any updates in the meantime?"

"I don't recall any updates beyond security stuff. I couldn't swear to it, but it probably would've been the same."

"Uh-huh," I said. "You mind if I take that mouse for a second?"

He hesitated, glanced at the notarized form again, and slid the mouse across the desk.

I scrolled through reverse-chronological lists of Judy's prescriptions, appointments, and diagnoses. The cephalosporin prescription was there, dated two days before her father's death.

"Is there anyplace on here where y'all would normally mention that she wasn't supposed to get cephalosporins?"

"Well, I gather she's not the one who's allergic to it—if she were, it'd be right there on the screen, and that box would be red." He pointed to a blank white box.

"Uh-huh. So what do y'all do when it's somebody else in the household who's deathly allergic?"

Dr. Perez sighed like the usual parade of stupid questions had started early today. "Mr. Munroe," he said, "we're not handing out chocolate bars laced with peanuts and shellfish here. We prescribe medication, which is for the person whose name is on the label, and normally we expect to rely on the child safety cap and common sense."

I laughed. "Fair point. But is there, like, a notes section, or anything?"

"There's a place for notes, yes."

I kept on scrolling down. "Oh, right there?" I had reached the bottom of the screen, which had a box labeled "Additional notes." Nothing was written in it.

He nodded.

"Well, it's a real shame there wasn't anything in there about that," I said.

"If she'd mentioned the issue to me," he said, "or to anybody previously, there would've been."

I walked out to the hospital parking lot, got in my car, and headed for the donut shop. I felt I had earned that perk by subjecting myself to the unconscionably early meeting with Dr. Perez.

I took the long way. I did not want to drive by the beach. I didn't need any reminders of my mistakes.

Back home with six bucks' worth of donuts and hot coffee, I shucked off my jacket and tie. I didn't need them, I figured, for the video call I was about to have. I'd only ever talked to this guy on the phone, but he was a computer and cell phone forensics expert, and in my experience, they tended to dress casually. Medical experts wore suits; computer experts wore black T-shirts featuring robots or anime characters.

I went upstairs to get LaDonna's file and my laptop, then brought them back down to the dining room. I liked to keep an eye on Squatter when he was outside. After setting up on the table, I gave him a treat and let him out the sliding door. The deck faced south, and it must've already been warm from the morning sun; he took five or six steps out onto it and then curled up for a snooze. I finished my own treat—I was a little too old-school to munch on donuts during a video call—and got logged in.

A minute later, a pale thirtysomething guy with a ponytail appeared on my screen.

"Morning, Adam," I said.

"Good morning to you, Leland."

Adam looked like he hadn't been out in the sunshine for at least a couple of years, and he was wearing a *Lord of the Rings* T-shirt. If he flew in from Pittsburgh to testify at LaDonna's trial, I realized, I might have to take him shopping for a suit.

After a little chitchat, I mentally started the clock. "Thanks for that PowerPoint," I said. "The maps make it real clear she couldn't have been at the hospital at the time." He'd sent a five-page presentation showing, on maps of Basking Rock, the locations of LaDonna's cell phone between 8 a.m. and midnight on the day of the second drug theft. It placed her at home all morning and then running a couple of errands in the afternoon. Her phone didn't get to the hospital until almost seven thirty that night—consistent with her statement that she'd traded her day shift for a friend's night shift.

"Well, you know how most people are. They need pictures. You can't just give the raw data to a jury, or even to the judge."

"Yeah, that's for sure," I said. "So what I'd like to do is attach your presentation as an exhibit to a declaration, which I'll write up for you to sign. You've done those before?"

"Declarations? Sure. Typically, the attorneys I've worked with will write it, and then I fix the technology aspect of it—is that how you work too?"

I chuckled. "Yeah, you're definitely going to need to correct whatever I write about the technology. But before we get to that, would you mind removing her street address from the maps? You can replace it with 'Ms. Winters's Home.' Because once I file this thing, it's a public record, and I don't want her home address out there for all and sundry."

"Absolutely, absolutely. Sorry, I should've thought of that."

"No problem."

"So when is this all due?"

"I'm hoping to file the motion today, if you can fix that address thing for me. And then her trial's in a couple of weeks. You still available for that, if need be?"

"Absolutely."

I'd drafted a pretrial motion to exclude the evidence of LaDonna's supposed log-ins to the dispensing cabinet. With Adam's declaration, together with the charge nurse's testimony that the passwords were visible to anybody walking by, I had an argument that the log-in evidence was unreliable and unfairly prejudicial. Under Rule 403, that meant I could ask for it to be excluded.

Since it was the core of the government's case, though, I knew LaRue would fight like hell for my motion to be denied. He was one of my least favorite kinds of prosecutors: a true believer, convinced in every case that he was on a moral crusade.

A lot like Ginevra Barnes. I still hadn't talked with her about Judy's case, but she'd had that same type of crusader attitude when I'd dealt with her before.

That reminded me of something. "Adam, on top of the cell phone stuff, you're a big computer science guy, right?"

"I like the way you phrased that," he said, smiling. "I should put that on my business card."

"Yeah, that or 'boy genius.'"

He laughed. "I might be getting a little old for that one."

"Well, that's up to you. But let me ask you something. And before I put my foot in my mouth, bear in mind that I'm pretty much the exact opposite of a tech guy, so I'm probably going to ask this wrong. But are you one of those hacker types?"

He raised an eyebrow. "Uh… in what sense?"

"I mean, like, if I gave you a laptop that we didn't know the password for, would you be able to get into it so we could see what's on it?"

"Oh! Yeah, that's— Sorry if I hesitated there. I thought you were going somewhere else with that."

I chuckled. "Right, like, can you hack me into the Pentagon? No, man, I'm in South Carolina here. I'm not that sophisticated."

"You don't have to knock the South just because I'm a Yankee. I'm happy to take a look at the laptop. What's the operating system?"

"I don't know. Nothing fancy, I wouldn't think. This was the laptop of a sixtysomething businessman. Not a real technical guy."

"Okay, so some version of Windows, probably. And is it on, or has it been off for a while?"

"Off, I'd guess. The owner died more than a year ago, and his widow has it, but I don't think she's been using it. Actually, I know she hasn't, because she said she didn't know the password."

"Right. Would it be a safe assumption that there might be something on this laptop that you'd want to use as evidence in a lawsuit? Or a criminal case?"

"Criminal case, yeah."

"Got it. So what I would do is take a forensic image of the hard drive —that's a fancy way of saying I'd make a perfect copy—and then I'd put the laptop itself in cold storage, basically, and do all the work I'm going to do on the image. Running my searches, decrypting anything that's encrypted, and so forth—all that's done on the copy. Because I need to be able to tell the court that I haven't made one single change to the original hard drive."

"Sounds good. Shoot me an estimate on that, and I'll FedEx you the laptop."

"Oh, no. Absolutely do not do that! I'll send you a Faraday bag, and you can ship it back to me in that."

"A Faraday bag?"

"Yeah, it's… Picture a normal laptop bag, except this one's made of conductive material that basically acts as a shield. It prevents the laptop from sending or receiving Wi-Fi signals, Bluetooth, GPS… The whole idea here is, we want to preserve it exactly how it was whenever the owner last touched it."

After we finished the call, I looked at my phone. Terri had texted me the previous day. I hadn't read it. I still wasn't up to reading anything from her. I felt like a fool.

But clients paid me to keep them out of jail, not to feel good about myself. Terri was my PI, and she was a damn good one. It was my job to get over whatever else I had hoped she might be.

I opened the message. It said she'd arranged to have lunch with LaDonna's ex-boyfriend, the hospital janitor, on Friday—in other words, today—and could I join her?

I looked at the clock. I could.

I met them at the steak house in town, and by the time I arrived, they'd already been served. Desmond had suggested the restaurant. Apparently, he felt he might be able to overcome his reluctance to speak with us if the conversation came with a twelve-ounce sirloin, three sides, and a glass of whiskey.

I sat down and ordered a burger. Terri, I noticed, was having the same.

"Desmond was just telling me about the hospital," she said. "He's worked there for sixteen years."

I whistled like I was impressed. Desmond smiled. He was a little heavy, but a good-looking guy, maybe forty years old.

"I bet you know that place better than the doctors do," Terri told him.

"Oh, no doubt about that, no doubt at all," he said, sawing off a hunk of steak. "Yeah, I seen some things."

"I'm sure you have."

He put the meat in his mouth, chewed and swallowed, and gulped most of his whiskey to wash it down.

"You want another one of those?" I asked.

"Sure thing."

I nodded. "I'll tell the waitress when she gets back with my food."

"I bet nobody up at that hospital can keep a secret from you," Terri said.

"No, they can't. That is the truth. And you know what, we make the right deal, I could be a resource for you. Folks suing the hospital, folks who just got questions—there's stuff I could find out for you, real easy. Because I got access everywhere. I know that place backward and forward."

"I bet you do," Terri said.

"Yeah," I said. "That's something to think about."

I was pretty sure no deal I could possibly make with him would pass muster under the ethics rules. He seemed like the talkative type, though, and sometimes all those folks needed was attention with a dash of admiration. If that's what he wanted, we could provide it.

The waitress set my burger down, and I ordered Desmond another drink.

"I didn't realize you got to go all over the hospital," Terri said. "Like, every department?"

"Just about," he said, nodding. "Not the, uh—they got the maternity unit, and then the level one and two nurseries attached to that. And that wing's got its own staff. Mothers and babies, you know, that's a whole different thing. But for the rest, yeah, that's all me."

"What, everything from—I don't know—cardiology to the CCU to oncology?"

"Well, they only got the outpatient oncology," he said. "Folks come in, sit in their chairs for a couple hours on a drip, getting their chemo. You need more than that, you've got to go up to Charleston or down to Savannah. But yeah, I'm in charge of the outpatient. And cardiology, and... you name it."

"Wow, I bet everybody there knows you," she said.

"Yes, they do." The waitress set his drink down, and he said to her, "Thank you, ma'am. And thank you," he added, raising his glass and giving each of us a nod.

I raised my ice water, and Terri raised her tea. Then we got down to eating for a minute.

I made some headway on my fries before saying, "You know what, Desmond, I'm actually curious about a doctor you got over there. That cardiologist, Dr. Kassel? You know him?"

"Do I *know* him?" Desmond sounded a little offended. "The guy who's— The doctor who gives every press conference and has his face on the billboards? Do I *know* him?"

Terri gave me a look and said, in a tone like I was being schooled, "He *did* tell you two minutes ago that he works on the cardiology unit."

Since I had inadvertently taken on the bad-cop role, she was stepping up to play good cop. It was a classic technique.

"I did say that," Desmond said. "Yes, I did."

"You probably see him almost every day." She sounded impressed.

"Him and his boss, Mr. Thibodeau. Yes, I do. I must talk to him every week or so, man to man. I've known him since he got there. I showed him his way around."

I didn't react, but I was skeptical. I didn't see why the head of janitorial would be in regular contact with the CEO and the hospital's most high-profile doctor. The place wasn't *that* small.

"So what do you think of him?" Terri asked.

Desmond finished chewing a bite of steak and said, "Dr. K? Well, you know. I got thoughts. I got my opinion. I don't know that I need to come out and say all that, though."

"No, of course not," she said smoothly, as if anything he did was fine with her. "You don't need to do anything you don't want to at all."

"No, ma'am, I don't." He took a sip of his whiskey. Setting it down, he looked at something in the middle of the table—not so much looking at it as resting his eyes on it, relaxing—and shook his head like he was recalling a catalog of disappointments in the past. "He ain't how he looks on the billboards," he said. "That big old handshake and smile, and putting his arm around little kids for the camera? He ain't like that. I can tell you that much."

Terri nodded slowly, like what Desmond had said was deep.

"Anyway." Desmond picked up his fork again to stab at the steak. "They say not to bite the hand that feeds you, and I'm not going to. You got something else you wanted to hear about?"

Something in Terri's face told me it was time to back off. We could ask more about Kassel later, maybe. If Desmond was willing to meet up again.

I grabbed a piece of bread from the basket. "Yeah, this case we've got, with Ms. Winters? We're just making sure we cover all the bases, reaching out to folks that knew her, that kind of thing."

"Oh, yeah, I knew her," Desmond said, chuckling. "For a little while. I've known a lot of the ladies up there."

"Mm-hmm. You get around," Terri said, with a sly smile.

"I do, I do."

"When was it you started seeing her?"

He thought about that for a second. "I went on vacation around Memorial Day, for a week. So I want to say it started right after that."

"And it went on until, when, August?"

"I don't know, sometime in the summer." He shrugged. "You know. Not meant to last."

"She a good woman?" I asked. "Honest?"

"Well, I had no problem with her. Except she was maybe a little uptight. But I still got to go up on the stand, you know, and say what I got to say."

"Mm-hmm," Terri said. "And what's that?"

"What I saw." He reached for the bread. "Because I might've seen her take a little something, that one time."

There was a hint of bravado in his voice that put me on alert. I got the sense he was enjoying this part of the conversation a little too much—the veiled threat of testifying, the idea of making us squirm.

I wasn't going to give him what he was looking for. I'd known enough bullies to be aware that folks of that sort only did more of it if they got a rise out of you. I relaxed, leaned back in my chair, and took a bite of my bread. "This is real good," I said. "You mind passing me the butter?"

Terri slid the dish across the table. As I smeared butter on my bread, I said to Desmond, "Anyway, apologies for all the questions, but we've got to cover our bases. You know how things work."

He was disappointed at my lack of reaction. I could feel it. I kept my eyes off him and raised a hand, signaling the waitress.

"You know," he said, "there's some folks that are hoping I remember what I saw." The pitch of his voice had risen a little. He seemed to really want another dose of attention.

I ignored him. The waitress stepped over, and I asked for the check.

Terri knew what game we were playing. She was the good cop again. She said, with warm interest, "Oh? Who's been asking you about that?"

Desmond leaned back, threaded his fingers together, and rested them on his stomach. He wasn't going to give up his dirt until he felt the full weight of our attention on him.

I put my bread down and looked at him with an expression of interest and respect.

"There's somebody pretty important at the hospital who doesn't like her. Man whose business she could not keep herself out of, back when she worked there. I told her to watch out, but that woman did not know how to stay in her lane."

"My goodness," Terri said, shaking her head. "Dr. Kassel?"

"Well, he wasn't a fan either," he said. "But I meant Mr. Thibodeau."

15

JANUARY 11, 2023

I parked outside LaDonna's home. Wednesday was her day off this week, and I had news.

Her house, which she'd told me she'd bought right before her daughter was born, was painted a cheerful light blue. It was small even for a one-story, but it was cute, and the yard was well kept. The sunny porch was immaculate, with nothing on it but a pink tricycle parked in the corner, a planter with some kitchen herbs, and a row of seashells lined up along the railing.

I rang the bell. Inside, a little girl's voice called for her mommy. LaDonna appeared—the door had fake beveled glass at the top—and unlocked a deadbolt and chain to let me in. She tried to introduce me to her daughter, but the girl scampered off to another room and then peeked out, smiling, from one side of the doorway. For a second, I saw big dark eyes and high pigtails with pink beads on the ends, but when I smiled back, she ran off again.

"I'm sorry," LaDonna said, laughing. "She's real skittish of people she doesn't know."

"In this world, that's not a bad thing."

"I guess not."

She showed me to her dining room table and got us both some tea. Before we got down to business, she excused herself for a moment, and I heard her in the next room talking with her daughter. A familiar TV theme song started playing, and she came back.

"Is that *Sesame Street*?" I asked. "I don't think I've heard that tune since I was a kid."

"Yeah, it's on DVD now. All the episodes from the seventies and eighties. I like the more traditional shows. Not all this video game stuff kids watch these days."

"Good call."

She sat down, took a sip of tea, and said, "So, what's the news?"

"I got a call from LaRue this morning. That motion I filed the other day must've scared him a little, because he's offering you a plea deal."

She nodded, taking that in. "Okay," she said, "if it scared him, does that mean he thinks we might win?"

"Well, he knows it's a possibility. But it goes both ways. Until the judge rules on the motion, which he probably won't do until right before trial, neither side knows who's going to win. So we've both got an incentive to come to an agreement. That way the judge won't be able to hit us with something worse."

"Something worse?" she said. "Losing a case because his evidence is full of holes is worse, from his point of view, than—" She looked at the doorway to the room her daughter was in. Lowering her voice down close to a whisper, she said, "Worse than putting an innocent woman in prison?"

I gave a halfhearted shrug. The world was what it was. I wished we could change that, but I'd never seen a wish accomplish much.

"Okay," she said. "What did he offer?"

"He would go down from the five felony counts and three misdemeanors to only one felony."

She looked away for a second, letting the indignity sink in. "And I'd have to get up in court and say I... committed that?"

I nodded.

"And then I'd be a felon. For life."

"Yeah."

"And is there any... time?"

"Six months."

She winced.

It was not my job to talk her into this deal, but I wanted her to have all the facts. I said, "If I could just lay things out so you have the full perspective..."

With a quick nod, she let me know she'd listen.

"Okay," I said, "so let's start with the case he filed. He charged you with multiple counts for each theft. So for three thefts, we're looking at three felony counts for allegedly taking the vials of pain meds, and that's under Section 843 of the United States Code. Plus, there's two felonies for false statements about healthcare matters under Section 1035, because he says you changed the patient records to cover up those thefts. And then we've got the three misdemeanors for simple possession."

"And the, uh, potential sentence..." She paused to glance at the doorway to the next room. Then she said, "If you could answer without saying the word J-A-I-L, I'd appreciate it. Just the numbers, please."

"Uh-huh. Well, to kind of put these things in two different piles, a misdemeanor is any charge for which you can't get more than one year. And felony means a charge for which you can get more than one year, although obviously some felonies will get you a lot more than that. So, with those three misdemeanor counts, the absolute max there is three years."

She took a deep breath, like she was bracing herself to hear the rest.

"Bear in mind," I said, "it's real unusual for a first offense to get the maximum. So the numbers I'm saying really are the absolute worst, not what I would expect to happen in real life. So, for the three counts under Section 843, the max there is four years on each count—"

Her mouth tightened, and she closed her eyes.

"Now, typically you'll see those sentences run concurrently, meaning you serve them at the same time. So somebody who gets two years on this and three years on that would really only be looking at three years total, since the first two years count toward both sentences."

I was trying to reassure her, at least to some extent, because I didn't want to do LaRue's dirty work for him. He might've felt it was his job to scare LaDonna into taking his plea deal, but it certainly wasn't mine.

"How much time is it on the other felonies?"

"Under Section 1035? Those two counts carry a max of five years each."

She stood up quickly, went to the window, and looked out at her yard. The tightness in her back looked like anger to me, so I wasn't surprised at the quiet fury in her voice when she said, "Mr. Munroe, I have followed all the rules. I worked hard in school. I got a professional degree. I bought this home for my baby to grow up in, because it's in a decent school district. I did everything I was supposed to do, but…" She took a deep breath. I figured she didn't want to say more when her daughter was right in the next room.

"It isn't fair," I said.

She gave a bitter laugh. Outside the window, the palm tree in her yard was swaying in the wind. Its tall, skinny trunk was bent like an archer's bow.

"I heard a speech once," I said. "Matter of fact, I think it might've been Martin Luther King. He said, the moral arc of the universe bends toward justice—"

She cut me off with, "He died a long time ago. Shot down in cold blood."

"That's true," I said after a moment. "But I'm still inclined to think he was right. Thing is, he also said that the arc is long. It is real damn long. And my job, in your case or anybody else's, is to make it bend sooner. To get it where it's supposed to be, in time to make a difference."

"That's a noble thought." Her tone still had some bite to it.

And I deserved it. I wasn't the one who might end up serving time for something I hadn't done.

My heart lurched, the thing it had been doing lately, and my stomach lurched along with it. I tried to remember if I'd ever felt like this before when I was sitting down, not exerting myself at all. I made a mental note to call my doctor, but then realized I didn't have one. I'd never gotten around to finding a doctor after moving back to Basking Rock.

"I have to… consider that offer," LaDonna said, in a tone of absolute disgust. "For my baby girl's sake, I have to make the right choice. If I accepted his terms, would I be able to… get visitation?"

I figured she'd used that word in order to make it harder for her daughter, if she was listening, to understand. I tried to do the same with my own terminology.

"Well… that depends. There's no federal facility in South Carolina for women, so—"

"What?" She turned to face me. "Not in the whole state? Why not?"

I paused to think of an explanation that didn't use the words "jail" or "prison."

"The reason is, female convicts only make up around 7 percent of the federal correctional population." In the other room, I heard her daughter singing along with the TV. Since we didn't seem to have a four-year-old eavesdropper, I went back to plain English and said, "About every bad thing you could name is mostly done by men."

That struck a chord. I didn't know what LaDonna's past was, but I could see she had no trouble accepting that that was the truth.

"Okay," she said. "Then where's the nearest women's facility?"

"It'd probably be either Tallahassee or West Virginia. I can ask LaRue."

"Two states away? What is that, five hundred miles?" Her face flashed with a hurt that made me think she might cry, and she whipped around to look out the window again. "Don't ask him," she said, her back to me. "Don't ask him one damn thing."

"No, ma'am," I said. "I won't."

"I'm taking my baby girl to the beach today. Taking her to play in the sand and have fun." The defiance in her voice made it sound like she was prepared to drive her car right over anybody who got in the way of that plan.

"That sounds good," I said. The temperature was in the high sixties, but with her trial only weeks away, I knew she couldn't wait around for warmer weather. "Shouldn't be crowded, on a weekday."

She kept on looking out the window. "This might or might not be news to you," she said after a moment, "but that moral arc you were talking about is different for people like me. There's a doctor I reported in June, and he was still working when I left. No consequences. That audit they did must've skipped right over him."

"Who was that?"

"Dr. Ainsworth. An ear, nose, and throat guy. I had a patient get read-mitted to the CCU with complications a couple of weeks after he did a surgical procedure on her."

"What'd he do wrong?"

"Nothing that I know of, medically. Complications happen. But she'd already gotten her bill for the surgery, and she was real worried about it. I told her I wasn't the one to talk to for that, but she showed it to me anyway, and I saw he'd billed her for a more complicated procedure than what he'd done. I don't know anything about reimbursement rates, but I do know a complicated procedure costs more than a simple one."

"How'd you know he did a simple procedure?"

"I was there. He did it right there in the room. Local anesthesia."

"Who'd you report him to?"

She turned around to face me. I could see she was a little surprised by my level of interest. "Well, I talked to him first, when he rounded on her to see how she was doing. I thought it was just a mistake on the bill, and he'd want to get it fixed, but after, out in the hallway, he got real snappy with me. Some doctors you can't talk to—they don't like it. Surgeons, especially. So I reported it up the chain."

I was trying to figure out if it made any sense to think there might be a connection here. Employers did sometimes retaliate against whistle-blowers, but framing somebody for multiple felonies felt like a stretch. Especially since this doctor's name hadn't come up at all in the investigation Terri and I had done.

"At your work," I said, "who knew about that? I mean, the fact that you'd reported him."

"Besides him and the administration? I don't know. I might've mentioned it to a friend on the unit."

"Did you ever happen to mention it to Desmond?"

She winced. "I told him a lot of things." Her voice was at about half its usual volume, and she was looking at the floor. Her embarrassment about that misguided affair was palpable.

"I'm sorry," I said. "But I've got to ask."

"You know, he did say something once." She was squinting up at the far wall like the recollection was just coming into view. "I mentioned it, and he... I think what he said was, he liked me, he didn't want me to run into any trouble, so I should learn to stay in my lane."

"What did you think he meant?"

"Just... stay out of it. But I was, like, I already reported it. I don't need your commentary. You know? Maybe *you* never read the policy manual, but I did, and I did what it said I was supposed to do." She was getting more annoyed as the memory of the conversation came back to her. "Anyway, he didn't like that. He thought I was disre-specting him, saying since he's in janitorial, he didn't understand what my responsibilities are. Which, I'm sorry, but he *didn't* understand."

"Of course not," I said.

"He can be real arrogant."

"Yup."

She peered at me, her eyes narrowing. "Did you talk to him?"

"Yep. My PI and I met with him the other day."

"Okay. So you saw how he is?"

I chuckled. "Yeah, I saw how he is." After a second, I added, "He ever tell you he was friends with higher-ups at the hospital?"

"Oh, he told you that?" She sounded amused.

"Is that one of his standard stories?"

"Yeah. You'd think they gave him rides to lunch in their Mercedes." I laughed, and so did she, but then she said, "He exaggerates a lot, but I did see him talking to a few of them sometimes. He—it was gross, honestly, because he would use that to, like, reel a woman in. As in, go out with me, and I'll put in a good word. I'll help you in your job."

I made a disgusted sound. "When you say talking to those higher-ups," I said, "how do you mean? Saying good morning, that kind of thing, or—?"

"No, more than that. It was like they were... not *friends*, but, you know, work friends."

"Huh. And which higher-ups are we talking about?"

"Oh, the CEO, the guy on all the billboards, the... I don't know. A few different people."

"You mean Thibodeau? And Dr. Kassel?"

"Yeah, them, and some others."

I thought for a second. "Did you ever see Thibodeau or Kassel being work friends with other people on Desmond's level?"

"I don't know. I don't think so. Why are you asking about this?" Then her expression changed. "Oh."

"Yeah. I'm trying to— Well, two things. Number one, I'm trying to figure out what happened here—"

"You think *Desmond* set me up?"

"Maybe. Did that ever occur to you?"

"Well… honestly, no, because… Look, I didn't break up with him. I should have, and I'm disappointed in myself that I didn't, but no. He just… moved on. That's how he is: one woman to the next. So I didn't feel like there was any reason for him to be… vindictive, or…"

Out of the corner of my eye, I saw her daughter coming back from the other room. She flashed past me and hid behind her mother's legs, hugging her around the hips. "Mama," she said, "I'm hungry."

"Okay, baby." LaDonna looked at me. This was not to be discussed in front of the child.

I took my empty tea glass to the sink and said goodbye to both of them.

As I closed the front door behind me, I glanced at the tricycle again. This was a good home. I knew there was nobody else who would care half as well for that child. And no prison sentence would be short enough to keep that girl in LaDonna's custody.

16

JANUARY 13, 2023

S itting with Terri on a couch in Judy's stark white living room, I tried to explain why I hadn't told Mrs. Reed about Tawny Lee or the story that she'd told us.

"I don't update your mother about your case or our investigation. She's not my client, you are."

Judy was looking across the coffee table at me with puzzlement, like I was a machine that had stopped working. I got the sense that she wished she could turn me off and back on again to see if that fixed the problem.

"Here's the issue," she said. "My mother and I don't discuss the things my father did with other women. And I don't want her to hear about that stripper and Dr. Kassel for the first time in the courtroom, when I'm up there on the stand."

"When you're up on the— Wait, what? That's not how she would hear it."

"Not if you explain it to her first. That's what I'm saying."

"No, what I mean is, that's not something you could testify about. That would be hearsay."

She shook her head like I must have misspoken. "How is that logical?" she asked. "I have to be able to tell my whole story. How can a jury make the right decision otherwise?"

"Sure, if you testify"—something I sincerely hoped to avoid—"you tell *your* story," I said. "But information about what other people did, without your involvement, isn't your story."

"Of course it is. I'm the one who's been charged. Everything to do with my father's death is part of the story I've got to tell."

I was at a loss. Judy seemed to have no clue what hearsay was. Every other client I'd ever had knew something about that, whether from watching crime shows on TV or from their or their friends' personal run-ins with the law.

I took a sip of coffee, trying to gather my thoughts. It was good, strong stuff. We'd arrived shortly after breakfast, and Judy had pointed us to her espresso machine.

Terri looked up from her laptop. "Judy, can I share something I've picked up over the years?"

"Of course."

"What I've noticed is that for most people facing criminal charges for the first time, one of the hardest things to come to terms with is that they're not in control. Not at all. It's like you got caught in a hurricane. You can't get up there on the stand and make it go away any more than you could tell a storm to change course. It follows its own rules. All you can do is hunker down, protect yourself, and... you know, navigate it. Which is what we're trying to help you do. So maybe think of us as something like the National Weather Service."

From Judy's face, I thought the first hint of understanding was dawning on her.

"Yeah, we've mapped it out," I said. "We're looking at all the vulnerabilities, so we can tell you, like, here's something we really need to work on protecting, and that thing over there, we don't."

"And one thing you're right about," Terri said, "is that we need to drill down into what was going on with Alanna and Dr. Kassel. We might never figure out exactly what happened here, but the more we can find out about them, the better."

"That's right," I said. "If we can show that Alanna was seeing both your father and the doctor who... well, bare minimum, failed to save his life, then that's great. It's wild, as stories go, but it's memorable, and it could go a long way toward raising reasonable doubt in the jury's minds."

"So," Judy said slowly, "we need to get that stripper up on the stand to talk about that?"

"No, the strip—I mean, Ms. Lee, she can't tell the jury about Alanna's... escapades, with your father or Kassel or anybody else, because that's hearsay too. Unless Ms. Lee saw them together, which I don't think she did. If she only knew about it because your father told her, she can't testify about that."

"Then who can? I don't expect either of them will admit to having an affair."

"Oh, no," I said. "I'm pretty sure they won't. And that's fine. It's actually better if they deny it, right up there under oath in front of the jury, and then I confront them with the evidence showing that they lied. Because after that, the jury won't believe anything else they say."

"So that's what I've been working on," Terri said, clicking something on her laptop. "Alanna keeps a real low profile, incredibly low for this day and age, but I was able to get a few pictures of her walking from her house to her car."

"You did?" I said. "Isn't she in a gated community? How'd you manage that?"

"Well, I had to use a drone."

I started laughing. "This woman," I said to Judy. "Don't ever cross her. She is something else."

Terri smiled but kept her eyes on her laptop screen. "I also got photos of Dr. Kassel, which was easy. That man would put his face on postage stamps if he could. And then I ran them both through this service I subscribe to, which does a reverse image search with facial recognition. So..."

As she set her laptop on the coffee table and turned it around, I asked, "What, do you work for the CIA now?"

She laughed. "Anyway, I found this."

We were looking at what appeared to be a teenage girl's or college student's selfie, taken outdoors on a sunny day. Most of the frame was filled with the girl's pink bangs and dramatic eye makeup. Terri clicked a couple of times, zooming in on the top left corner of the frame. Two small faces came into view: Alanna and Dr. Kassel, who must've been across the street when the selfie was taken. They were facing each other, and I could see part of a stone doorway between them.

"Damn," I said. "Where was that? And when?"

"It came off this girl's Insta," she said, "so the location metadata was stripped. Which is too bad, because if I knew where it was, I could run searches for other photos taken in that area. But at least we know it's the right time period—she posted it on June 5, 2021."

"Two weeks before my daddy died?"

"Mm-hmm. So now we at least have some evidence that they knew each other back then."

Judy, gesturing to the laptop, said, "You mind if I take a closer look at that?"

"No, of course." Terri handed it over.

While Judy scrutinized the screen, I asked Terri, "So how does that work, that image search thing? What's it do that I can't do myself on the internet?"

She shrugged. "You can't put two different people's pictures into a search engine and have it find photos of both of them together."

"Good lord."

"It's pretty cool."

"I mean, it's useful. But I'm still coming to terms with the fact that privacy doesn't exist anymore."

"Oh. Yeah, that part's a little weird."

Judy, still looking at the screen, said, "Oh, I know where this is. It's about 300 yards from here, over that way." She pointed roughly southwest. "See, look at this."

She turned the laptop around. She'd zoomed in to show about three feet of the stone frame of the doorway Alanna was standing in, part of a black iron railing, and a few blue tiles.

"That's one of Franklin Mosely's townhomes. Those turquoise tiles were his signature for a few years in the 1890s. There are hardly any of them left, since they never did stand up well to hurricane debris. But on that place they're in a recessed entryway, and it's north-facing, so they were protected."

Her tone was casual. She might as well have been showing us a picture and pointing out the features—the flags, the tall columns, the president standing on the South Portico—that made it obviously the White House.

Terri and I looked at each other. The astonishment in her eyes made me realize that I'd never shown her the map of the French Quarter that Judy had drawn. "Judy's got a deep knowledge of our local— what did you call them? Architectural assets?" I said.

"That's one term you could use for this townhome, yeah," Judy said. "And the interesting thing is, there's another one a few streets over that he built in the same year, which originally looked almost identi-cal. But it's on a corner facing southeast, so it took some pretty savage hits from storms over the years. Then it got a whole new facade in the sixties, so that pretty much killed its historical value. Although the foundation is still worth looking at. I wish more builders had used Mosely's techniques when it came to that—he really knew his way around flood protection."

Terri was staring at Judy. I was pretty sure she still hadn't blinked. "Do you just happen to know a lot about that... was he an architect? That Mr. Mosely?"

"Yes, he was," Judy said briskly. "Although not one of the most important ones of his era. On that street, I'd say he ranks third."

"On that *street*?" Terri asked. "You know all the architects on that street?"

"Buildings are easy to remember," Judy said. "I've never understood why most people don't pay much attention to them."

Terri looked at her for a second. "My goodness, Judy. I'm sorry, I don't think I've gotten to know you as well as I should have."

"You haven't asked me very many questions. If you'd like to, I'm happy to schedule a time to talk."

Terri gave her a slow nod. "Yeah. Let's do that. Um, in the meantime, though, can you show me that street on a map? Or that building? I'd like to run some searches on the address."

"Oh, of course. I'll type the address into Google, and you can take it from there." She swung the laptop back around, typed something, and pushed it over to Terri.

A minute later, Terri had the property record up. "It's owned by something called Property Advisement LLC."

"Were they shooting for the most generic name possible?" I asked.

Terri typed for another minute, then rolled her eyes at the screen. "The secretary of state's website says that entity is owned by two other LLCs. Huh."

That rang a bell—or not so much a bell as an alarm.

"Remember that case we had early in the pandemic?" I said. "The one where we found all those LLCs nested inside each other, and—"

"Oh," Terri said, her face turning serious. "Yeah."

I turned to Judy. "We had a case where following a trail of LLCs ended up in a breakthrough. And Roy's the one who helped us do that —Roy Hearst, who I used to work for—because he knows that kind of stuff inside and out."

"That sounds good. Go ahead and hire him. Or if that's not how lawyers work, I'll hire him."

"Okay. I don't happen to know his billing rate—"

"I'm sure it's fine."

. . .

197

At six o'clock that evening, Terri and I met Roy at his golf club. He was waiting for us at the bar. After some enthusiastic catching up with Terri, he walked us across the restaurant to the private room he'd reserved for us.

We got our dinner orders placed, the waitress brought our drinks, and then Terri excused herself for a minute. As soon as the door closed behind her, Roy said, "Leland, are you okay? You're still not taking my vacation advice, are you."

There was no sense denying it. He'd told me a long time ago that a person would fall apart without at least one vacation a year. But when I was growing up, vacations had never been in the budget, so making time for them didn't come naturally.

"I take it from your suntan that you went someplace nice over Christmas," I said.

"The Bahamas. You should try it." He leaned back in his chair and looked at me, shaking his head. "I always thought you worked too much."

I shrugged. "I've got back-to-back trials coming up. The first one starts in six days, and then Judy's is a little over a week after that. Not a lot of time for relaxing spa treatments, or whatever else you'd recommend."

"What I'd recommend is not making the mistakes I made when I was your age." He took a sip of his gin and tonic and set it back down. "So I'll say it one more time, and then I'll stop." He looked me in the eye. "Number one, don't work too hard. And number two, don't let a good woman go." He gave a meaningful nod in the direction Terri had gone. "Right? Nothing ventured, nothing gained."

"Yeah. Or in my case, something ventured, nothing gained."

"Oh." He deflated a bit. "Damn. Well, I'm sorry to hear that."

"Thanks."

He looked past me, and his face lit up. " Terri! Come take a look at this before our food arrives."

He pulled a Redweld file out of his briefcase.

"I had to chase some of this up to Delaware and send a runner to their Division of Corporations," he said. "And then the other thread led to Wyoming and Nevada, so I paid for some help there. If Judy cared about money, she would not like today's bill. But what we've got here is pretty good." He took some papers out of the Redweld and slid them across the table. I started reading.

"At least you didn't have to chase it down to the Caymans this time," Terri said.

"True. That would've taken a while."

"Well, I'll be damned," I said, seeing Alanna's and Kassel's names on the documents. I looked at Roy. "So what's the situation, exactly?"

"Well, you've got the LLC that owns the building," he said, taking the document back and flipping to the last page to show us a chart that looked something like a family tree.

"Then," he said, going up a generation, "this other LLC owns the first one. Both of them are registered in South Carolina." He went up another generation. "Then there's two more LLCs that own that second one. They're in Delaware. And each of those two Delaware ones is owned by another one—this one here's in Nevada, and as you can see it's owned by that mistress you were concerned about. And then this Wyoming one is owned by the doctor."

Terri said, "So basically, they own this building together."

"Yup. They've set up all these shell companies like one of those Russian dolls, you know..." He gestured to show dolls nested inside each other. "But when you take it apart, it's the two of them hiding in the middle."

"What's the point of having their companies in those random other states?" I asked.

"Oh, it's not random. They clearly got good legal advice as far as where to incorporate. Those states all provide a little more protection than most, in terms of privacy. That's why I had to hire runners— some of the information I wanted isn't available online."

He looked up and smiled at the doorway again. The waitress was coming in with our food. She served us, gave the usual helpful spiel, and left us alone again.

I started in on my shrimp while Terri and Roy compared notes on their steaks. After a few bites, I asked, "About that Russian doll setup they've got, why'd they bother? I mean, what's the point, when it didn't even take you one day to figure it out?"

"It only took me a day because you told me what address to research. If I were just trying to figure out if those two people owned any real estate together—that would be damn near impossible."

"Is there any legit reason somebody would use that kind of setup?"

He shook his head. "Nobody does that with an ordinary business transaction. You don't need three or four layers of LLCs to hold a piece of real estate. And doing it that way is a real pain in the ass. Maybe for some multinational with ten thousand employees that kind of structure makes sense, but if I see a small company doing that, or in this case individuals, I've got no reasonable conclusion other than that they're trying to hide something. Maybe they're concealing assets during a divorce, maybe it's a tax thing, or criminal activity... but normal, it is not."

"When was it that they set all this up?" Terri asked. "I know they bought the building about a year ago, so not that long after the victim's death."

"Yeah, and all of these LLCs were created eighteen months ago or so. Presumably for the purpose of stashing real estate away without their names being attached. It'd probably be a good idea to run a name search on each of the LLCs to see if any of them own other properties, but I didn't have time for that today. Here, you keep this." Roy handed me the Redweld.

We dug into our food again—it was excellent—and started chatting about things that were less important and more fun. An hour or so later, when Roy went to the men's room, Terri got back to business.

"I'm thinking I ought to do a stakeout," she said. "On that building. Because what Roy found is great, but all it proves is that those two started some kind of business relationship around the time the victim died. Which could be a coincidence, so we definitely need more."

"Right. It may look fishy to us, but I can't see a jury reacting in horror if I bust out this LLC stuff in court."

"Mm-hmm. I'm not sure how well they'd even understand it. Scandals are kind of like jokes: if you have to explain them..."

"Exactly. This paperwork isn't some private detective's motel adultery photo."

I laughed, but she didn't. "No, that's literally what I want to get," she said. "That's the point of a stakeout."

"I thought that only happened in movies. You know, photos through a crack in the blinds of some guy getting it on with his side piece."

"Oh yeah, that's real. The crack in the blinds, or the passionate clinch as they're stumbling into the room..."

"People *do* that?" I said. "What's the point of sneaking off to some motel if you're going to start making out before you're even in the room?"

"What can I tell you? Lust makes people stupid."

I laughed harder than I had in a while. We both did.

"Anyway," she said, "for this to work, I have to ask you to do something you're not going to want to do. Is there any way you can postpone your meeting with the doctor?"

I deflated. It had been hard enough to get Kassel to return my phone call; arranging a meeting had been even harder. "I really don't want to give him the chance to change his mind."

She nodded sympathetically. "What I'm afraid of," she said, "is that something about your conversation might make him nervous. If he thinks you're on to him in any way, he'll watch his step for a while. And that's the opposite of what we want. For me to have any chance of getting compromising photos of them, we need him relaxed and careless."

"Dammit," I said.

She was right. We both knew it.

17

JANUARY 16, 2023

E mma Jean refilled my glass of tea—I was back in the living room where Judy had played piano, but this time neither she nor Terri were there—while Mrs. Reed recovered her composure.

I took a sip. The late-morning sun was slanting in the windows. I could spend about another forty minutes here; after that, I needed to grab lunch and head for the hospital to meet with Dr. Kassel at one. Terri and I had gotten what we needed, although not in the way we'd expected to.

When Mrs. Reed got ahold of herself, she looked at the paper in her hand, then back at me. "Are you sure this is real?"

"As sure as I can be. My computer expert found it on your husband's hard drive."

I didn't mention what Adam had found in Conway's emails: photos, apparently taken by a PI that Conway had hired, of Alanna and Kassel in that passionate clinch Terri had mentioned. Six days before he died, he'd forwarded them to Alanna, threatening to share them with Kassel's wife.

The document we were looking at was two pages long. I'd printed out a copy for Mrs. Reed. At the top, it read: "Amendment to Conway H. Reed Revocable Living Trust Dated April 8, 2009."

"I can see that's a notary's stamp there," she said, "but did you check if it's real?"

She was still in denial, but only barely.

"Yes, ma'am. I called the notary, and she confirmed it."

She took a deep breath and closed her eyes for a second.

The amendment was dated two months before Conway died, and it changed the living trust beneficiary from Mrs. Reed to Alanna Carpenter.

What that meant in practical terms, I didn't know, because Conway's laptop didn't have a copy of the original trust document on it. The trust was more than a decade older than the laptop, so that was no great surprise. But it was a problem, because a trust could contain just about anything: three dollars, a racehorse, a real estate portfolio. So I had come to see if Mrs. Reed had a copy.

She did, but she didn't need to refer to it. She apparently had it all but memorized.

"This is the trust he created after my accident," she said, shaking her head in stunned disbelief. "About eight months after, when... the dust had settled, I guess you could say, and we were starting to see what the road ahead was going to look like. We went and redid our estate planning, with reciprocal trusts and pour-over wills. So this trust... I think it contains everything that was in his sole name. So probably everything but this house, our joint account, and the trust fund he created for Judy."

"I'm real sorry," I said. "This is a hard thing to find out."

She nodded.

I wasn't going to delve into Mrs. Reed's finances unless I had to—that would be intolerably rude. If she hadn't yet noticed the amputation of all those assets, I figured, that must mean there'd been enough in the joint bank account and Conway's life insurance to keep her going thus far. Everything else was still in limbo while the estate was being dealt with, so it had fallen to me, rather than the executor, to drop this bomb.

So I wasn't going to pry, but I needed to assess Alanna's motive to kill. I didn't remember much from my estates and trusts class in law school, but I did know a revocable trust could be changed at any time. It was right there in the name. You could make somebody the beneficiary of millions on Tuesday and take it all away again on Wednesday —unless you died before you had a chance to change the document.

Given her financial background, Alanna had to know that too.

"Mrs. Reed, please believe that I wouldn't ask this if I didn't think it might be important to Judy's case, but do you happen to know roughly what the value of that trust would be?"

"As of today? I couldn't tell you. But back when we did our estate planning, I seem to recall Conway saying it was on the order of thirty million."

"Uh-huh. Well, thanks. That's good to know."

Even a woman as wealthy as Alanna Carpenter might kill for that kind of money. And it was probably a lot more now. I was no financial wizard, but I knew that the fortunes of rich men tended to grow.

I was about to ask something else, but Mrs. Reed spoke up first. "Emma Jean," she said, "would you mind taking that picture down for me?" She gestured to the photo of Conway on the wall.

"Not at all," said Emma Jean, heading over to it.

"And if you could go through the house and get all the other photos of him…" She trailed off, looking out a window.

Emma Jean lifted the framed picture off its hook and turned around, holding the side with the photo against herself—I thought she might be trying to spare Mrs. Reed the sight of it. "Where would you like me to put them?"

"I don't know," Mrs. Reed said. "I really don't."

"There's some room in the garage."

Mrs. Reed nodded. "Yes, that sounds good. Judy can go through them there and see if she wants any. Then we can… What day is trash day?"

"Thursday."

"Okay. Thank you."

Emma Jean carried the photo out of the room, and I let Mrs. Reed sit with her thoughts.

After a minute, she looked up at me and said, "I know what this trust amendment must mean for Judy's case. That's the only good thing about it. I'd like to have you talk with the executor."

"That'd be good. I'll fit a call in whenever I can, but if he wants to talk on Thursday or Friday of this week, it'll have to be after hours. I've got a trial during the day." LaDonna's trial was the next emergency on my agenda.

"I'll tell him that. But I am going to need to fight this. Confidentially, I don't have that much money left. Maintaining this home is expensive, and when I think of all the modifications to make everything accessible… I couldn't imagine having to do that all over again somewhere else." Mrs. Reed shivered. "Living with a spinal injury is very expensive. Emma Jean's salary alone is over sixty thousand a year, and then there are medical expenses and so forth."

"My goodness, I'm sorry to hear that." Remembering the eleven dollars an hour that LaDonna was making at a similar job, I added, "I have to say, I really respect that you're paying Emma Jean a good wage. That type of work isn't always paid right."

"Oh, I wouldn't dream of doing otherwise. She is the best aide I have ever had. For the first three or four years after my accident, I can't even tell you how much of my energy was taken up with finding and training new aides, dealing with the unreliable ones…" She shook her head. "I bought one girl a car, because it was always car trouble that kept her from coming or made her get here late—or so she said. But it turned out, it wasn't that."

"It's got to be hard, finding the right person."

"It really is. So once I found Emma Jean, my goodness. What a relief. She's just perfect. Oh!"

She looked past me with a surprised but friendly expression. I turned and saw Emma Jean in the doorway. She was holding a smaller picture, presumably of Conway, although once again she was holding it so we only saw the back. "I'm so sorry," she said. "I didn't mean to overhear. I just had a question about this picture, because Miss Judy's in it too—"

"It's fine, honey. Maybe put those ones in a guest room, and we'll go through them when I'm feeling a little less down about things. But don't worry—I was only telling Mr. Munroe what a gem you are."

Emma Jean looked simultaneously embarrassed and moved. To me, she said—chin down, quietly, but in a rush—"She won't say it herself, but Mrs. Reed is wonderful. She doesn't judge anybody's background. She respects folks for what they are." She fled the room without waiting for a reply.

"I wish everybody dealing with a disability like this could have someone even halfway like her around to help," Mrs. Reed said. "But even if you can find them, which is hard enough, most people can't afford them. That's the whole reason I started my charity."

"That's a real good thing you do," I told her. Terri had researched the charity for me. Through some type of financial magic involving trusts and training and free legal advice, it helped South Carolina paraplegics and quadriplegics in lower economic echelons avoid the poorhouse and the nursing home.

"It's a *necessary* thing," she said. "As for myself, I'm going to have to get those assets back so that I don't end up needing the services of my own charity someday. But I don't want to interfere with Judy's case at all. So I'll wait until you give me the go-ahead."

"Oh, I think you can get started right now. That's not going to harm Judy. It might even help."

"How so?"

"Well, I don't handle civil lawsuits, so don't quote me on this, but I seem to recall that if you file one against Alanna, you'll be able to demand a whole lot of documentation and other evidence from her. Who knows, you might find something that helps Judy."

For the first time since my arrival that morning, Mrs. Reed smiled.

Terri met me at my house for a quick review before we headed to the hospital to meet with Dr. Kassel.

On my home office corkboard, Alanna now had a string connecting her to Kassel. Below them was a picture of their building in Charleston—I'd written "$4.68M" on it in ballpoint pen; that was the price they'd paid for it—and below her was a copy of the first page of Conway's trust amendment.

We sat in chairs, looking up at the wall.

"So what's your vote?" I asked. "Jealousy and fear? Or greed?"

"You mean did he do it by himself, or did they do it together for the money?"

"Uh-huh."

Terri hesitated. "Well, I haven't met her yet," she said. "I still don't have a sense of who she is. And I can't take her low profile as evidence of guilt, because she's been low profile for years. Since long before she met Conway."

"Yeah. But what's your gut telling you?"

She sighed and shook her head. "Almost every time I've seen... I'm not even going to call them love triangles. Lust triangles is more like it. Anyway, whenever I've seen a triangle where one of the people was killed and the other two stayed together afterward, that's usually how it was. They got rid of the third wheel together."

"Yeah."

"But this was a real weird way to do it—the hospital thing. That's what I'm stuck on. It's not something they could've planned."

"Yup. Maybe they had a different plan, but then Conway came to the ER and Kassel seized his chance."

She nodded slowly. "You going to subpoena him?"

"I think I'm going to have to. Otherwise I might not be allowed to ask him about this at all."

At the hospital, we parked and went up to Kassel's office. The waiting room was half-full, but the receptionist took us back into a small conference room. I was surprised to see somebody else there—not Dr.

Kassel, but a bland middle-aged man in what had to be a three-thousand-dollar suit. It was gray and understated, like he was, but something in the cut and fabric told me what it had cost.

"Harrison Thibodeau," he said, standing and offering his hand.

"Oh, hello," I said. His handshake was as nondescript as he was; not limp, but not the kind of aggressive squeeze you got from men who felt they had something to prove. "Leland Munroe. Terri, this is the hospital's CEO."

I introduced her, and they shook too.

Thibodeau gestured for us to sit. As I slung my briefcase on the empty chair next to mine, I said, "I believe you know my friend Roy Hearst. He mentioned you when we were golfing a few weeks back."

"Oh, yeah. Roy's a hell of a golfer."

"That he is."

"Say hello to him for me, if you will."

"Of course."

The door opened, and Dr. Kassel came in, apologizing for his lateness. He was about six two, with dark hair and an easy smile that looked to me like about twenty grand's worth of cosmetic dentistry.

"Dr. Kassel's been a busy guy lately," Thibodeau told us. "Lot of catching up to do after going off on vacation and coming in—what was it—top five in that triathlon?"

Kassel waved him off. "Oh, it was just a winter triathlon. They're not as hard."

Another reason to dislike Kassel added itself to my pile. It was as if somebody had assembled a perfect man from the raw parts: movie-star looks, half-million-dollar salary, high-status job, and now this.

"I know you're both very busy," I said, "and I don't want to waste your time. We're here for a real simple reason. Now, I've read the coroner's report in this case, of course, but that's an after-the-fact forensic reconstruction, if you will, of what might've happened to poor Mr. Reed. What I'd like to get a sense of, Dr. Kassel, is how he looked to you, as a physician, in his last moments."

Terri and I had decided not to ask Kassel anything about his connection to Alanna. We didn't want him to smell danger and find some way to avoid getting up on the stand. I knew that wouldn't be hard; a doctor could easily fake a medical issue that would justify failing to show up in court. Back in Charleston, as a prosecutor, I'd had a doctor no-show on me, and the case had proceeded without him. The testimony I'd wanted him for came in, but it was read out in monotone by the IT admin responsible for the records. That was the last thing I wanted to see happen here.

"Well," Dr. Kassel said, "he looked very typical for a man in his sixties who's having a heart attack. I don't recall anything out of the ordinary in that regard."

"And I believe," Thibodeau said, "there's ample detail in the medical records. To perhaps save time here, can I inquire, is there any particular issue you're hoping Dr. Kassel can help you zero in on?"

I was not clear why the CEO was at our meeting. The hospital's general counsel would've made sense, but Thibodeau wasn't a lawyer. I'd looked him up at some point. He was a healthcare administrator with an MBA. Granted, given Basking Rock's size, he had to be aware that I was representing two different people with ties to his hospital. Perhaps it was curiosity that had him sitting across from us today. Not that I would share anything with him about either case.

"Actually, yes, Mr. Thibodeau, thank you," I said. "What we're trying to pinpoint is exactly when Mr. Reed might've taken the antibiotic that unfortunately ended his life. So I'm hoping to get a sense of when certain symptoms arose, and where he was in the process when he arrived at the hospital."

Thibodeau nodded. "I must watch too many of those TV shows," he said, "but I think I understand your point here. If you can nail down the time of, in this case, Mr. Reed taking a pill, you can eliminate some suspects or implicate others."

"That's about the sum of it, yes."

"That's very interesting," he said. "I certainly don't mean to trivialize anything about this—a man died here, a pillar of our community, and this case could hardly *be* more serious—but I just find that so interesting, what y'all do."

With a smile, Terri said, "A lot of folks agree with you there. That's why there's so many of those crime shows on TV."

Thibodeau chuckled. "I'm sure you're right."

He seemed, I noticed, to be taking up a lot of the time we'd scheduled for this meeting, which had me thinking that his presence was due to more than curiosity. Particularly since Dr. Kassel had hardly said a word.

Thibodeau squinted out the window like a thought had just occurred to him. "But *are* there any other suspects? I'm sorry; that's not my business at all, is it."

"Well, no," I said, "but I can't blame you for wondering. We're all human beings. In the face of something like this, it's natural to want to understand what happened."

"People ask me about this case all the time," Terri said.

"Oh, I'm sure they do," he said.

"It's pretty high-profile here in town," I said. "I've overheard folks in restaurants speculating about—well, a little bit of everything. Probably the most undignified is the chatter about the fact that Mr. Reed had a mistress." I was watching Kassel as I spoke. His jaw muscles tightened for a second.

Thibodeau sighed and shook his head. His expression seemed to say *What a shame.*

"Anyway, it'd be real helpful if you could put some thought into what the window might've been for when he took that antibiotic."

"I would have to check on that, I'm afraid," Kassel said. "Because at the time, obviously, we were treating him for his heart attack. But I'm happy to look back at the records."

"If you could, that'd be great. Save us some time at trial. Some lawyers ask witnesses to look at records right there on the stand, and that's not my approach—it's real dull for the jurors. But anyway, if you could look at those, that could be a real help in terms of including or excluding suspects. Knowing who Mr. Reed was... uh, spending time with that morning... and what activities he was involved in that might have triggered that heart attack..."

I put a little flavor into the word *activities*—enough, I hoped, for Kassel's imagination to go where I wanted it to. He wasn't looking at me anymore. He was staring at the table and nodding like he was thinking hard about the medical issues.

"Well, my goodness," Thibodeau said. "Sounds like you've got quite the interesting case."

"Indeed. Oh, and I ought to let you know—I apologize in advance, because I know y'all have already had to deal with some paperwork in the run-up to this trial—but I'll be sending over a subpoena for you, Dr. Kassel."

Thibodeau nodded. "I believe we already got one of those for you from the solicitor, didn't we, Dr. Kassel?"

"We did. And I'm happy to cooperate. It's part of my duty as a citizen, isn't it. Although I really don't recall that much."

"He's a busy man," Thibodeau said. "Lot of patients every day."

"Oh, of course," I said. "And I'm sorry about all the paperwork, especially because mine is pretty redundant. Although I suppose that, as a hospital, y'all are used to a ton of paperwork."

Thibodeau chuckled again. "Oh, yeah. Like you would not believe."

After a little more chitchat, we said our goodbyes. Terri and I rode the elevator down in silence and walked across the hospital parking lot without saying a word. Once I'd driven out of the lot and it was more than certain no one could overhear, I said, feeling pretty satisfied with myself, "Well, I think he'll show up for the trial."

Terri laughed. "If he thinks he can stop you from implicating his girlfriend?"

"That's the beauty of it," I said, stopping at a light. "I don't know how he feels about Alanna now. But whether he wants to save her or throw her under the bus, he's got to testify. If he wants to save her, he'll say the window for taking the pill was after Conway left her house that morning. If he wants to implicate her, he'll say it was while Conway was with her. And I don't honestly care what he says—I just want him on the stand."

"I like that," she said. "Although you maybe rubbed his nose in it a little hard. What 'activities' triggered the heart attack…"

"Well, you know how it is. If you want an oyster to make a pearl, you've got to open it up and jam some sand in there."

18

JANUARY 19, 2023

A t eight fifteen Thursday morning, an hour before we were scheduled to start jury selection for LaDonna's trial, I was sitting with her and Ms. Baker in our war room around the corner from the courtroom. I gulped the last of my coffee, said goodbye to them, and headed out for the hearing on my motion to exclude. Judge Nicholson preferred to hold evidentiary hearings immediately before trial, with only attorneys present.

The guard was just unlocking the courtroom door. I nodded to him and went in. Since trial was before a different judge than the preliminary hearing had been, we were in a different courtroom, although it continued the theme of polished cherrywood and dark blue carpet adorned with stars. The arched white ceiling overhead, with its classical plaster details, told anyone who came in that they were in a temple of the law.

Five minutes later, after LaRue had arrived, the bailiff went through the same "All rise" formalities that he did when the public was there, and Nicholson, who at forty-eight was on the young side for a federal judge, took his place on the bench.

"In the matter of United States of America versus LaDonna Marie Winters," he said, "I understand the defendant has moved in limine to exclude the testimony of the government's computer forensics expert concerning some alleged log-ins on a device at the subject hospital. Is that correct?"

LaRue and I, both standing at our tables, said, "Yes, Your Honor."

"All right. Now, I've read both parties' briefs, and I've got some questions. But I'm going to allow counsel to state their main points for the record. Counsel?"

It was my motion, so I went first. "Thank you, Your Honor. The issue here is that this evidence is unreliable, for reasons I'll get to in a moment, and unduly prejudicial to my client. As such, it should be excluded under Rules 403 and 702. The government's burden in this case is to prove beyond a reasonable doubt that Ms. Winters, on the dates alleged in the indictment, stole the vials of medication at issue and altered certain patient records to make it appear that the medication had been prescribed to them. However, their evidence that she was the perpetrator is so unreliable and unfairly prejudicial that it must be excluded. If I may ask Ms. Thompson, could we please see Defense Exhibit T-1?"

The clerk pulled up the photo of the dispensing cabinet from the preliminary hearing.

"As Mr. LaRue acknowledged at the preliminary hearing, this photograph was taken in the critical care unit of Basking Rock Hospital. What we're seeing here is the dispensing cabinet where medications are stored. This was the very cabinet that apparently, according to an audit, the medications were stolen from. Now, to get the medication out, you've got to log into the dispensing cabinet by entering a username and password on the screen there, which, as we can see, is about the size of a desktop computer screen. And as we can also see, the dispensing cabinet is sitting out in the main hallway. Matter of fact, it's right next to a public bathroom."

I kept eye contact with Nicholson and let that sink in.

"And as we learned at the preliminary hearing," I said, "from the government's own witness, a nurse by the name of Candace O'Malley, that screen there is a touchscreen, and you log in by typing on a keyboard on the screen. Not a real, physical keyboard, but a picture of one that appears on the screen. Mrs. O'Malley also admitted that passersby can see the log-in information as it's being typed, which, as I'm sure Your Honor will appreciate, essentially makes everybody's password insecure. So as a result, forensic evidence that Ms. Winters's log-in was used is not a reliable basis for concluding that Ms. Winters is the one who used it."

Nicholson was nodding in a "Let's get this over with" way, so I sped up. He'd read a more formal version of everything I was saying in the brief.

"And finally, Your Honor," I said, "this is not a mere theoretical concern. We have testimonial and forensic evidence that on one of the three specific occasions when the government's expert will testify that somebody standing in the hallway of the critical care unit typed Ms. Winters's log-in onto that screen, Ms. Winters wasn't even at the hospital. She was more than two miles away, at her home."

"Isn't that actually good for your case?" Nicholson asked.

That was not what I wanted him to take from this. He wouldn't exclude the evidence if he saw it that way.

"Well, Your Honor, it raises reasonable doubt, to say the least. But that's because it essentially proves that the log-in evidence is unreliable as far as telling us *who* logged in. Since that evidence doesn't have any real probative value, the prejudice clearly outweighs it."

"Any and all evidence against your client is prejudicial, Mr. Munroe. That's why the government wants to present it to the jury. What I'm not seeing here is why this particular evidence is so unduly prejudicial as to deprive your client of her due process rights."

"Well, Your Honor, I would say the guardrails provided by the Federal Rules of Evidence were put there in large part to protect due process rights. That's one of the key underlying principles. So when the government's evidence is such that it can't meet its burden under Rule 702—in other words, it can't show that this evidence is reliable and helpful to the jury—then admitting that evidence does implicate due process. In other words—"

"I read the briefs, counsel," Nicholson said. "Thank you. Now, Mr. LaRue?"

LaRue smiled at the judge like the two of them were on the same team and had been through this type of hearing before—which they undoubtedly had.

"Well," he said, "as Your Honor pointed out, the defense will have the opportunity to raise the issue of reasonable doubt with the jury. And I'm sure the defense will vigorously challenge the government's computer expert when we put him on the stand. In sum, Ms. Winters will have every opportunity to put on a robust defense. Now, in the interest of time, I won't reiterate the government's brief here, but I do want to highlight one thing about Mr. Munroe's argument."

He turned my way and looked at me for a second like he was taking stock of my character. He did not seem favorably impressed.

"I couldn't help but notice," he said, turning back to Nicholson, "that Mr. Munroe claimed to have evidence that on only *one* of the three occasions when opioid medications were stolen under Ms. Winters's log-in, Ms. Winters was allegedly not present. He doesn't mention anything about the other two occasions. I take that to mean he's got no such evidence as to them. But instead of wanting to go to trial and fight this fair and square, with the government putting on our evidence and Mr. Munroe putting on his, what he's asked Your Honor to do is throw out *three* pieces of crucial prosecution evidence—to not even let the jury hear about them—on the basis that some testimony from a defense witness that we haven't even heard yet will supposedly undermine *one* of those three pieces of evidence. And I would submit, Your Honor, that that's not fair."

LaRue was good. He was wrong, but he was good.

Nicholson gave me a quick nod that told me the hearing was over.

"I'll take the defense motion under advisement," he said. "I'm not inclined to exclude the evidence at this point, and in fact, I don't believe I can properly do so on the record before me. But, Mr. Munroe, you're free to renew it during trial if you think you've built up a record supporting it."

Back in the war room, I told LaDonna the news. I thought I'd prepared her for the fact that we probably wouldn't prevail on this motion, but apparently I hadn't. She started blinking, and then her composure cracked. She turned to Ms. Baker and burst out sobbing.

I stood there while they hugged.

After a minute or two, LaDonna found the will to speak. "Can I still take that plea deal?"

"I can ask."

"It's six months," she told Ms. Baker. "I can do that if I have to. But I don't know how to tell my baby. I don't know who's going to—who's going to take care of her while I'm gone."

That triggered more sobbing. Once LaDonna had calmed down again, Ms. Baker asked me, "For that deal, what's she got to say she did?"

"It'd be a guilty plea on one of the felony theft charges."

Ms. Baker narrowed her eyes. "A felony is for life."

"It stays on your record, yes."

"She'd lose her nursing license."

"No!" LaDonna said. She looked horrified, even though we'd already discussed the impact on her license more than once.

People faced with stakes this high sometimes slipped into denial; I'd seen it many times. I had to make sure she understood. "Yes," I said. "It would at least be suspended for a good long while. And it could be revoked."

LaDonna looked from her to me and said, frantically, "But I can't *do* that. How am I supposed to raise my daughter on eleven dollars an hour? How does that pay for a place to live and a car to get to work? I'm already about to lose my house!"

"That's not a plea deal," Ms. Baker said. "You lose your license, that's a life sentence."

It took a couple of hours to get a jury seated. LaRue seemed determined to keep mothers off the jury, and I was just as determined to keep them on. He got rid of the only nurse in the pool, but he ran out of peremptory challenges before he could strike the healthcare aide. She asked to be excused because she couldn't afford to take time off work, but Judge Nicholson refused, telling her the trial was only scheduled to take two days.

I let a few older jurors go, because I thought the younger ones might have a better grasp of the computer and GPS evidence.

We broke for lunch, came back, and Judge Nicholson gave the jury a grand speech about the importance of their service. Then he all but put them to sleep with his legal instructions, and we began.

"This case is about lying," LaRue began. He let that sink in. "This case is about stealing." He looked at them, one after the next. "This case is about a fundamental breach of the public trust."

He painted them a portrait of nursing—"one of the highest callings there is"—and then he looked at LaDonna and said, "There was a time, I really do believe, when Ms. Winters was worthy of her uniform. Her patients could trust her. Basking Rock Hospital could trust her."

He looked back at the jury and said, "But that changed. That changed. And that is why the United States District Court for the District of South Carolina has had to call you here today."

He went on to describe each of the three thefts in vivid detail, starting with the dates and times that LaDonna logged in. He acknowledged there was no evidence she abused drugs herself; he said she'd done it "out of the oldest motive, one the Bible speaks of: greed."

The jury was riveted. The healthcare aide glanced at LaDonna and shook her head in dismay.

When LaRue was done with his story, I told mine.

I agreed with him that nursing was one of the highest callings. I agreed that all three thefts had occurred. "But what Mr. LaRue didn't tell you," I said, "is that when the government went into Basking Rock Hospital to investigate these thefts, they didn't find any security footage showing Ms. Winters committing even one of them. They didn't find any medication on her person or in her belongings. They didn't find any empty pill bottles with her fingerprints on them. They didn't find any of that. What they found was that the person who committed these crimes—

the person who wanted the drugs to use or to sell, who would stoop so low as to do this—used her password when they did it."

I asked the clerk to put up the photo of the dispensing cabinet and walked the jurors through where it was located and how it worked.

"So other nurses could see you logging in. Nurses' aides, respiratory therapists, phlebotomists, and X-ray techs could see it. Janitorial staff could see it. Visiting family members could see it. Patients could see it. But Mr. LaRue wants you to believe that none of those people used Ms. Winters's log-in to steal these drugs. He wants you to believe that Ms. Winters, a dedicated nurse with no prior record at all, decided to steal drugs one day—and decided the best way to do it was to log in under her own name."

I went on in that vein and returned to my table feeling pretty good.

But then LaRue called the DEA agent who investigated the thefts. Agent Rodriguez was unusually good on the stand. He didn't have the stiff, jargon-filled monotone that I was used to hearing from cops. Rodriguez brought the government's case to life. His only mistake was some hearsay, when he related something that he'd been told by a former colleague of LaDonna's.

I could've objected, but I let it go. Objecting would only draw the jury's attention to what he'd said. In any event, objections weren't how you won a trial. You could win that way on appeal; if Nicholson overruled an objection of mine, letting in something that he shouldn't have, and LaDonna got convicted, then some federal appellate judge might eventually overturn the verdict. But that would take years. To prevent her from losing her home to the bank and her daughter to social services, I had to win here and now. This wasn't law school, it was real life.

"Agent Rodriguez," LaRue said, "have you worked on other cases where a healthcare worker used their own log-in to steal pharmaceutical drugs?"

"Yes, I have."

"Have you worked on cases where a healthcare worker used their own electronic ID badge to get access to pharmaceutical drugs?"

"Yes, that too."

"So that's a thing that happens? People do that?"

"Yeah." Rodriguez shook his head. "It surprised me, too, earlier in my career."

"Why did it surprise you?"

"I thought people were smarter than that."

A couple of jurors laughed.

"Especially healthcare workers," Rodriguez continued. "But in all seriousness, sometimes people get desperate. And sometimes they don't understand how the computer system works."

"I see. And apart from your professional knowledge that sometimes people do use their own log-ins to commit federal crimes, was there anything particular to this case that gave you confidence that you'd correctly identified the perpetrator here?"

"Yes, there was. Because I didn't only find that the thefts took place when Ms. Winters was logged in. I also found that some patients' medical records had been changed under her log-in."

"And what did that tell you?"

"Well, contrary to what the defense attorney said earlier, that tells me it's unlikely that it was the janitorial staff or a patient visitor who logged in under Ms. Winters's password. Even if they knew how to operate a dispensing cabinet, in terms of getting the drugs out, they most likely wouldn't know how to access and edit a patient record. The people who know how to do that are generally the nurses."

"And can you explain for the jury what you mean by 'edit'?"

"Yes, I mean change the information that was there."

"Change in what way?"

"Well, what both these edits did was make it appear that the patient had received their prescribed dose of medication when they actually hadn't, because it had been stolen."

I barely heard the next question. A flash of lightning had just illuminated Judy's case. I needed to talk to my computer expert.

I scribbled *Call Adam* on my notepad and put my focus back on LaRue. After eliciting more detail on how professional the edits looked, he said he had no further questions.

Nicholson looked at the clock. It was almost four thirty. He announced that the trial would resume in the morning and let the jury go.

I walked with LaDonna and Ms. Baker to the courthouse parking lot, reassuring them both, and we saw LaDonna off. As I escorted Ms. Baker to her Oldsmobile, she said, "I got something I want to talk with you about. You remember where my house is?"

"Uh, around the corner from your daughter, right? Off of Douglass Drive?"

I'd represented her daughter, Simone, in the early days of the pandemic, so we'd had some team meetings on Simone's veranda.

She nodded and gave me the full address.

"I'll see you there," I said.

As soon as she pulled away from the curb, I texted Adam. He was coming to the courthouse tomorrow for his turn on the stand, but I needed to talk to him now.

He called back when I was about halfway to Basking Rock. I got right to the point. "Would it have been possible for Judy's doctor to prescribe a safe medication, and the hospital pharmacy gave her that, but then somebody went back into the system later on and changed the record to say she'd been prescribed cephalosporin?"

"I mean... yeah, somebody with editing privileges could do that. But you're talking about two different records, right? One in the hospital system, where the doctor put in the prescription, and then one in the pharmacy system showing what they gave her?"

"It's two different records, maybe, but it's the same system. At least I think it is. She saw the doctor at the local hospital, and then she went to the hospital pharmacy to pick up the meds."

"*Oh.*"

That was a small word, but he said it like it was big: loud and full of meaning.

After a second, he continued. "Okay, that's... yeah, that could be huge. I'm sorry, it never crossed my mind that both those things could be on the same system, because... I guess we don't do it that way here. I've never heard of anybody picking up their prescription at a hospital pharmacy."

"Yeah, you're city slickers up there. You probably even have a Walgreens or something."

He laughed. Then he got back to business. "Okay, so here's how it works. Electronic records, which is what these are, sit in a database somewhere. And that's got a front end, which is the screen a doctor or a pharmacist would type stuff on, or select things off a drop-down list,

225

however it's set up. And then it's got a back end, which is the coding and the tables and the guys who know what information goes where."

"Tables?"

"Maybe picture it as a giant chest of drawers. If the doctor types an order for—what's another antibiotic? Say, penicillin, then 'penicillin' goes into the 'what medication got prescribed' drawer. And the pharmacist can see in that drawer. When you start working at a new job and you get a log-in to their system, on the back end it's going to give you access to certain drawers and not others, and it's going to say what your access is. Like, can you put something in this drawer, or are you only allowed to look into it and see what's there? Or are you not even allowed to look?"

"Uh-huh. Okay, so obviously the doctors can put something into the medication drawer, and I guess nurse practitioners and maybe some others."

"Yeah, and if it's all the same system, then you probably only have to change what's in the medication drawer once to have it automatically change in both places. I mean on the doctor's side and on the pharmacist's. And from that point on, if somebody checks the records to see what drug was prescribed, that's what it'll say. Whatever drug you changed it to."

"Is there a way we can find out if that's what happened?"

"Well, depending how things are set up and how modern the database is, some of those drawers are what's called auditable. Maybe all of them. And that means you—or, not you, but somebody who has access—can pull up a history of every time somebody put something in that drawer or changed what was in there. That's actually what the investigators did in LaDonna's case, to find out who opened the dispensing cabinet. Or, I mean, whose log-in was used to open it."

"Goddamn. Okay, thank you much. I'm going to do what I can with this, but for now let's refocus on LaDonna's trial. I'll see you at the courthouse tomorrow."

As I took the exit for Basking Rock, my head was spinning. What Adam had said was compelling—now I knew that it absolutely could have happened—but a bigger question remained: Who would've wanted to change Judy's records that way, and why?

If Mrs. Reed's lawsuit against the hospital had been a serious threat, maybe somebody would've been unscrupulous enough to change Judy's records in order to shift blame from the hospital to her. The timing of the change—if there was a change—would be important. If it happened while Mrs. Reed's lawyers were still in settlement talks with the hospital, I'd need to investigate that angle.

I parked outside Ms. Baker's house, a small midcentury one-story with a lavish garden—she was a wizard with plants. She had me sit in the living room and brought me sweet tea. We skipped the usual prolonged Southern inquiry into each other's well-being; she wasn't the type for that. From the first time I'd met her, I'd noticed she regarded the world with a jaundiced eye and did not put much energy into making others comfortable.

"Mr. Munroe," she said, "I did not like how the trial went today. And that's not your fault, but I'm concerned, so I've decided I need to tell you something."

"Oh?"

"Yes. Now, you know I used to work up at the hospital, and I don't anymore. When I left, I told LaDonna she might want to come with me. She didn't, and I understand that. It's one of the best-paid nursing jobs around here, and the place I went isn't. She's got a baby to raise. But I thought we both ought to leave, and now I know I was right."

When she didn't go on, I asked, "Why was it that you left?"

She looked at me for a second. Then she said, "When my daughter was facing her trial, I told you something in confidence. You gave me your word that whatever I said would remain private—that we had a covenant. You kept that covenant, and I'm going to need to ask for that again."

My answer didn't take much thought. I wanted to hear what she knew, and if confidentiality made it hard for me to put the information to use, I figured we'd talk that through. "Okay," I said. "I promise you that."

"Because I'm not getting up on no witness stand. If you put me up there, I'll say I forgot. I'm old, Mr. Munroe. I've got another three, four years before I can retire, and I just want to get there in peace."

"Understood. I won't ask you to testify. I won't involve you at all."

"Okay. So I want you to know, you need to watch out for that Mr. Thibodeau."

"Oh? Why's that?"

She looked off to the side like she was trying to think where to begin. "I used to work with a woman there," she said. "The most senior nurse we had. She took me under her wing and gave me guidance when I was just starting out. She was there for more than thirty years. And I once overheard her talking to him. She'd noticed something— we both noticed it. Overbilling, charging patients for things they didn't need or for things they never even got."

"Uh-huh. And… how'd he respond?"

"At first he was all 'Oh, never you mind. You take care of the patients; I'll take care of the business.' He's real polite when he wants to be. But she kept pushing. She'd been there a lot longer than he had, and she knew how things were supposed to be."

228

I waited, but she didn't go on. Finally, I asked, "So... what happened?"

She shook her head. Her mouth was pressed into a tight line. "Mr. Munroe," she said, "he ruined her. All kinds of trumped-up disciplinary things, and moving her shifts around, night shift and day shift one after the other, just to make things hard for her. It got her so tired she made a bad mistake. A medication error, and it killed a patient. And that was it for her. That was more than she could take."

"That's awful," I said. "How's your friend doing now?"

"She's gone. She went to the Lord."

"Ms. Baker, I am so sorry."

"Well, you know. Can't expect much in this world. At least she's in a better one now."

I sat with that for a second. "So what you're saying is, that's why all this happened to LaDonna. Because she reported something like that? A padded bill?"

She nodded. "If she'd told me about that bill beforehand, you better believe I would've told her not to report it. Just stay out of it. Keep your head low. But she didn't tell me until after she'd done it."

We talked a little more, and then I got up to leave. I was almost to the front door when a question came to mind.

"Ms. Baker, when you worked at the hospital, did you know a man named Desmond Brown?"

19

JANUARY 20, 2023

The next morning in court, I did a short cross-examination on Agent Rodriguez, and then the onslaught began. A federal prosecution is a freight train, ten thousand tons of the law plowing toward you down the tracks.

LaRue called the next witness—the hospital auditor who discovered the thefts—and had him go through his meticulous investigation step by step.

To show the jury the human cost, he called one of the patients whose records had been digitally altered so it looked like she'd received her pain meds when in fact she had not. She described, at times in tears, her night of relentless pain.

He called the hospital pharmacist to explain what the stolen drugs were and how they helped patients—or how they would have helped patients, if only they hadn't been stolen.

With the hospital IT manager, he went over, in exhaustive detail, every bit of digital evidence that pointed to LaDonna.

The sheer amount of information that he hit the jury with seemed designed to convince them that whatever misgivings they might have, there had to be something to this case. I'd talked to jurors before, in post-trial interviews, to understand why they'd reached the verdict they'd reached. More than once, jurors who'd voted guilty told me that was how it felt.

These jurors knew that this was only going to be a two-day trial. They knew nobody had died. But we were all sitting in this majestic building while a federal prosecutor hammered them with fact after fact, and I was sure it was making them feel like, to merit this much effort, there had to be at least some truth to the accusations.

Before we broke for lunch, I got the auditor to admit he hadn't compared the dates and times of the three thefts to LaDonna's time sheets. He'd only looked at the shifts that were scheduled, not the shifts she'd actually worked.

"So if she wasn't there at the time your audit found her log-in was used, wouldn't that mean the theft must've been committed by somebody else?"

"Objection," LaRue said. "Calls for speculation."

It was sustained. I wasn't going to be able to get anywhere with this argument until I put my expert on and got the GPS evidence on the record.

I did get the IT guy to admit that a person's log-in could be used by anyone who knew it, and that without video, eyewitnesses, or two-factor authentication, there was no way to be sure who had logged in. So I'd knocked a few pieces of coal off the federal freight train. And I'd begun to understand why the feds almost always won.

. . .

Over lunch with LaDonna and Adam in the war room, we planned out our afternoon. I was going to have her testify first and then close with him. I'd chosen that order in case she fell apart on cross, although I didn't tell them that. If she held her own with LaRue, fantastic. If she didn't, at least Adam would—he was an experienced expert witness—so we could end on a good note.

They also didn't need to know what I'd learned from Ms. Baker. When she knew Desmond, she'd said, he was a functional opioid addict. As long as he got his fix, he could get to work on time and live his life without too much trouble. I already knew from Terri's background research that he'd been arrested for possession of fentanyl. The fact that just last year he'd apparently stolen money from his girlfriend and a pill off a patient's tray made me think he might still have that problem.

Desmond was on LaRue's witness list, but so were a few other people I didn't think he'd have time to call. Witness lists almost always included people who ended up not testifying; you had to cast your net a little wide, in case the other side did something unexpected and you needed to put up a witness who could respond to it.

I wouldn't have called a guy with a drug-arrest background unless I was desperate, so I was surprised, when we resumed after lunch, to hear LaRue call him. Beside me, LaDonna stayed straight and still in her usual military posture, but I could tell she was confused.

Desmond was dressed for a special occasion. His black suit coat had a gloss that made me wonder if it was made of satin. He got sworn in, and LaRue ran him through his professional background, emphasizing his access to nearly all areas of the hospital and his familiarity with how it ran.

"And in the course of your work there," LaRue said, "did you become acquainted with a nurse by the name of LaDonna Winters?"

"Yes, sir, I did."

"And do you see her here today?"

"I do. She's right there." He pointed.

I waited for LaRue to ask about the nature of Desmond's relationship with LaDonna, but he didn't. Strategically, I couldn't think of a good reason for him to leave it out. I wondered if Desmond hadn't told him.

LaRue had the clerk project a picture of one of Desmond's time cards on the screen, and I realized what was coming. He had Desmond authenticate it—"Yes, those are the hours I worked that day," and so forth. It would've been boring as hell, except that the date on the time card was the day of the first theft. There was only one reason for LaRue to establish that Desmond was at work that day.

"And what happened during your shift that day?" LaRue asked.

"Well, I did my work, you know, as usual, except for one thing. Over in the CCU, when I was cleaning out the bathroom, I looked up from what I was doing and saw Ms. Winters by the dispensing cabinet."

"Was that unusual?"

"That she'd be there? No, nurses use that thing a lot. But I *saw* something. I saw what she did."

"And what was that?"

"She pocketed something. She pulled it out of the drawer, and it went straight in her pocket. And she looked around, all furtive, like. When she saw me in the bathroom doorway, she kind of froze."

"She froze."

"Yeah, like she was uncomfortable. And then she just walked away."

Beside me, LaDonna was sitting ramrod straight, silent, with her fists clenched in her lap. I could almost feel her vibrating with rage. I was

233

glad she was angry. If a juror glanced over, that wasn't a bad emotion to see on her face. Anger was a natural reaction to outrageous lies.

While LaRue elicited more details about what Desmond had supposedly witnessed, I thought through how to handle his cross.

When my turn came, I got up. "Afternoon, Mr. Brown. Good to see you again." I looked at the jury and explained, "Mr. Brown and I have met before. I interviewed him as part of my investigation into this case. He and I both live down in Basking Rock."

I had to disclose to the court that I'd met him, but I preferred to do it by telling the jury. I looked at them as much as I could throughout the trial, because most of the time, their reactions mattered more than the judge's.

I walked over to the stand and said, in an accusatory tone, "Mr. Brown, I noticed that when you were talking to the jury just now, you didn't tell them that you had a romantic relationship with Ms. Winters. But you did have one, didn't you."

My tone had made him a little defensive. That was the point.

"Well, yes I did, but—"

"Matter of fact, you started seeing her right around Memorial Day last year, didn't you."

"Yeah, like I told you before, right around there."

"And that was only six or seven months ago, correct?"

"Yeah, I guess."

"So it's not like you forgot that you used to date her, is it."

"No, I didn't forget, I—"

"You didn't forget. Thank you."

I could feel LaDonna silently hating me for telling the whole court-room that she'd slept with this fool. I hadn't been able to explain to her why I needed to. There were no time-outs between the direct and the cross. You just had to get up and do it.

"Isn't it true, Mr. Brown, that your relationship with Ms. Winters lasted for around three months?"

"About that, yeah."

"And that little story you just told, according to your time sheet, it happened on July 8, correct?"

"Yeah, that was the date."

"And you started dating around Memorial Day. So on July 8, she was your girlfriend, correct?"

"Yeah, she would've been, yeah."

"Any particular reason you left that detail out?"

"Man, I didn't leave it *out*, I—" He was getting frustrated. That was good.

"Mr. Brown, you told us that whole little story, with all those details about where you were and what Ms. Winters was supposedly doing, and you never mentioned the fact that she was your girlfriend at the time, correct?"

"That's correct, but like I'm trying to explain—"

"These are yes-or-no questions. We don't need an explanation."

"Yeah, we do, because you're making it sound like—"

"Like you're hiding something, right?"

"Objection," LaRue said. "Badgering the witness."

"I'll withdraw it. Mr. Brown, isn't it true that the reason you're up here telling a story that could put your ex-girlfriend in jail is that your relationship ended badly?"

"Man, that's not what this is!"

"Isn't it true that the *reason* your relationship ended badly is that she found out you were an opiate abuser with—"

"Objection!"

"Your Honor, this goes to the witness's credibility."

Nicholson looked at LaRue.

"Your Honor," he said, "this is way beyond the scope of my direct."

Nicholson said, "I think that's his point, though, isn't it?"

In federal courts, unlike South Carolina state courts, what I could ask on cross depended on what LaRue had asked on direct. Only the topics he'd raised, plus matters relevant to the witness's credibility, were allowed. Nicholson got it: by not raising the fact that Desmond and LaDonna had had a relationship, LaRue had made Desmond seem more credible than he was.

"Yes, Your Honor, it is," I said. "It's about Mr. Brown failing to tell the whole truth."

LaRue had no answer. "Overruled," Nicholson said.

Desmond had, unfortunately, calmed down a little bit during this hiatus. But goading him didn't matter as much anymore. I just wanted the jurors to hear enough to decide he wasn't credible.

"Mr. Brown," I said, more slowly, "isn't it true that Ms. Winters found out you had a history of opiate abuse, with two arrests for possession of fentanyl?"

He didn't say anything.

"Isn't that true? Yes or no."

Looking at his lap, in a near whisper, he said, "Yes."

"So you've struggled with an opiate habit, correct?"

"Yes."

"I'm sorry, I'm not sure the jury could hear that."

"*Yes.*"

"And you testified that you've been near that dispensing cabinet while Ms. Winters was using it, correct?"

"Yes."

"You probably clean that bathroom a lot, don't you."

"Pretty often, yes."

"So, pretty often, you're near the dispensing cabinet when nurses use it?"

"I mean, the bathroom's right there."

"So, yes?"

"Yeah."

"But you're accusing *her* of being the one who stole the opiates?"

"Yes, I am, because—"

"Just so we're clear, the type of drugs that were stolen from that cabinet are the same type you've had abuse issues with?"

"Look, that was in the past."

"These thefts were in the past too. But thank you. No further questions."

I knew that Desmond's drug arrests and substance abuse struggles had nothing to do with the breakup. I knew my questions were misleading. But there was no other way to get the truth about him in front of the jury.

As I walked back to the defense table, I made eye contact with LaDonna. She wasn't angry anymore.

LaRue did a redirect on Desmond, but there wasn't much he could salvage. After that, to my surprise, the prosecution rested. I thought my case was on cruise control, gliding into the home stretch.

LaDonna did great on direct. I asked her if she had stolen any medication from her place of work. She looked at the jury, head high, and told them with absolute conviction that she had never done, and would never do, anything like that.

And she didn't fall apart too badly on cross. It wasn't her fault that LaRue managed to catch the curve ball I'd thrown him with my cross of Desmond and hurl it straight between my eyes.

"So you were dating Mr. Brown at the time of the thefts, weren't you," he said.

"Yes, I was, unfortunately."

A couple of the women jurors laughed. LaRue gave an *I've-been-there* shrug and said, "Yeah, most of us make some mistakes in our dating lives, don't we."

"Yes, we do."

The women jurors were now smiling at LaRue, enjoying this line of questioning.

"Sometimes, pretty big mistakes."

LaDonna looked wary. I could tell she sensed he was trying to trap her.

"Like dating a drug addict," he said. "That's what you did, isn't it?"

She hesitated. I'd told her not to say any more than she had to on cross. "Unfortunately, yes," she said.

"For three solid months, correct?"

"About that long, yes."

"And you had access to his drug of choice, didn't you."

"I had access to what the doctors prescribed for my patients."

"And that included the type of drugs your boyfriend was addicted to, correct?"

After a second, she said, "Yes."

"Did you ever feel he was using you for drugs?"

"No, that's not what—"

"And you got tired of that, so you broke up with him?"

"No!"

"You didn't get tired of it?"

"That's not what I meant!"

By the time his cross was over, the jurors had a whole new story about why LaDonna might have taken the drugs.

I didn't do a redirect, because LaRue apparently thought that she'd broken up with Desmond over his drug use. I knew she'd kept on dating Desmond until he took up with someone else, and I didn't want to keep her on the stand long enough for LaRue to find that out. Breaking up with a man over his drug use was a better story to leave in the jurors' minds.

Instead, I went straight to Adam, and he was solid. The jury liked him. He had a knack for explaining complex technology in an accessible way, and I could see that they truly understood what he told them about the GPS evidence. LaRue only asked him one question on cross—whether the GPS evidence showed that LaDonna was at the hospital at the times of the other two thefts—and he had to tell the truth: she was.

But I was confident he had convinced the jury that on the day of the second theft, LaDonna wasn't there. Someone else had used her log-in.

And that was all we had. I rested, but LaRue made a shrewder move.

"Your Honor, in view of some of the unexpected testimony we've heard today, the United States would like to call a rebuttal witness. It shouldn't take but a few minutes, and then we can let the jury retire to do their duty."

With Nicholson's permission, he called Agent Rodriguez back to the stand.

With his best witness talking to the jury again, LaRue had a field day. In five minutes, the jury heard that Rodriguez had interviewed Desmond for hours and had excluded him as a suspect, with documentary evidence backing up part of that decision: on the date of the third theft, Desmond had been out sick. "I don't come down here to the United States District Court, and swear on the Bible to tell the truth, in order to put the wrong person in jail," Rodriguez said.

The prosecution rested.

20

JANUARY 23, 2023

On Monday morning, LaDonna's jury was still out. That was a good thing, because I was busy trying to fix the mistake I'd made in Judy's case. Because I didn't understand how databases worked, and because I hadn't made sure that my expert knew that the hospital and the pharmacy shared the same computer system, I had failed to subpoena crucial evidence. Hidden deep in what I imagined as the flashing green ones and zeros of that system, there were, Adam had told me, audit trails. If Judy's medical records had been changed, the proof would be there.

I was sitting in my kitchen, on hold with the hospital's legal department, watching Squatter snooze on the deck. I'd drafted up a subpoena on Thursday night, right after talking to Adam, and gotten it over to the hospital Friday afternoon. But with Judy's trial starting in one week, I knew I might not get the evidence in time.

The secretary came back on the line. "I am so sorry," she said, "but he's heading into a meeting right now. So he's asked me to refer you to our CEO, Mr. Thibodeau."

"Okay, thank you." I took down the number she gave me. When I called it, I got another secretary. She took a message.

I was making another pot of coffee when my phone rang. I lunged to answer it, spilling most of a bulk container of ground coffee on the counter.

It wasn't Thibodeau. It was Judge Nicholson's clerk, telling me the jury was back with a verdict.

A little less than two hours later, we were in the courtroom, standing as the jury walked to their seats. LaDonna hadn't said more than two words to me since we'd arrived. I didn't expect her to. She was terrified.

When we were all seated, Nicholson said, "Good morning, everyone. I'll note for the record that all jurors are present. Ladies and gentlemen of the jury, have you reached a verdict?"

The foreman, a fiftysomething plumber, said, "Yes, Your Honor."

"Okay, Madam Clerk, if you could please take the verdict?"

His clerk stood. "Mr. Foreman, I'll be reading you each charge in the order it appears on your verdict form, and if you could please read back to me what y'all wrote down for that one."

"Yes, ma'am."

"With regard to the allegations concerning July 8, 2022, on the felony count of obtaining a controlled substance by misrepresentation or fraud under 21 US Code section 843(a)(3), how do you find?"

"Not guilty."

I felt a couple hundred pounds of pressure remove itself from my shoulders. The jury had not believed Desmond's testimony. Maybe the evidence of his own drug problems and his relationship with LaDonna had made them think he'd logged in as her to steal it himself. Whatever their reasoning had been, the other felony and the misdemeanor for that date had to come back not guilty too.

They did.

"With regard to the allegations concerning July 24, 2022, on the felony count of obtaining a controlled substance by misrepresentation or fraud under 21 US Code section 843(a)(3), how do you find?"

"Not guilty."

Adam's GPS evidence had saved us. The other felony and the misdemeanor for that date came back the same way. I could feel waves of relief coming off of LaDonna. I wondered if she was going to cry.

The clerk asked the same question for August 13, 2022.

"On that count," the foreman said, "we find the defendant guilty."

Beside me, LaDonna gasped.

As the foreman read out guilty on the misdemeanor for simple possession, LaDonna sank to her knees on the starry blue carpet and started to wail. "My baby," she cried. "My baby, my baby!"

Ms. Baker hurried toward her from the pews, but the bailiff stopped her. LaDonna kept crying out for her daughter.

Most of the jurors averted their eyes, but one of them—the healthcare aide—was watching LaDonna. Her mouth was trembling. She looked like she might start crying too.

"Your Honor," I said, "I would ask that you poll the jury." I looked back at the jurors. I made eye contact with the healthcare aide for a second; then she looked away. "We need to know whether each person on the jury reached this verdict freely and of their own accord."

Nicholson said, "Madam Clerk, if you will?"

"Yes, Your Honor. Mr. Foreman, is that verdict your verdict?"

"Yes, ma'am, it is."

"Juror number four, is that verdict your verdict?"

"It is."

She went down the line. Juror after juror answered yes.

"Juror number seven, is that verdict your verdict?"

The healthcare aide looked down at her feet.

"Juror number seven?"

She didn't answer.

Nicholson said, "Juror number seven, please answer the question."

She looked up at him like she was afraid he might hit her, and then back down.

"Juror number seven, is there a problem?"

"Your Honor, I'm sorry, I told you at the start I shouldn't be here."

"Excuse me?"

She met his gaze again. "I told you I couldn't afford the time off work. It's been three days now."

"Yes, it has. What we're asking about right now, though, is your verdict."

I spoke up. "Your Honor, I'm concerned that this juror's financial worries may have led her to go along with the other jurors so that she could get out of here quickly and get back to her job. Would Your Honor please question her on that?"

He nodded. "Juror number seven—"

She broke down.

"That's true, Your Honor." She wiped her nose with the back of her hand. "I'm sorry. I'm sorry. But the foreman here told me they'd wait on me all week if that's what it took. They can afford to sit here all that time. I can't."

Nicholson took that in. After a moment, he asked, "Would further deliberations make it possible for you to render a verdict in this case?"

She looked completely baffled. "What does that *mean*?"

"If I sent the jury back to talk about this some more—"

"Your Honor, I can't do that. I told you from the start, I can't afford to do that. But I will never believe that this woman did those things. I heard what she said up there, and I will *never* believe that."

Judge Nicholson looked at her for a minute. Then he sighed loud enough for his microphone to pick it up. The sound of his breath filled the courtroom. He swiveled his chair to look at me and LaRue.

"Counsel?" he said.

LaRue was looking at his desk.

"Counsel," Nicholson said, "do you see any reason I should not declare a mistrial?"

LaRue looked up at him and shook his head.

I was speeding back to Basking Rock when my phone rang.

"Mr. Munroe! So glad I caught you. This is Harrison Thibodeau."

"Afternoon." I put the car on cruise control. "Thanks for the quick callback."

"No problem. So, I gather you sent us another subpoena for that Judy Reed case."

"Yeah, this one's for some electronic records. Nobody's got to physically come in to court or anything."

"Uh-huh. Okay. You'll have to forgive me; I don't quite grasp all the legal details here, and unfortunately, my GC is out of the office today."

His general counsel's secretary had told me he was heading into a meeting.

In a light tone, I said, "I hear you. Well, it's probably more of an IT thing, anyway. These are just some electronic records that y'all can probably throw on a thumb drive and get over to me pretty easily. I'm happy to swing by and pick them up."

"Oh, that'd be great. However, the timing here is just..." He laughed. "See, our head IT guy is on vacation this week, and it's kind of a skeleton crew down there. But I assure you, we're working on this just as fast as we can."

"Uh-huh."

"Okay, then. Well, I'll let you go. Goodbye."

He hung up.

At home, I started a pot of coffee and went online to give myself a crash course in the law of healthcare fraud. Most cases were tried at the federal level, and the United States Department of Justice had a vast array of case summaries on their website. I hadn't realized that nursing homes, hospitals, owners of dialysis clinics, and almost any other healthcare business could make millions by padding bills or prescribing tests and procedures that patients didn't need.

I went on Westlaw and pulled up a forty-page treatise on Medicare and Medicaid fraud. I needed to have some clue what I was looking at, legally, before I picked up the phone.

When I'd finished reading it, I looked at my watch. It was too early to call Cardozo. It was a little dicey to call him about LaDonna's case at all, even though it was technically over for now, and I certainly didn't want to call him about it when he might still be at the office.

I whistled for Squatter and took him out for a walk. My new neighborhood was cute, even though the sidewalks were brand new and blinding white, and most of the trees were still small. I preferred the decaying charm of old Southern towns, so this new subdivision would probably never quite feel like home. But it had good security, solid infrastructure, and a fenced yard for my dog, all at a price I could tolerate. Squatter toddled alongside me as we went down a slight hill.

I wondered how LaDonna was doing. I'd had to help her up off the courtroom floor and explain real quick what a mistrial meant. She'd nodded as if she'd heard what I was saying, but I knew she couldn't possibly be processing the details while her body was still flooded with adrenaline and who knew what all other stress hormones. After the jury was dismissed, Ms. Baker drove her home, and I imagined her playing with her daughter right now, or getting ready to start cooking dinner. Chicken nuggets, maybe. That's all Noah would eat when he was that age.

"Hang on, buddy," I said, pulling back on Squatter's leash. "You got to wait for the car."

Squatter didn't understand intersections. He didn't understand a lot of things. So knowing how the world worked and protecting him from it was my job. He was one of the earthly creatures I had deemed myself responsible for.

There were a lot of those.

If juror number seven hadn't spoken up, LaDonna would've been taken away in handcuffs to spend the night in the local women's correctional facility, awaiting transfer to whichever federal prison had room for her. She probably would've gotten three to five years.

And that might still happen. After seeing her and Ms. Baker off, I'd gone back upstairs to wrap things up with LaRue. As we stood on the white marble floor outside the courtroom, with the sunlight pouring in, he'd said, "I'm sure you're aware that we normally do refile charges in this type of situation. But we've got procedures, so I've got to take this back for the office to review. I'll be in touch."

Some types of mistrials killed the case for good, thanks to the double jeopardy clause, but a hung jury was not one of them.

A couple of hours later, after eating a microwaved burrito in front of the TV news, I called Cardozo.

It had been a while, so we shot the breeze for a minute. We'd been friends all through law school, and he became a federal prosecutor in Charleston around the same time I went into the same line of work for the State of South Carolina. Unlike me, he hadn't disgraced himself and been forced to resign.

When we'd caught up a bit, I said, "So, I've got a case for you, I think. Not you personally, but whoever in your office handles health-care fraud."

"That'd be Simon or Teresa. I can put you in touch. What's the scoop?"

"Well, first," I said, "you've got to promise not to come down to Basking Rock and close our little hospital. It's the only one we've got."

He laughed. "Even if we do, somebody else will buy it up and reopen. There's not much else you can do with a hospital building."

"Okay. I'm sure we can put car accidents and having babies on hold in the meantime."

"Naw, I'm messing with you. I doubt it would close. We had a health-care fraud case last year that put a chiropractic clinic out of business, but with a hospital, you probably just have to take the garbage out. Escort it to federal prison, and then the hospital's board will bring in a fresh new crop of uncorrupted personnel. Problem solved."

"That sounds good. Now, full disclosure, this relates to that case of mine that your office was prosecuting."

"*Was* prosecuting? How'd that go?"

"Oh, you haven't talked to LaRue?"

"I never talk to LaRue. I unfortunately have laryngitis every time I see him. I have to step away."

"He's not my favorite guy either. But we got a mistrial today."

"And now he's dragging that turd back here for review?"

"So he told me."

"Okay. Well, I was not aware of that when you called," he said airily. "And as of now, I think that case is technically not active. So what's the deal?"

"Well, for the basic outline, we've got a nurse with no priors accused of stealing opiates from work. There's three thefts under her log-in, but we've got GPS proof that for one of them, she wasn't even at the hospital when it happened. And security was terrible—it was real easy to see people's passwords when they logged in. So the reason I'm calling *you* is, she's been there for ten-plus years with no issues, and these accusations came down all of a sudden right after she reported a physician for padding his bill."

"Aha. Why do I feel like I've heard this before? Is there some website where crooked healthcare administrators share their playbooks with each other?"

"Maybe so," I said. "Anyway, your Mr. LaRue seems intent on torturing my nurse some more, if the office lets him, but I think there's much bigger fish to fry."

"Not to mention, fish that are actually guilty. What you're describing is basically Simon and Teresa's break room conversation almost every single day."

"Great. If they want to consider taking this on, I can tell them which rocks to look under. The biggest one is the CEO. And he's got this janitor guy with a little bit of a drug problem. I'm speculating, but I think he might be letting that guy skim some pharmaceuticals here and there for personal use, as long as he does it under the log-in of whoever they want to pin stuff on."

"That's... probably not even a unique setup. Yeah, I'll see which of them is the least busy, or the most interested, and put you in touch."

Things looked brighter when I got off the phone. For LaDonna, anyway.

For Judy, I knew one thing: Thibodeau was not going to give me the audit trail. For a second, pacing around my living room, I thought about filing a motion to compel. But I knew the judge would deny it. Thibodeau's lawyer would go in and say the hospital was doing its very best to gather this complex technical information, and if they weren't able to do it in time for my trial next week, that was my fault for not asking for it earlier. And he'd be right.

I was getting a little frantic. I wanted a cup of coffee—having a cup in my hand helped me relax, like cigarettes did for smokers—but it was almost nine at night, way too late for that. And I didn't own any decaf. I didn't consider it coffee.

I decided to make some hot chocolate. I got the milk out of the fridge and yanked open a drawer to grab a measuring spoon. It was the wrong drawer, though. After a few months in this house, I still wasn't all the way used to where everything was. This drawer had a mess of pancake flippers and ladles in it.

I didn't slam it shut. I stood there looking at it, because I could feel an idea coming to me.

What if the stuff in that drawer was all I had to make hot chocolate with? If I had to figure out a way, I'd look closer at everything in there and think on how to use it. You could use a ladle as a spoon. And it might be awkward, but you could also use it as a cup. Hell, if you wrapped something around the handle to keep it from burning your hand, you could even hold it over the stove and use it as the pan.

The evidence that Terri and I had already gathered was all I had to defend Judy with. I had to figure out a way. No magic subpoena was going to drop justice into my lap.

I put the milk back in the fridge and went up to my office. I was going to read that autopsy report again from cover to cover. And I was going to learn everything I could about cephalosporin.

21

JANUARY 30, 2023

At seven thirty Monday morning, Judy appeared at the front door of my office. We were all meeting there before going to the courthouse for the first day of trial. Terri and Dr. Hargroves, already sitting in the waiting area, were both on their second cups of coffee.

"Good morn—" I began, but Judy cut me off.

"My mom will be right in," she said. "Emma Jean is parking. You know, this is awfully early for my mom. She had to be up at five a.m. so she could get through her morning routine in time."

"Well," I said, "there's no love like a mother's, is there."

Judy looked at me blankly. "Her love isn't the issue. The point is, she shouldn't have to go through this. Are you going to be able to take her needs into account tomorrow?"

I counted to three in my head, slowly, before responding. I'd read someplace that that was a good strategy to keep yourself from getting annoyed. "What I might suggest," I said, "is that she meet us over at the courthouse at eight thirty or quarter to nine. What we're doing here is more of a team strategy meeting. It's optional for her."

"But she wants to be here."

"Okay. Just so you know, you and I can't talk about anything confidential in front of her. We don't want to risk waiving attorney-client privilege. So if we need to discuss anything like that, here or down at the courthouse, we'll need to step away."

"That's fine. But what I'm saying is, she wants to be here for our morning meetings all through trial, so we'll need to start later."

"The court ordered that trial would start at 9 a.m. every day, so we have to be there by—"

Terri came over to extricate me. "Judy, hello! Did you see Dr. Hargroves over there? Isn't this the first time you've met in person?"

"Yes, up to now we've only talked on Zoom. So he's testifying today?"

"No, the prosecution goes first," Terri said. "But he flew up early so he could watch the trial and hear whatever the coroner and the emergency room doctor have to say. That way, he can help us strategize how to respond."

Judy nodded. "That's a solid call. I'm curious about what they'll say too. I brought my laptop to take notes. If either of them says something stupid or contradicts himself, I'll let you know."

I opened my mouth to say what I thought of that idea, and then I closed it again. They went over to chat with Dr. Hargroves.

I was prepared to steal that laptop and hide it if I had to. Even if the judge allowed it, I was absolutely not going to let a woman on trial for her father's murder sit in front of the jury tapping away on her computer.

At a quarter past eight, we said goodbye to Rachel and headed out. Terri loaded our file boxes into her Subaru, but since my office was only four blocks from the courthouse, the rest of us walked.

Seeing Mrs. Reed navigate the route in her wheelchair, I realized how many unnecessary obstacles she faced. Corners with no curb cuts, sidewalks jacked off-kilter by the roots of giant trees. At one point she had to go nearly a block out of her way, cross the street at the only place she could, and catch up with us several minutes later. It was like a physical equivalent of the justice system: for some, the hurdles went unnoticed, while other folks got slowed down or stopped in their tracks.

By eight thirty, most of the team was in our war room, and I was in the courtroom with Emma Jean, getting Mrs. Reed settled in. The front row of the spectator's pews was the only one with enough space for her wheelchair, so I was glad she didn't mind being conspicuous.

"Emma Jean," I said, "would you mind making sure Judy's laptop is off?" I'd told Judy that Judge Davenport didn't allow laptops for anybody but lawyers and reporters—a rule I'd made up out of thin air to avoid wasting more time arguing. I had endured her protests as to why that was unfair, until her mother finally prevailed upon her to let it go.

Emma Jean reached into the tote bag hanging from the back of Mrs. Reed's chair and pulled out the laptop. She opened it and said, "The screen's not coming on."

"Great, thanks."

Behind me, I heard the click of a woman's heels. A familiar voice said, "Morning, Leland."

I arranged a smile on my face and turned around. With her perfectly sprayed helmet of blonde hair, our assistant solicitor looked like an earnest newscaster on small-town TV.

"It's been a long time, Ginevra. I hope everything's good now with your family."

"Well, thank you. We're okay. You know the Lord never gives us any more than we can handle." She smiled, and I caught a glint from her sparkly pink lipstick.

I couldn't quite bring myself to agree with her views on the Lord.

"So, anyway," I said, "let me introduce you to my client's mother, Margaret Reed. And this is her assistant, Emma Jean Johnson. Ladies, this is Ginevra Barnes, who's serving as prosecutor on this trial."

"We've met, during her investigation last year," Mrs. Reed said. She gave Ginevra a gracious smile. "I do hope you understand why I can't support what you're doing here at all. My husband's death was an accident."

Emma Jean just glared until Ginevra went away.

By ten to nine, we were all in our places. Terri and I were at either end of the defense table, with Judy between us. The rest of the team was in the first two rows behind us. Ginevra's side had a similar setup, although with fewer people. Davenport's bailiff, a tall Black man with shoulders that spoke of copious weightlifting, stood a few yards in front of us, keeping an eye on things.

I could hear the courtroom door opening every five or ten seconds, and when I looked back, I realized why. When a local heiress is accused of patricide, it is news. Gawkers and tragedy groupies gather in the hope of seeing horror up close. I spotted Shannon Pennington, our local true-crime podcaster, and several excited-looking women with her that I took to be her fans.

For a second, I regretted that I hadn't advised Judy to hire a big PR firm to help guide her through this situation. This level of scrutiny was hard for anyone to deal with. Then it occurred to me that if her mother had to yell at her to get her to put her laptop down and not act like some amateur reporter during her own murder trial, no PR firm could've made much headway.

Over the next few minutes, the door opened less and less often, and the rustling and whispering behind us subsided. Up front, a woman hurried out of a side door, head down like she didn't want to be seen, and took her place at the court reporter's station. Seconds before nine o'clock, the bailiff boomed, "All rise," as Davenport came out the other door with his clerk.

When he got up on the bench, the bailiff called, "The Honorable Lucius G. Davenport presiding. Court is now in session."

Judge Davenport got right to business. He was not an affable guy. He pulled his microphone closer and said, "Good morning, ladies and gentlemen. In view of the number of spectators, before we proceed to voir dire, I'll instruct all those present on some ground rules. If you're unable or unwilling to comply, please escort yourself out before proceedings begin."

He glanced over at the court reporter, saw her typing, and continued.

"As I'm sure you all know, today's proceedings will be the first day of a murder trial. We therefore must behave in a manner that's respectful to the deceased, in addition to being respectful toward the jury that will shortly be seated and toward the Constitutions of the United States and the State of South Carolina, including the rights and presumptions that they grant to the accused. Any noise, commentary, or inappropriate behavior will result in your immediate removal by my bailiff, Mr. Jackson. All cell phones and similar devices should be turned off right now and must remain off whenever court is in session, which means whenever I am in the courtroom." A rustling rose behind me as dozens of spectators reached for their phones.

Davenport kept talking in the same vein for another minute. When he was done, the courtroom was quieter than I would have thought possible. He looked at the bailiff and asked him to bring in the first twenty members of the jury pool.

Davenport always did the voir dire himself, so for the next ninety minutes, he read out the questions that Ginevra and I had prepared, over and over, to prospective juror after prospective juror. Almost all the members of the jury pool had heard about this case, and three claimed to know someone who was involved. Those three were immediately excused. Eight more were let go because their family obligations—stay-at-home mother of toddlers, woman serving as the sole caretaker of her Alzheimer's-stricken mother, and so on—made jury duty impossible.

I used a peremptory to get rid of an angry-looking patriarch, and Ginevra used one of hers to toss a young woman with blue hair. She used another to excuse a local lawyer. It was an article of faith to which all lawyers subscribed that you never wanted a lawyer on a jury. The idea was that they would overthink everything and argue the other jurors into submission.

We knew what we were like.

By a quarter to eleven, we had a jury: four men, eight women, racially mixed. Despite what the Constitution promised, it wasn't a jury of Judy's peers. None of the jurors even remotely approached her economic bracket, and all of them had simple careers that I could understand.

Judge Davenport announced that the trial would begin at eleven sharp.

. . .

After the break, Davenport gave a short speech about the jury's purpose and responsibilities. Then Ginevra stood for her opening statement.

"Ladies and gentlemen of the jury," she said, "my name is Ginevra Barnes, and it is my honor and my duty to represent the State of South Carolina. On behalf of our fair state, I thank you for your service here today. As you heard from His Honor a little while ago, this is a murder trial. The most heinous crime there is. One of the oldest teachings of our civilization, a teaching we all know, is 'Thou shalt not kill.' But as the evidence will show, in this case, an ungrateful daughter, driven by greed—this woman, defendant Judy Reed—violated that commandment. On June 18, 2021, Judy Reed killed her own father."

The jurors followed Ginevra's pointing finger and looked at Judy.

I had advised Judy that if the jury looked at her, she should briefly make eye contact with one or two of them and then look down. I wanted her body language to convey that she understood how serious and sad this situation was.

She wasn't doing that. She was staring straight ahead. The anger in her posture hinted that she thought this whole thing was obnoxious and unfair.

"Ladies and gentlemen," Ginevra said, "the State of South Carolina shares your shock. We share your values. To murder the father who raised you, the man who gave you life, is a dark and terrible crime. As we are taught by the Bible, Exodus 21:15, 'Whoever strikes his father or his mother shall be put to death.'"

Ginevra nodded to the clerk, and her first exhibit appeared on the screen: a photo of Conway on horseback, smiling and tanned, against a cloudless blue sky. Judy saw it and looked away.

"This, ladies and gentleman, is Conway Reed. He grew up here in the countryside just south of Basking Rock. He married a local girl at twenty-four, worked hard all his life, and he became a wealthy man. He bred horses, including one you may have heard of: a colt named Basking Rock Dreams that ran in the Kentucky Derby nine years ago, bringing the eyes of the world to our town. Mr. Reed also came to own a substantial amount of real estate. As you will hear, by the time he died, he was worth tens of millions of dollars. And that, ladies and gentlemen, is why his daughter killed him."

Another nod to the clerk, and the photo of Conway was replaced by an old news headline with a photo of him and Mrs. Reed standing beside Judy, who must've been seven or eight years old. She was dressed in equestrian gear, holding a trophy.

Despite her proud parents on either side of her, Judy didn't look like a proud kid—or any kind of kid. The only childlike thing about her was her size. She wasn't smiling or showing any interest in her trophy. She was staring at the camera with slight irritation, like she had work she needed to get back to.

I figured Ginevra was using a picture from the news because Mrs. Reed had refused to give her any family photos for her presentation. Usually the relatives of murder victims cooperated with the prosecution, but that wasn't happening here.

"This is Conway Reed," she said, "his wife, and Judy back in 2001. As an only child, Judy was close with her parents, and they gave her everything a little girl could want. But it wasn't enough for her, ladies and gentlemen. For some people, nothing is ever enough."

Ginevra contemplated the photo for a second and then turned to the jury.

"In this trial, you will learn something that Judy Reed has known since she was a child. You will hear testimony, from a doctor who treated Conway, about a weakness that he had. Conway had a life-threatening allergy to a common type of antibiotics called cephalosporins. They're sold under names like Keflex, Rocephin, and more. Some of you have probably taken them yourselves. They've cured a lot of diseases and saved a lot of lives. But Judy Reed knew her father could not take them. If he took them, he could die."

The clerk, noticing Ginevra's cue a little late, replaced the picture on the screen with what looked like a stock photo of pill bottles.

"For Judy's entire childhood," Ginevra said, "at every doctor's appointment where antibiotics were discussed, her mother made it clear that they shouldn't give her any type of cephalosporins. The danger to Conway was too great to even have them in the house. But you will hear testimony from Dr. Perez at Basking Rock Hospital that on June 15, 2021, when Judy Reed was in town staying with her parents, visiting from her home up in Charleston, she went to urgent care and got a prescription for cephalosporin. For the first time in her life, she went to the pharmacy and picked up a whole bottle of those pills, knowing that even one of them could kill her father. Three days later, he was dead. And you will hear from the county coroner that what killed him was… cephalosporin poisoning."

She paused, turned, and looked at Judy. The jury followed suit. Judy kept staring straight ahead, like all this was beneath her.

"Judy Reed poisoned her father, ladies and gentlemen. She took his life stealthily, like a snake in the grass. She did it because, as his only child, she'd been expecting to inherit tens of millions of dollars. And as you'll learn, things were happening in Conway's life that made her fear that he was going to change his will. Because although Conway was married to his wife, Margaret, for nearly forty years, in 2007 Mrs. Reed suffered a terrible accident. She is sitting right over there."

She pointed. I heard Judy huff in irritation. She didn't like having her mother dragged into this.

"In 2007, Margaret Reed was left permanently disabled after a horse-riding accident. Conway stayed with her, and he took care of her. They were legally married until the day he died. But they no longer had marital relations, and there came a time, after Judy was all grown up, that Conway decided he wanted that in his life again. He met a woman, and he was planning to marry her. Her name is Alanna Carpenter, and you will hear from her during this trial."

A photo of Conway and Alanna appeared on the screen. From the background and her fancy hat, they looked to be at a horse race.

"As you can see, Miss Carpenter is much younger than Conway was. She was thirty-one in this picture and thirty-two at the time of his death. She was young enough to bear him children, ladies and gentlemen. Young enough to bear him... more heirs."

I could see it dawning on a couple of the jurors what that meant.

"Judy Reed," Ginevra said, "could see her inheritance slipping away. Conway's new wife would be the beneficiary of things that Judy thought she was entitled to. And if they had children, every new child would shrink what was left for her even more. But Judy knew something else about Conway. She knew that, as a sixty-three-year-old man, he had a little issue with his blood pressure, and he took pills for that every day. You'll hear from a pharmacist, Dr. Walker, about the kind of pills Conway took."

At her cue, the clerk put up a photo of two medication capsules side by side. They weren't quite identical; they were slightly different shades of blue.

"You'll hear that Conway's blood pressure pills were the same size and almost the same color as the cephalosporin pills that Judy brought home. As Dr. Walker will explain, that's a capsule of his blood pressure medication on the left there, and Judy's type of pill on the right. You can see for yourself that a person could easily mistake one for the other. And that's exactly why, for Judy's entire life, her mother never allowed any type of cephalosporin in the house. But on June 15, 2021, Judy went and got some, and she brought it to her parents' house. As you'll hear, she brought her cephalosporin home in a bottle that looked completely different from Conway's pill bottle. Her bottle was orange, and his was green. Hers was small, because she was only prescribed a ten-day supply, and his was large."

The clerk switched to side-by-side photos of two different bottles, generic photos that looked like they came from the manufacturer's website.

"You will hear that these are the types of bottles that Conway's and Judy's pills came in," Ginevra said. "Nobody could mistake them for each other. So Conway did not pick up the wrong bottle by accident. By the close of evidence, I think you will agree that the only thing that could have happened here is that Judy Reed put one of her cephalosporin capsules into her father's pill bottle. She put it there, and she waited. And she didn't have to wait long."

Turning to face the jury, she continued, "Now, I will be the first to admit that this is circumstantial evidence. I can be completely transparent with you, because the State of South Carolina has nothing to hide. And I want to tell you something now that you'll hear again when Judge Davenport reads you his jury instructions: Circumstantial evidence is valid evidence. It is real. Contrary to what they may say on TV shows, as jurors you can rely on circumstantial evidence. That is the law."

I could have objected—she wasn't supposed to teach a law class in her opening statement—but it wouldn't have looked good. After all, she was correct. I kept my mouth shut.

"And again, you'll hear this in your jury instructions, but it's important to keep it in mind throughout the trial: there are two types of evidence." She held up two fingers. "They're called direct and circumstantial. Direct evidence is something you saw with your own eyes, or you heard the gunshots, that type of thing. Let me give you an example. If you look around this courtroom, you'll notice that the only windows are those little ones way up there." She pointed. "We can't see out of them from down here, can we. That means none of us can get direct evidence of what the weather's like. We do get direct evidence that it's daytime, because we can see the sunlight up there on the ceiling."

The jurors were all looking up at it.

"But we don't have direct evidence of whether it's raining or not. We can't see that. If somebody walked in that door," Ginevra said, pointing down the aisle, "and he was wearing a wet raincoat and carrying an umbrella, and as he passed by you some water splashed off his umbrella onto you, that would be *circumstantial* evidence that it's raining outside. We can't see the rain ourselves, and we didn't see him coming in through the courthouse door either. But we can still conclude that it must be raining outside, and he must've come in pretty recently."

A text from Terri popped up on my laptop screen: *She's good.*

I typed back: *Unfortunately.*

"We can do that because we know what rain is, and how it looks on your coat, and how the world works. We are allowed to decide what must have happened based on nothing but circumstantial evidence. That is the law. That's why, if you look in the casebooks, you will see murder trials where the victim's body was never even found. Killers have been tried for murder and sentenced, based on circumstantial evidence, without the victim ever being found."

Judge Davenport shifted in his seat. It felt intentional, like he was letting Ginevra know that was all the law-class teaching he was prepared to tolerate. She moved on.

"The other thing I want to note, ladies and gentlemen, is that Conway Reed was not a perfect man. I've never met a perfect man, and we won't be hearing about one during this trial. So if the defense points out his flaws, please bear that in mind. Now, Conway did support his wife and daughter to the very best of his abilities, and he did stay married to his wife for nearly forty years."

She stopped and looked at the jury.

"But he was not faithful to his wife. He was not even faithful to his new girlfriend. That is a failing, for sure. However, the law does not require fidelity before it will protect the sanctity of human life. So I would ask you not to let the defense distract you with whatever they may say about Conway. His life mattered—his life was a sacred thing —no matter what he did or didn't do. So on behalf of the State of South Carolina, I am asking you to look at all the evidence, both circumstantial and direct, and then apply it to enforcing the most ancient law we have: thou shalt... not... kill."

22

JANUARY 30, 2023

W e broke for lunch after that. With all of us in the war room trying to eat our sandwiches, it was a tight fit, and it didn't help that Judy, her mom, and Emma Jean were quite upset by Ginevra's opening statement. I couldn't blame them, but I was not in a hand-holding mood. Terri and I exchanged a look. Then she nodded and turned to them, sympathizing and offering words of reassurance.

I asked Hargroves, "You mind taking a little walk with me? Let's bring our lunch."

We went down the hall, taking bites of our sandwiches as we walked. I had a cup of coffee in my other hand, and he had an unopened can of Coke in his pocket. I took him around a couple of corners and down another hall into a quiet annex. The two courtrooms there weren't in use today, but they were locked. All that was left was the men's room. We went in, and I checked the stalls. We were alone. I got a paper towel and laid it across the windowsill so we could set our lunches down.

"I like to show my experts the high life," I said.

He laughed. "This is fine with me. After being a medic in Vietnam, most anything else seems fine." He cracked open his Coke and added, "That woman's one hell of a lawyer. We've got an uphill climb."

"I know. And normally I'd be rehearsing my opening statement right now. But I went back and read a bunch of stuff last night, and I've got a question for you. I don't think I fully appreciated how many different cephalosporin drugs there are, or even that they're different."

"It's a big family, yeah. And the different generations are effective against different types of infections."

"Uh-huh. Now, it's been twenty-odd years since I last took a chemistry class, and I can't say I was paying much attention at the time. So I apologize if I ask stupid questions. But am I correct in thinking that they're all cephalosporins because on some level they all work the same in a patient, but if you look at them under a microscope—or whatever it is that y'all use for your tests—you can tell them apart?"

He winced like I was not quite on target. "Well, putting it that way isn't real accurate. Especially the part about the microscope." He smiled. "But I see where you're going. On some tests, different cephalosporins look the same. They've got a characteristic ultraviolet absorption spectrum, for instance. The coroner ran one of those, among other things, to figure out what drugs Conway had in his system. And then there's tests we can use to tell them apart from each other. That said, the tests the coroner ran on Conway's blood came back consistent with cephalexin"—the particular cephalosporin that Judy's medical records said she'd been prescribed—"and that's one of the most common forms of it that's out there."

"Are there ways the coroner could've drilled down farther?" I asked. "If it came back consistent with cephalexin on one type of test, but he wanted to double-check? I mean, if he wanted to eliminate the possibility that it was any other form of cephalosporin."

"Yeah. Let me think on this a second." His fluffy white eyebrows drew together in concentration and then disappeared into his bangs.

I munched my sandwich and took a sip of coffee.

"What I'm thinking through," he said, taking a swig from his Coke, "is what equipment I have back at my lab that could figure that out in the least amount of time. And that my intern knows how to use."

"You think he can get this taken care of before my opening?"

We both snorted.

Back in the courtroom, I stood up and introduced myself to the jury.

"This morning, Mrs. Barnes told you a story," I said, stepping out from behind the defense table and walking slowly toward the jury box. "She told a very dramatic story about how she thinks Conway Reed might have died. It was a story worthy of a Hollywood screen-writer. It was a story about some of the darkest forces in the human heart, and it was fascinating. If it were on TV, I'd probably watch it."

I stopped walking. "But as I stand here in this courtroom with y'all today, I don't know who that story was about. I don't know any money-hungry heiresses whose hearts are dark with greed." I gestured toward Judy. "I do know Judy Reed, though. She's sitting right there." She turned her head and looked, for a quick second, at the jury.

"Now, Judy Reed is a scientist. She's a type of scientist that I'd never even heard of before I met her, a geographic information systems consultant, or GIS consultant, as you may hear one or two witnesses say. She does things like analyze historic buildings and the land they're sitting on, and look at the building materials that were used, and determine what needs to be done to preserve those buildings for generations to come. State and national monuments, that kind of thing. She will talk your ear off about things like soil drainage and

267

weather patterns and the properties of the mortar that builders used back in the eighteenth century. Apart from her family, that sort of stuff is pretty much all she cares about. And speaking of her family, sitting there behind her is her mother, Conway's widow, Margaret Reed."

Mrs. Reed nodded to the jury. Her expression had the exact gravitas that I'd asked for from Judy.

"Mrs. Reed, as you can see, is in a wheelchair. She had a terrible accident that left her paralyzed from the chest down. Her condition makes it very difficult and time-consuming for her to get out of the house. Matter of fact, she had to get up at five o'clock this morning, with the help of the home health aide sitting there beside her, to get to court on time today. She did that, and she'll be doing it again every day for as long as this trial lasts, because—as you'll hear when she testifies—she doesn't think Mrs. Barnes's story is true. She is here to support her daughter."

I paced along the front of the jury box to bring the jurors' eyes back to me. "I'm not going to take up too much more of your time talking, because I think we ought to let you start hearing from witnesses. But one thing I'll mention, although I'm sure that as Americans you already know about this, is reasonable doubt. Under the law, you cannot convict Judy Reed of this crime unless you think the evidence shows that no reasonable person could doubt that she is guilty as charged."

I stopped walking. "So let me tell you why it's *very* reasonable to doubt that." I started back the other way, looking at them.

"Here's what's missing," I said. "You're not going to hear any evidence at all about Judy touching her father's pill bottle or even knowing where he kept it. There's no evidence of that. And you're not going to hear anything about DNA or fingerprints or blood spatters—none of that type of evidence is in this case at all. You're also not going to hear that any of Judy's own pills were missing. And you're

268

not going to hear that her cephalosporin was found in her father's pill bottle, because it wasn't. You're not going to hear any of that, because that evidence doesn't exist."

I looked the jurors in the eye, one after the other. "But you are going to hear Mrs. Barnes's story, and you'll hear that first, because in our legal system, the prosecutor always goes first. So I want to tell you just two more things about Judy before I hand things back to Mrs. Barnes. The first thing is that, financially speaking, she is not like you and me. Due to her good fortune at being born into the Reed family, as well as to her own hard work as a GIS consultant, Judy Reed is set for life. She lives in a four-thousand-square-foot historic mansion in Charleston's French Quarter that was bequeathed to her by her grandmother. She earns six figures every year working in a very specialized scientific field. Her father could've left all his money to charity, and it wouldn't have made any difference to her lifestyle."

I looked back toward the defense table and said, "In that respect, though not in all respects, the Reeds are very fortunate people."

I turned and nodded to the clerk. "The second thing I want to tell you, I'm going to do with a picture. They say a picture's worth a thousand words."

The clerk brought up my only exhibit: the drawing of the French Quarter that Judy had done, minus the arrow pointing to her house. I didn't want the whole courtroom to know exactly where she lived, so I'd asked her to photoshop that out and change the color of her rooftop so it was the same as the others.

"This is a picture Judy drew for me of the French Quarter. To me, that is amazing—the level of detail, the accuracy, everything. There's twenty-three buildings in that picture. I counted. And what's all the more amazing is that Judy drew them all from memory. She drew this straight from her own mind."

Out of the corner of my eye, I noticed one juror's head pop back in surprise.

"This picture surprised the heck out of me. I couldn't even draw my own front porch with anything like that level of detail. When I saw this, I realized that it's not just her finances that make Judy different from you and me. Judy's brain is different. Her personality is different. She is not interested in the same things most of us are. She's not driven by the same needs and motives that most of us are driven by. She is a true one-off."

I turned back to face the jurors. "So I don't know who Mrs. Barnes's story was about, but I can tell you this: it wasn't Judy Reed."

Ginevra requested a twenty-minute break, so I took the opportunity to meet with Judy and her mom. I ushered them into the war room, and Terri took Emma Jean to the vending machines for a soda.

I closed the door behind me and said, "I just wanted to run through a couple points in case Mrs. Barnes manages to get through the coroner and the detective faster than I expect her to. If she calls you, Mrs. Reed, it could happen at any point after that."

Ginevra had subpoenaed Mrs. Reed, which was no surprise, since she'd witnessed her husband's collapse and could speak to Judy's whereabouts at the time.

"I am ready for her," Mrs. Reed said, voice tinged with anger.

"Oh, I know you are. What I want to do is set your expectations as to me. Now, I'm allowed to ask you about anything that's relevant, but there are a lot of things I'm not planning to ask about, and I want you to understand why."

In South Carolina state court, I wasn't constrained by the scope of Ginevra's questions. I had much more latitude than I did in federal court, but that didn't mean asking every question I could was a good idea.

Mrs. Reed nodded, so I went on.

"First off, I'm not going to ask you about Conway's trust amendment, and if Alanna is called, I won't ask her about it either. There's a risk that if the jury sees that amendment, they'll take it to mean that your relationship with Mr. Reed had completely broken down. If they think there was no affection left between the two of you, your faith in Judy's innocence won't mean much. And I've got no way to prove that Alanna was aware of the amendment, so it's not going to convince them that she had any motive to kill him.".

She looked disappointed, but she nodded.

Judy was indignant. "I thought witnesses were supposed to tell the *whole* truth!"

"The whole truth about the questions the lawyers ask, yes."

"But—you're purposely making sure the jury doesn't hear the whole truth about Alanna! Why?"

"I… just *explained* why."

"Honey," Mrs. Reed said, "people see things in different ways. We've got a whole lot of context that the jury's never going to have."

Judy huffed. "The only ways to see this are the right way and the wrong way."

"That may be," Mrs. Reed said. The resignation in her voice told me she'd had a lot of conversations like this. "So, then, what he's saying is, these jurors would see that information the wrong way. That's why he doesn't want to show it to them."

Judy shrugged with annoyance, but she stopped arguing.

I looked at my watch. "We ought to get back."

Mrs. Reed pushed the joystick on the arm of her wheelchair and turned toward the door. Then she pushed it again to turn back to me. "Mr. Munroe, what you said out there just now about my daughter... It meant something to me." There was real emotion in her voice.

"Well, I'm glad."

She looked at Judy with a smile of such understanding and love that I would've been speechless if it had been my turn to talk. I'd seen that look on my wife's face long ago—she gazed that way at Noah sometimes.

"Most folks just don't get you," Mrs. Reed told Judy. "Most folks never will. But he's starting to, isn't he."

Back in the courtroom, Ginevra called the county coroner, Dr. Madison, to the stand. He was a squat man in his fifties with a résumé a mile long; Ginevra walked him through it to impress his qualifications on the jury. Semirural counties like ours didn't usually have coroners of his caliber. He'd worked as a forensic pathologist in Atlanta for a decade before moving to Basking Rock, his wife's hometown.

After establishing Madison's expertise, the gruesome part began. Ginevra had the clerk display a photo of Conway's body in his hospital bed, taken by one of the transporters who'd been dispatched from the coroner's office to pick the body up. For the next forty minutes, Dr. Madison walked us methodically through every step of his investigation, with photos: lung tissue, the tongue, the maculopapular rash. He explained all the tests he'd done, and the jury got to see his lab notebook with the notes he'd made during the investigation.

"My role," he testified, "is to determine two things. Number one, the cause of death. The answer might be a gunshot wound, a heart attack, or, as in this case, anaphylactic shock due to cephalosporin exposure."

"And what's your degree of certainty that cephalosporin was the cause of death?"

"Oh, that is conclusively determined. I don't see any factual basis for doubting that at all."

"Okay. And what is the second thing you've got to determine when you investigate a death?"

"The second thing is, what was the manner of death. That's a technical term, but it simply means, was this death due to accident, homicide, suicide, or natural causes, or is the reason undetermined?"

"Was the manner of Mr. Reed's death undetermined?"

"No, it was not. That's a finding you'll see where, for instance, the body has been exposed to the elements for so long that it's no longer possible to figure out what happened. Which, obviously, was not the case here."

"So, what did you do to determine his manner of death?"

"It's a process of elimination. We immediately excluded natural causes, because death by cephalosporin exposure isn't natural. And I excluded suicide, because there was no evidence at all pointing in that direction. No note, no history of depression, nothing along those lines."

"So that left you with accident or homicide?"

"Yes. I excluded accident for a number of reasons. First off, I was informed by detectives that Mr. Reed had spent most of the morning at his home before collapsing at about 11 a.m. My testing showed he was not under the influence of any intoxicating substance when he died. So this is a man who appears to have been exposed to cephalosporin at his home, in broad daylight, at a time when he had all his wits about him."

"And why is that important?"

"Because the only known source of cephalosporin in his home was his daughter's prescription, and nobody with his wits about him could have mistaken her prescription bottle for his own."

Ginevra had the clerk project the same photo of the two pill bottles that she'd used in her opening. "So what did that tell you?"

"It told me Mr. Reed did not pick up and take a pill from his daughter's bottle by accident."

"Is that why you determined this was homicide?"

"That's part of it. There's also the fact that Mr. Reed's blood pressure medication came in the form of a light blue capsule, and so did his daughter's cephalexin."

The photo of the capsules appeared on the screen.

"When I pulled up photos of the dosage forms—the pills, that is—I realized that Mr. Reed could easily have mistaken her capsule for his own... but not if he saw the bottle. That would only have been possible if one of her pills was in his bottle. There's only one way her pill could have gotten into his bottle, and it's not by accident."

"So that's how you determined Mr. Reed's death was a homicide?"

"Together with all the other evidence, yes. When you exclude the other possibilities, you're left with whatever truth you're left with."

I saw a couple of jurors nodding like that made sense to them.

· · ·

There wasn't much I could do on cross. I raised the issue Hargroves had flagged about not being able to pinpoint the time at which Conway had taken the pill, but it didn't get me far. Madison said that in a man with prior severe allergic reactions, it was unlikely that he could walk around for long with a cephalexin capsule in his stomach; the allergic reaction would happen pretty quickly. All I got out of him was that it was "unlikely, but not impossible" that Conway could've taken the pill more than an hour or so before his collapse.

Ginevra called the police detective next. The timing was bad. It was past four o'clock, so I knew I wouldn't get to cross him today. The jury would go home with whatever Ginevra got out of him in their heads.

And what she got was devastating. Detective Blount was always good on the stand. He was a tall, strong, square-jawed guy with ramrod posture. As he was sworn in, I saw a couple of jurors adjusting their own posture, sitting up straighter. Blount could have that effect. I didn't like him, but there was no denying he had some charisma.

After running through his credentials, Ginevra got into the meat of the case. We saw doorbell camera footage of Conway staggering down his front steps and photos of the Reeds' driveway with yellow police tape around the spot where he fell. In one of the photos, Judy was standing near the Tesla looking bored; her mother was up on the porch behind her, tears shining on her face.

"Detective Blount, could you explain for the jury how you went about investigating Mr. Reed's death?"

"Yes. To clarify, it took nearly two months before the coroner's report came back conclusively stating this was a homicide, but some concerns arose on that first day, when I was informed by the coroner that Mr. Reed had a distinctive rash that suggested the heart attack may not have been the cause of death."

"And that would be the maculopapular rash that Dr. Madison discussed today?"

"Yes. I can also tell you that, in the twenty-two years that I have been a police detective in Basking Rock, I've responded to many homicides, as well as suicides and accidental deaths, and I've seen more family members than I could possibly count reacting to the news that their loved ones had died. Based on that experience, I had questions in my mind about Judy Reed very early on."

"And why is that?"

"Well, if you look at that photo up there, you can see from the time stamp that it was taken at 2:19 p.m. That's about three hours after Mr. Reed was rushed to the hospital and an hour after he was declared dead. Now, people don't all react to death the same way. Not everybody cries, for instance. Some people get angry. Some fall apart and have to be sedated. But the one common denominator that I see, no matter how the survivor feels about the individual who died, no matter what their relationship was, is shock. A sudden death is a shocking thing."

All the jurors looked up at the photo again. In it, Mrs. Reed's stricken expression made Judy's lack of interest stand out more. Judy might as well have been waiting for a bus.

"A sudden death," Blount repeated, "is a deeply shocking thing. Unless you were expecting it."

Ginevra nodded, letting that sink in. "So did you focus on Judy Reed immediately?" she asked.

"No. There are protocols we follow to make sure we find all the evidence and follow up on all the leads. We look at every remotely plausible suspect. A man's death is important. We do *not* want to make a mistake."

"Of course. So what protocols did you follow here?"

"We interviewed all the members of the household, first off. So Mrs. Reed and Judy Reed, who both witnessed Mr. Reed's collapse, and Mrs. Reed's assistant, who I believe I see sitting over there. She was folding laundry on the other side of the house at the time, so she wasn't technically a witness. Then we interviewed Mr. Reed's business associates, his doctors, and his…" He searched for the word. "Paramour, girlfriend—that would be Ms. Alanna Carpenter. All of this is routine. It's protocol, it's how we make sure we cover all the bases."

"And did you tell the people you interviewed that you were investigating this as a homicide?"

"No. We don't come right out and tell anybody that it was a murder. Or an accident or anything else. We don't want to prejudice their answers, so until the coroner's report came back and the family was of course informed that it was homicide by cephalosporin poisoning, what I told them was that we were conducting a routine investigation into Mr. Reed's death."

"And was there a point where you came to consider Judy Reed as your primary suspect?"

"Yes. After the coroner's report came back, I went out with one of my deputies and we reinterviewed the household members and Ms. Carpenter."

"But not Mr. Reed's business associates?"

"Based on our previous interviews with them, we considered it unlikely that they would've provided him with medication or had access to his medication. Because of the rash that the coroner pointed out to me, I had asked them initially if they were aware of Mr. Conway having any allergies, but they all credibly stated that they were not."

"What did you learn during this later part of your investigation, after the coroner's report?"

"All four of these women knew about Mr. Reed's cephalosporin allergy, and they all denied having any such medication around the time of his death. But after I reviewed their medical records from that time period, I saw that only three of them had told the truth."

"And which of them was lying?"

"Objection," I said. I knew I'd be overruled, but it was a bad look to let the word *lying* go by without a challenge.

"Overruled. Detective Blount, you may answer."

"Judy Reed was lying. Her medical records showed that she'd gotten a prescription for cephalosporin three days prior to Mr. Reed's passing."

"Did you ask her about that?"

"Of course. And she denied it. I had the medical record printed out, I put it in her hand, and she looked at it and just said, 'Obviously that's wrong.'"

When he quoted her, he used a tone that was familiar to me: Judy dismissing the views of lesser mortals.

"What was your next step?"

"I sent one of my deputies down to the pharmacy to check, and their records showed Judy Reed picking the prescription up. I asked her about that, and she said that the records must be wrong. The hospital was wrong, the pharmacy was wrong—all of this evidence, according to her, was wrong."

"And based on that, what did you conclude?"

"What she told me was ridiculous," Blount said. "Absolutely ridiculous." He looked at the jury. "I've been a police detective for twenty-two years. In that time, I've learned that when somebody lies to me during an investigation, that is a sign of guilt. And when I put evidence in front of them that *proves* they're lying, and they tell me a ridiculous story to try and extricate themselves from that web they've weaved..." He shook his head.

"What does that mean, in your experience?" Ginevra asked.

"There's only one reason to do that. And that reason is guilt."

23

JANUARY 31, 2023

On Tuesday morning, I wasn't feeling well. I didn't usually have problems with my nerves during trial, but I did now. One of my hands was shaky, and my heart lurched a couple of times. I finished my second cup of coffee and decided not to have any more. I had to balance out the need for mental clarity with whatever was making me feel out of whack.

Ginevra spent another two hours on her direct of Detective Blount. My cross didn't last long. I had nothing to dilute the impact of what Blount had said, and I didn't want the jury to bask in his charisma any longer than necessary, so I kept things short.

After lunch, Ginevra called Dr. Kassel to the stand. He testified for half an hour about Conway's medical state, the efforts made to save his life, and the belated realization that it was anaphylaxis, not the heart attack, that was killing him.

"Not a day goes by that I don't kick myself about that," he said, looking down. "He was having a heart attack, and as a cardiologist, that's what I was focused on. Heart attacks kill so many men his age. But I do take some comfort from the fact that, in the hospital's review of his case, they found that by the time he reached the emergency room, given the severity of his allergic reaction, there was nothing we could've done."

"I can imagine, Dr. Kassel," Ginevra said. "I appreciate how hard your job must be."

When she was done, I went over and handed the clerk a thumb drive with most of my exhibits. The impeachment exhibits—ones that I would surprise Kassel with if I caught him lying on the stand—were in a Redweld folder on the defense table.

They included a through-the-motel-window shot of Kassel and Alanna half-dressed on a messy bed. The PI that Conway had hired to tail them had done a good job. I was looking forward to this.

"Good morning, Dr. Kassel," I said. "I only have a few questions for you. First off, to make sure we understand what happened when, hospital records show that Mr. Reed arrived in the emergency room at 11:39 a.m., correct?"

I looked at the clerk, and she put the record on the screen.

Kassel took a look. "Yes, that's what it says."

"And because the paramedics had determined he was suffering a heart attack, you had already been called, correct?"

"Correct."

"Okay. So before he got there, you knew he was on his way?"

"I would have, yes."

"And I imagine you took a look at his medical record while he was in transit, just to get the lay of the land, so to speak?"

"Oh, yes. With a heart attack in progress, you want to be ready to treat the patient as soon as he arrives. Or any emergency, really."

"So that the jury understands how all this technology works, can you take a look at this and tell us if this is more or less what you would've seen?"

The clerk put up my next exhibit, a screenshot of Conway's medical record. The box for allergies, right near the top, was red and said "Cephalosporins."

Kassel nodded. "Yes, that's how it would've looked."

"So before he even got to the hospital, you knew a few things about him: male, age sixty-three, having a heart attack right in the ambulance, and allergic to cephalosporins. Correct?"

"Yes, that's correct."

"And did you recognize his name?"

"I'm sorry?"

"Well, it says 'Conway Reed' at the top there. Did you recognize that?"

"Should I have?"

"Are you saying you didn't?"

After a pause, he said, "He was fairly well-known around town, because of his success in horse racing. So I suppose it may have rung a bell."

"Okay. But he didn't run in your social circles?"

"Oh, no. I don't have much free time, given my work commitments, and when I do socialize, it's generally with family, other physicians, or the leaders of the medical charities that I work with."

"Uh-huh. And where did Alanna Carpenter fit into all of that?"

"I'm sorry?"

"How did you come to know Mr. Reed's girlfriend, or fiancée, Alanna Carpenter?"

Kassel looked me dead in the eye. This look was not good news. We recognized each other as enemies.

Just before his pause got too long, he said, "Now that you mention it, I believe Ms. Carpenter did some type of consulting for Basking Rock Hospital. And I believe I met her in that capacity."

"Okay," I said, nodding as if I already knew that. I went over to get my Redweld folder, brought it back, and said, "So you met Mr. Reed's girlfriend. About how long before Mr. Reed's death did you start sleeping with her?"

Two people spoke at once: Ginevra objecting and a juror calling out to the Lord. Kassel said nothing.

Judge Davenport gave me a lethal glare. "Counsel, I trust you have some basis for this line of questioning?"

I opened my mouth to say "Absolutely, Your Honor," but nothing came out.

I looked around.

The last thing I saw was Terri's face.

I woke up in the dark. There was an antiseptic smell. I blinked and saw a ceiling with sound-absorbing tiles, a whiteboard on the wall, the silver rails of a hospital bed. Something was beeping.

A young, Black nurse came in. Across the hall, I saw another nurse and a dark window. I wondered what time it was.

"Oh, hello, Mr. Munroe!" The nurse smiled. "I'm Britney. Do you know where you are?"

"Basking Rock Hospital?" It was hard to talk. I cleared my throat.

"Yes. Do you remember what happened?"

I shook my head.

"I guess you were in court today, and you collapsed with what's called an arrhythmic syncope. That means fainting because your heart wasn't beating the way it's supposed to. But fortunately, our chief cardiologist was there to help you. He rode here with you in the ambulance, and he's actually working the night shift tonight, which he doesn't normally do, so that he can take care of you."

I stared at her. Then I said, "Can you get me my phone?"

"Oh, I'm sorry. We don't have phones in the CCU. Most of our patients are too sick to use them."

"I meant my cell phone."

"I'm not sure that made it over here with you. Hopefully somebody in the courtroom picked it up."

I shifted, and something pinched my arm. An IV needle was taped to the inside of my elbow, with its plastic tubing curling away behind me. That arm was strapped to the bed railing.

"You're getting IV magnesium and potassium," Britney said.

"Why's my arm tied to the bed?"

"Oh, that's a restraint. When patients get distressed, we don't want them ripping out their IV."

"Can we get that taken off now?"

She smiled. "If you promise me you won't flail around."

"I promise."

I watched a nurse push a cart past in the hall as Britney was unstrapping me.

"What is it that's wrong with my heart?"

"Atrial fibrillation." Her voice was serious. "Let's just say you're real lucky to be here."

I did not feel lucky. I had a pit in my stomach at the idea of spending the whole night in Dr. Kassel's care. "Britney, is there any way you could make a quick phone call for me?"

"It's actually shift change right now," she said, "so I'm a little busy. There'll be a new nurse after eight o'clock, and she should be able to do that. Your call button is right there on your blanket."

Once she'd left, I sat up a little to see if I was dizzy. It wasn't too bad. I twisted around, trying to see the IV behind me, but I couldn't.

For a minute, I fiddled with the buttons on the side rail. A nurse went past in the hallway, and I stopped, in case getting out of bed wasn't allowed.

When I finally got the rail down, I swung my legs over the side and checked for dizziness again. So far, so good.

I shuffled back to the IV pole and turned it so I could see what was marked on the bag. It was wrinkled and hard to read, but the top word did look like "Magnesium."

I knew how IVs worked. Any drug they hung on there would go into my veins. They could change it as I slept. It seemed obvious to me that you could inject something extra into the IV bag, if you wanted.

A man's voice behind me said, "Evening, Mr. Munroe."

I turned around.

In court, I'd been looking up at him in the witness box. He was tall, so I was still looking up at him, but now he had his white coat on and I was barefoot in a hospital gown. I didn't even have underpants on.

"You should get back in bed," Dr. Kassel said. "You could collapse again at any time. This thing can be hard to get under control. We're doing everything we can."

He had the same look in his eyes as he'd had in court. It did not match his words of concern.

I had told the whole courtroom, including the numerous reporters in the gallery, that he'd cheated on his wife. And he surely knew where else I was going with that. But I hadn't had time to put any evidence into the record.

I assumed the trial must have been put on hold when I collapsed. And someone would've explained to Kassel that when I got better, it would pick back up again where we had left off.

I needed time to think. I needed him gone.

I started getting back into bed. "Thanks for helping," I said. "I'll sit tight."

"You'd better. AFib can be rapidly lethal. If it causes a stroke…" He snapped his fingers to show how quickly I might die.

I said, as if I meant it, "Well, thanks again."

He nodded and went away.

I couldn't look up my condition on my phone. I couldn't call anybody. I realized I didn't even have anybody's number memorized. Terri, Noah, Rachel, Ruiz—everybody I normally dealt with, I called by touching their name on my phone screen.

One number was almost there. I had most of it. I hadn't gotten around to adding Hargroves as a contact, so I dialed him whenever I called, and his number had a pattern to it. The Atlanta area code was 404, and his number had some fours in it too. It was like part of a song stuck in my head. I tried to remember the rest.

A nurse I recognized walked past, and my heart lurched in a good way. "Keisha!" I called. "Hey, Keisha!" It was the nurse Terri and I had met at the community gardens on Christmas Eve, but she didn't seem to hear me.

I took a deep breath. I shut my eyes and tried to let Hargroves's number come to me.

A few minutes later, a woman said my name. I looked up. It was Keisha.

"Evening, Mr. Munroe! Sorry it took me a minute. I was running something to one of my patients. How you doing?"

"Not so good."

"I'm sorry to hear that. I was thinking of you the other day. Word got around about LaDonna's trial. I heard you ripped Desmond a new one, for real." She started laughing. "Oh my God," she said. "He was so mad. You should've seen his face when he heard some of us girls talking about it." She hung off the doorframe and belly laughed.

I started laughing too. It was contagious.

"Oh, *man*!" she said. "Man, oh man. After what he done, that did me good."

"That's what I try to do as a lawyer," I said, chuckling. "Just… spread the joy."

"And you did. You spread it good. A lot of us here are real happy about that. Now, what did you call me for? You need something?"

"Keisha, I need to…" I stopped myself. If I said I needed to get out of here, it might alarm her. "I need to call somebody. But I don't have my phone."

"Yeah, okay," she said, pulling her cell phone out of her pocket. "You just tell me the number."

"Well, that's the thing. Without my phone, I don't know anybody's number."

"Mm-hmm. That's technology, huh. You want me to call that detective friend of yours?"

I wanted that more than I wanted a million bucks. She must've seen it on my face. She started tapping on her phone screen. "I think she emailed it to me," she said, "to set things up so we could talk. What's her name again?"

I spelled Terri's name. Keisha searched her email and placed the call.

At twenty past eight, Terri and Hargroves showed up in my room. She'd suggested bringing him to see if he thought it was safe for me to leave. While she searched the cabinets for my clothes, he watched my heart trace on the monitor above the bed. Keisha's shift was over, and my new nurse didn't think she was allowed to show my chart to an outside doctor, so Hargroves asked her to call Kassel.

We waited and waited. Terri called Noah to let him know I was in the hospital, and Hargroves stood there with his hands in the pockets of his suit jacket, eyes fixed on the monitor.

Eventually he said, "I can't promise that you didn't have AFib earlier, but all I'm seeing is PVCs." I gave him a confused look, so he explained, "Premature ventricular contractions. They feel weird as hell, and in a bad case they can knock you out, but they won't kill you." He raised a warning finger. "Unless you're driving. You don't want to pass out at the wheel. Don't drive until you get this fixed."

Kassel didn't show up until almost half past ten, and then he and Hargroves argued about my heart for a while. Kassel insisted that my ECG on admission had shown AFib, but the nurse had gone to help another patient, and he claimed he couldn't pull up my record on her computer.

"As I'm sure you know," he told Hargroves, "it's very rare for PVCs to make a man lose consciousness. You were in that courtroom too. You saw him drop."

Hargroves nodded and said, "Rare's not the same as impossible."

Kassel let out an exasperated breath. Then he looked at me. "If you want to bet your life on this," he said, "I can't stop you."

It seemed like I was betting my life either way. I liked my odds better the farther I got from his care.

My clothes were nowhere to be found. With Hargroves and Terri flanking me, and an extra hospital gown to cover my backside, at 11 p.m. I walked barefoot to Terri's car.

24

FEBRUARY 2, 2023

It had been twenty-four hours since a Charleston cardiologist had stuck a bunch of electrodes to my chest and hung a Holter monitor around my neck. It was an ECG machine the size of a pack of cigarettes, and I was supposed to wear it for another two days. My heart health was the first topic of conversation when I walked into Ginevra Barnes's office at nine thirty Thursday morning. The second topic was Judy's trial.

At Ginevra's request, I had brought my Redweld. We reviewed the photos of Kassel and Alanna. Then I flipped open my laptop and pulled them up there, so she could see the metadata. The dates on the photos were from three different weekends in the two months before Conway's death. I also showed her his email to Alanna that the photos were attached to.

She sat back in her chair for a minute, apparently thinking things through. Then she looked at me. "I am inclined to step back and give this a little more investigation."

"Uh-huh," I said. "Meaning what?"

"At this point, I'm going to suggest a non pros, but without prejudice." Dropping the charges against Judy, in other words, but with the option to refile them later.

I nodded. "I'm obviously going to ask Davenport to make the non pros *with* prejudice. And even if I lose on that, if you do end up refiling, the jury is going to hear that the victim and his doctor were sleeping with the same woman, and the doctor knew that cephalosporins could kill him."

"I do realize that. It's very concerning. That's why I'm prepared to offer a non pros."

"Then let's do that. And we'll see which way Davenport wants it done."

"Yes, we will."

I started packing the damning photographs back into my Redweld. "By the way," I said, "please let Mr. Ruiz know I said thank you."

"Oh, this was not Mr. Ruiz's decision."

I stopped what I was doing and looked at her.

"He had to approve it, of course," she said, "but I told him that if the evidence you brought over supported what you'd been saying in court, then I didn't feel comfortable moving forward. As I'm sure you recall from your days at the solicitor's office, I have a duty to ensure that justice is done."

After that sank in, I started gathering up the photos again. "I hate to say it," I told her, "but I might have misjudged you."

She smiled.

. . .

After lunch, as Terri and I were driving over to Mrs. Reed's to celebrate, I got a call from Hargroves. He was back in Atlanta.

"Are you sitting down?" he asked.

"In the passenger seat of a Subaru, yes."

"My intern ran that test you wanted."

"Oh?"

"Yeah. He found that the drug Conway ingested wasn't cephalexin, it was ceftiofur. Since the trial got continued and you were indisposed, I didn't want to tell you until I could run it again myself and make sure."

"So it wasn't the medication Judy was given—or they claim Judy was given—at all? What was it?" I made an amazed face at Terri. She made one back at me.

"Ceftiofur is a cephalosporin that's used in veterinary medicine. Horses, cows."

"So… maybe one of his horses was taking it? How'd it get into *him*?"

"That I can't tell you."

At Mrs. Reed's house, I drank sweet tea while all the ladies drank celebratory mimosas. Mrs. Reed called me over to hug her more than once. When they ran out of mimosas, Judy uncorked a second bottle of champagne and Emma Jean brought more orange juice from the kitchen. Terri declined a third glass, explaining that she was my driver, and at Mrs. Reed's urging, Emma Jean drank it down.

Judy went to the piano and started playing. The tune wasn't classical, but I didn't recognize it until Emma Jean belted out the first verse. It was a Dolly Parton song. She sang the whole thing, bowed to much applause, and then went, laughing, into the kitchen while Terri attempted something by Whitney Houston.

I gathered up a few empty glasses, put them on a tray, and carried them into the kitchen. Emma Jean was leaning against the island, giggling tipsily to herself. There was a sink on the other side of the island, so I took the glasses over there and started hand-washing them. "My goodness," I said, rinsing out the first glass. "This must be such a relief to y'all."

"Oh, so much, so much. I can't even tell you. I just— Thank you, thank you so much. You've given Mrs. Reed her life back. I've known her for eleven years, and I've never seen her this happy."

"I'm sorry I had to upset her a couple of weeks ago, talking about that trust document I found."

"Oh, that was awful. What kind of husband does that?" She shook her head, stumbled a little bit, and grabbed the edge of the island to steady herself. "What an evil thing to do, and to such a wonderful woman!"

I soaped up a glass. "I suppose that must've been even worse than when she saw him down by the stables with Alanna."

"Oh, maybe. For me it was the same." She waved one hand extravagantly. "The way he was with that girl, I knew he was going to divorce her and leave us with nothing. I knew it."

I looked at her in surprise. She was gazing out the back window, shaking her head. Anger radiated off her. The words *leave us with nothing* echoed in my head.

I rinsed the glass and set it in the rack.

Emma Jean worked in this house every day. She'd known about Conway's allergy. How hard would it have been, I wondered, for her to find his pill bottle, open up one of the capsules, and replace his blood pressure medication with something else?

The music had stopped. I heard Terri saying something but couldn't hear her words.

I soaped up the next glass and asked, "Doesn't your nephew work at the stables? That must be nice. Do you get to visit him a lot?"

"Oh, sometimes, yeah."

"Does he ever help the veterinarians when they come out?"

Emma Jean didn't answer. I glanced up at her. Her expression was wary. "I don't know what you're talking about," she said, and she went back into the living room.

I turned my head, watching her go, and saw Judy in the doorway.

She came up to me and said, quietly, "Why were you asking her that?"

I looked behind her to make sure nobody else was nearby. "Judy, my medical expert called today. He ran a test, and he found something great, which was that the type of cephalosporin that killed your dad wasn't the same type as what you were—that is, what the hospital *said* you were prescribed."

"That's excellent. So the prosecution will have to admit they have no case against me."

"Yes, probably, but here's the thing. What he found was that it was a type that's used in veterinary medicine. In horses."

I glanced behind her again. We were still alone.

"I don't quite know how to put this," I said, "so I'll just spit it out. I have some concerns. Does Emma Jean's nephew ever help the vet? Would he have access to veterinary antibiotics?"

Judy stared at me. After a moment, she said, "Emma Jean is the best healthcare aide my mother has ever had."

"I know, but—"

"If my father had been one-tenth as loyal to my mother as she is, she wouldn't have had anything to complain to you about just now. She probably would've liked him."

"Okay…"

"So what you were suggesting is something that I don't think we need to explore. At this point, it doesn't matter," she said.

"As your lawyer, I have to say it might matter. I mean, if Mrs. Barnes gets the non pros without prejudice, we might need to use the information about the drug to keep her from deciding to refile the case."

Judy gave me another long look. "I think you had mentioned," she said, "that as the client, I get to decide my risk tolerance."

"That's true."

"Okay. Then I'll take that risk. You don't have to share those test results with her, right? Legally?"

"No, I don't."

"Good. So I'm instructing you not to. My mother needs Emma Jean. Without her…" Judy shook her head. "It's water under the bridge, Mr. Munroe, and it needs to stay that way."

From the living room, her mother called, "Come play some more music, honey! I thought of something I want to sing!"

"Be right there," Judy replied. She asked me, "Is there something you'd like to sing? My mom would enjoy that."

I shook my head. "I can't think of anything."

. . .

On the car ride home, I told Terri.

"Wow," she said.

We drove for a minute in silence.

"You couldn't tell Ginevra if you wanted to," she said, "could you."

"Nope." She knew the attorney ethics rules almost as well as I did. "And not just Ginevra. Without Judy's consent, I can't tell anyone outside my own case team."

"Well, okay then."

"I don't know how I feel about letting a murderer off like that. Possibly two, if the nephew knew she took one of those pills, and why." I stared out the window. After the accident, Noah's rehabilitation had damn near bankrupted me. I would have cut off my own arm to be able to give him the level of care Mrs. Reed had. If Emma Jean were to be arrested for Conway's murder, she wouldn't be the only one being punished. "But the rules are clear, and so was Judy."

Terri shook her head. "This has sure been an *interesting* one."

When we stopped at a light, she looked at me and said, "I hope after this, you'll finally take a freaking vacation."

"Does it count as a vacation if you spend it in the cardiology ward? Because depending on what this Holter monitor finds out, I might need a little hospital stay."

"No. Okay, listen. We're going to the beach."

She didn't drive to the beach in town or the causeway where we sometimes walked our dogs. She took us a little ways down the coast, where there were more palm trees and fewer traffic lights. We parked outside a place called Ray's Shrimp Shack. Out front there were some picnic tables, and in back was a stretch of sand sloping gently down to the ocean. The sun was getting low, and everything looked golden.

We ordered baskets of fried shrimp and took them out the back door on trays. There were three picnic tables on this side of the place, too, but Terri took us farther down the sand, to a pair of deck chairs facing the water. We sat with our trays on our knees, looking at the ocean and eating our shrimp.

"I *know* after this case you can afford a vacation," she told me.

"Yeah. Hell, I could pay you, me, and Rachel to sit around doing nothing for three months."

"Oh, that sounds nice."

Halfway to the horizon, a big white ship was going past. "Maybe I should go on a cruise," I said. "You want to come?"

She chuckled. "I don't think my boyfriend would like that."

I shook my head. "Who is this guy, anyway? I need to meet him."

"You do *not* need to meet him."

"I guess it's not that serious, then. That's good."

She looked at me, smiling. "Leland," she said, "go to the Caribbean or something. You'll like it."

"I was joking about the cruise," I said. "I couldn't enjoy a cruise. I'd spend the whole time worrying that they were smuggling drugs in the cargo hold. Or that my waiter was involved in human trafficking."

"My God, you are in deep need of a break."

I sighed. The sky was getting darker. "Yeah, maybe."

We fell silent for a bit. The waves crashed on the shore.

"I'll still be here when you get back," she said.

"You promise?"

"Mm-hmm. I could even watch Squatter for you while you're gone."

"Oh, now I guess I'll have to go, or he'll be disappointed."

25

APRIL 7, 2023

I t was midmorning in Sedona, Arizona. Red cliffs loomed a few hundred yards away, the sky overhead was swimming-pool blue, and I was sitting beside Noah in an in-ground hot tub. He and Terri had plotted to force me into a vacation after I got the thumbs-up from the cardiologist. Noah had suggested going someplace completely different from what we were used to; he thought it would clear my mind. Neither of us had ever been out west.

Neither of us had ever experienced a guided meditation led by a New Ager with feathers in her hair, either, so he'd decided that we ought to. Now we were sitting in the water along with three other guests from the hotel—or "wellness resort," as it called itself, presumably to justify its prices.

Our eyes were supposed to be closed, but I sneaked a peek at Noah. He was inhaling deeply, as instructed by the woman on the other side of the hot tub, who had informed us that her name was Starchild. A few different types of cactus were growing out of the terra-cotta dirt behind her, one of them studded with hot pink flowers. I shut my eyes again.

Whatever her real name was, the woman's voice was soothing. If I could tune out her words—for instance, if I could stop going off on tangents trying to figure out what the heck a "spiritual vortex" was—maybe I could give this meditation a good faith shot, like Noah was doing.

Her voice had a warm thrum to it, like the water. As I slowed my breathing, she directed our attention to a chakra whose name and location I didn't catch. She told us to fill it with yellow light. I had never been clear on exactly what a chakra was, so I was at a loss for how to go about filling one.

The heat on my shoulders reminded me that I hadn't put any sunscreen on. I wished I could hit pause on the meditation and go get some. Sedona was in the high desert, with harsher sun than we had back home.

Thinking of home made me wonder where Terri was at that moment. Squatter was staying at her house. Maybe the dogs were romping in her yard while she and her boyfriend watched them from the deck. With a little luck, maybe Squatter would bite him.

I doubted that this was how meditation was supposed to work. My consciousness was not going on the trip that Starchild's website had advertised.

"That get you any more relaxed?" Noah asked as we walked back to our room in sustainable fair-trade flip-flops provided by the resort.

"Uh, sure."

He laughed. "Yeah, I don't know either," he said. "When she started talking about energy grids, all I could picture was electrical lines and power plants. I kind of lost the plot."

"That's my boy." The hotel's glass doors parted and let us into the lobby.

"It was more relaxing than tracking a subject in traffic, I'll give it that," he said.

"You've done that already?"

"Oh, yeah. I found myself a mentor, like you said." We got to the elevators, and he hit the button. "So I'm starting to get some decent work."

I didn't like the thought of my kid tailing somebody in his car. A lot of folks were armed, and nobody took kindly to being followed.

But he didn't like me worrying. "That's great," I said. "You think that chakra stuff would go over well back home? Maybe your mentor could arrange for you to lead a workshop on it at the office."

He gave me a look. "Yeah, and why don't you see about leading one in federal court?"

I smiled. I'd missed him.

When the elevator came, it was empty. As we rode up to our room, he said, "Speaking of court, I saw Mr. Cardozo the other week. He told me to tell you he's sorry about your hospital?"

I chuckled. He looked confused. "He's messing with you," I said.

"Was he talking about that doctor who got indicted? I saw something on the news, but I wasn't paying attention."

"Yeah, a few people got indicted. Insurance fraud, Medicare and Medicaid fraud. The works."

"Like, billing more than they were supposed to?"

"Mostly billing for procedures that weren't done, meds that weren't used, doctors that weren't there. Lot of poor kids on Medicaid got milked to put money in their pockets."

"*Doctors* did that?"

We got out on our floor.

"Yeah. I'll tell you more on the drive."

The road to the Grand Canyon wound between low red mountains dotted with scrub and what someone at the hotel had told me was sage. The air smelled like pine mixed with cinnamon, clean and warm. About twenty minutes into the trip, Noah asked me to pull over at a gray shack by the roadside with a hand-painted sign advertising Navajo jewelry.

As I parked, I said, "Didn't think you were a jewelry guy."

"It's for Isabela."

"Oh, you're still seeing her?" I'd thought he'd broken up with Ruiz's daughter months ago.

"Yeah. We got back together."

We walked in and looked at jewelry for a few minutes, and he bought her something pretty with turquoise on it. It was strange seeing him do that. He was still a kid to me, but I'd been his age when I met his mother. This trip was his first time out of the southeast and our first big trip together. I was glad I'd forked out the cash for it. If time kept moving as fast as it had been lately, with him seeming to be in a different phase of life almost every time I looked at him, he might soon be too old to let me pay his way—or too busy with his own goals to take the time for a trip.

When we got to the interstate, we started seeing billboards again.

"That doctor who got arrested, wasn't he the one on all the bill-boards?" Noah asked.

"Yeah."

"He did all that fraud stuff?"

"Him and the hospital CEO, and some woman they had doing financial consulting. Apparently, she and the CEO were the ones who came up with the scheme." I'd read the indictments. They were public, so I could talk about them.

"And they did this *why*?"

"Why do a lot of people do bad stuff? It brought them a few million a year. The CEO and the doctor got big performance bonuses and then funneled a bunch more through the financial consultant."

I didn't mention Kassel's affair with Alanna. That wasn't in the indictment.

"How'd they get away with it up to now?"

"Lot of ways. Part of it was, they had a guy on staff who knew most everybody, because he was in janitorial and worked all over the hospital. If he heard about somebody getting suspicious, he'd tell the big dogs and they'd take care of it. A few times, the way they took care of it was having him help them frame a nurse for stealing drugs."

"Goddamn." When I glanced over, he was shaking his head.

"Yeah, it's real bad," I said.

"Uh-huh. And there's more of it, like, everywhere I look. Plenty of people that I would've thought were completely normal, I get paid to investigate them and we find out... like... I mean, the things we find out are *bad*."

He had confidentiality rules he had to stick to—we both did—but I'd been following rules like that long enough to read between the lines. The tone of a word or the way a pause felt could tell you a lot about what was underneath.

"Yeah, I know what you mean," I said. "All I can tell you is, that's why when you do find somebody good, you hang on to them. Or, even if they're not staying in your life, at least help them out."

He nodded.

I didn't tell him that Cardozo's office had nixed a retrial for LaDonna. She was free. And I'd referred her to a firm that helped whistleblowers file suit under the False Claims Act. If that worked out, she'd get a share of the money that the feds recovered from the hospital fraud ring. For now, though, she was focused on getting a new nursing job. Ms. Baker had put in a good word for her at her place of employment, since LaDonna wanted nothing to do with Basking Rock Hospital anymore.

Mrs. Reed's case contesting the change to Conway's trust would take a while to wend its way through the legal process, but her lawyer was optimistic.

None of those legal details were public yet, so for now I could only celebrate with Terri.

We drove in silence for a while. The sky was an impossible shade of blue. A sign on the roadside said that we were now at an elevation of seven thousand feet.

My new cardiologist had told me to take it easy on this trip, because higher elevations could stress the heart. This far above sea level, there was almost 20 percent less oxygen in the air.

He'd meant I shouldn't do any strenuous exercise, but there was no risk of that. Noah's leg had never fully recovered from the car accident years ago, so we weren't going to hike down into the canyon or rappel down any cliffs. Instead, I'd booked us a hotel right on the canyon's rim, and I'd paid the premium for a room with a balcony overlooking it all.

The drive up from Sedona was a little over two hours, and by the time we reached the Grand Canyon, the sun had started setting. We parked and walked up the path to the edge. Scrubby trees on either side blocked the view, apart from some clouds lit purple overhead. That got my attention, and I didn't look back at the earth ahead of us until Noah said, "My God."

We'd passed the last tree. The landscape was astonishing, nothing but red rock from horizon to horizon. I couldn't tell if we could see for fifty miles or a hundred or a thousand. The sky was red and gold; the land below it was, too; and the canyon was a shadow of such immensity that I could see how people might think, seeing this for the first time millennia ago, that this was the place where the earth split right in two.

We didn't need to talk. We stood there until the sun went down.

END OF PRESCRIBING DOUBT
SMALL TOWN LAWYER BOOK 5

Defending Innocence

Influencing Justice

Interpreting Guilt

Burning Evidence

Prescribing Doubt

PS: Do you enjoy legal thrillers? Then keep reading for exclusive extracts from ***Small Town Trial*** and ***Defending Innocence***.

ABOUT PETER KIRKLAND

Loved this book? Share it with a friend!

To be notified of Peter's next book release please sign up to his mailing list, at www.relaypub.com/peter-kirkland-email-sign-up.

ABOUT PETER

Peter Kirkland grew up in Beaufort, South Carolina. As a kid, Peter loved history and learning about his area. One year in school, he was given a project to research a few South Carolina law cases and the precedents they set and their effect on people's lives. This research project lit the flame for his passion for law and creating a more equal justice system since. Soon after this, Peter began reading legal thrillers voraciously and enjoyed the legal maneuvering and justice found within. As an adult he has continued researching the law and understanding the system and its effects on individuals. A few years ago, he decided to try writing his own legal thriller.

Now a full-time writer, he uses his research, passion for justice, and real case studies to bring together courtroom dramas with deep, rich characters, and gripping twists and turns.

New to the industry, Peter would love to hear from readers:

ABOUT DALETH

Daleth Hall grew up in Ann Arbor, Michigan, raised by a handicapped single mother who instilled in her a deep love for truth, justice, and the written word. By the age of three, she was already reading and writing, thanks to her mom's guidance. After discovering that a creative writing degree wasn't enough to didn't pay the bills, she followed her brother into law school and has spent the past 17 years as a trial lawyer.

Early in her career, she worked high-stakes criminal cases—from murder to federal corruption—until but a colleague's close call with a colleague, who was when an ex-client escaped from prison and tried to hunt him down hunted by an escaped client, convinced her to switch to that civil litigation was a better path. Despite the shift, Daleth remains active in criminal justice, serving as a bilingual certified court interpreter and working pro bono to overturn wrongful convictions.

In addition to her legal career, she writes gripping legal thrillers, plays, and short stories.

Daleth would love to hear from readers who can contact her at Daleth HallWriter@gmail.com

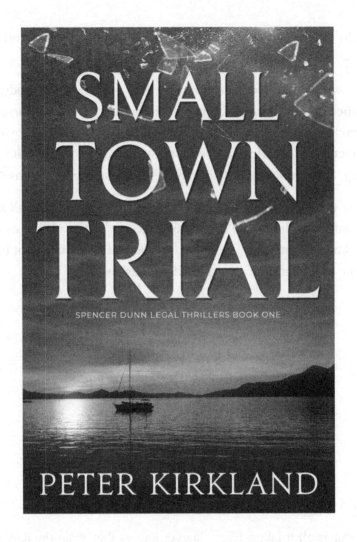

BLURB

Murder on a placid lake... Can Spencer Dunn keep his head above water?

When beloved mayor turned state senator Carlton Osborn is found dead on his boat, the local police suspect foul play. The only suspect is pregnant nineteen-year-old Amber Vega. And the only lawyer willing to take her case is Spencer Dunn. The hotshot attorney is eager to restore his reputation after a humiliating loss in court. But this case may be more than he bargained for....

Amber was caught red-handed on the boat with Osborn's body, and the police are determined to pin the murder on her. Even worse, she was having an affair with the senator, and was caught in a vicious argument with his wife. But the more Spencer digs, the less the story adds up. Something smells fishy, and it's not just Osborn's corpse!

Spencer will stop at nothing to uncover the truth, and he doesn't know the meaning of the word "quit". But if he can't unravel the mystery, prove Amber's innocence, and uncover the real killer, he might be the next one to find himself sleeping with the fishes...

Get your copy of *Small Town Trial*
Available January 23, 2025
(Available for pre-order now)
www.peterkirklandauthor.com

———

EXCERPT

Chapter One

One juror is all it takes. Every lawyer knows this, even the bad ones. Hell, *especially* the bad ones.

It was subtle but unmistakable. Juror number seven's lower lip quivered, and her eyes moistened every time I referenced the plight of the single mother: cast aside, emotionally blackmailed by a cruel ex-husband, beaten down by an unfair system. She felt it; she knew. Some of the others in the jury box seemed less sympathetic. Or maybe they were bored. It was difficult to tell. Perhaps their minds were already made up. I rested my hand on the exhibit shelf directly in front of number seven. Her own hands were shaking and tearing at a tissue in her lap as I spoke.

"So, you see, ladies and gentlemen, it is not as simple a matter as my colleagues for the prosecution would have you believe. As you were instructed when the trial began, for the crime of criminal restraint to occur, there must be both action and intent. In legalese, actus reus and mens rea."

I took a moment to look into a couple of jurors' eyes. It was hard for me to give this case my all when I thought it should never have been brought... but it had, and my client had agonized over it every day since.

"It means guilty actions and a guilty mind. The Maine family code stipulates that for what took place to be a crime, the noncustodial parent not only must take the child out of the state—that is the action —but he or she also must intend to take them somewhere where they cannot be found. In other words, the children are hidden away. That is the guilty mind, the intent. Do we have that here? Has the prosecution produced a single shred of evidence that even suggests that my client intended to conceal her children in a secret location in an attempt to deceive their father and keep them from him?"

I had no difficulty sounding sincere, at least. Shannon Maroney wanted nothing but the best for her kids, and she played by the rules. Which was more than I could say for some of my clients.

"No! We do not. We have absolutely none of that intent here. Not a scin-tilla. Not even a hint. First of all, my client was the rightful custodial parent when the trip north began. More importantly, these phone records," I continued, shaking the stack of papers in the air, "introduced as evidence and acknowledged by the prosecution, prove that my client notified, or attempted to notify, several people of the children's exact location, including Mr. Maroney. And we heard testimony from some of them: the girl's music teacher, several parents of school friends, Mr.

Engel, the boy's karate instructor. They all knew that Ms. Maroney and the children went to Canada to visit family, and that the visit involved an unplanned excursion to the family cabin. They were also informed that Ms. Maroney's father suffered a heart attack and had to be airlifted from that remote cabin to a hospital in Ottawa. We showed you copies of those reports: the Life Flight and hospital reports. I ask you, ladies, and gentlemen. If you were going into hiding with the intent to never be found, would you tell a half dozen or so friends and acquaintances exactly where you are? And would you attempt to inform the children's father as well?"

A few of the jurors shook their heads at this, including number three, a thirtysomething man who'd spent most of the trial looking at his smartwatch.

"In fact," I continued, pointing to the prosecution's table, "we are here for only two reasons. Firstly, Ms. Maroney's travel itinerary had to be changed through no fault of her own. Hasn't that happened to all of us? Secondly, we are here because Mr. Maroney thought it would be easier—or crueler—to file a complaint than to pick up a phone and reach out to any one of those people who knew exactly where his children were. He knew the names of the parents. He knew their routines. He took the kids to music lessons and karate practice. Why not call up the music school and ask if they had heard from his ex-wife? Or any of the parents who were notified—had to be notified—that the girl's birthday party needed to be canceled? But no. Let's beat the poor woman who's stuck in the wilderness, whose father was dead for all she knew, let's drag her into court. That'll make her regret getting a divorce. That will be a nice payback. And I submit that the prosecution, by bringing this matter to trial, is only enabling that sadistic behavior."

Okay, maybe that was too much. But I was right, and I was pissed. My client was being legally assaulted by a vengeful ex-husband. And a misguided and overzealous prosecution was the weapon he chose.

Why? I had no idea. Some DAs just get a bug in their britches, I guess. Or maybe the Fathers for Equal Rights lobby were big donors. Either way, it should never have come to this.

"In conclusion, ladies and gentlemen of the jury, I'm afraid we've dragged you down here for nothing. We're wasting time that you could use for better purposes. You have been shown conclusively that, while my client did indeed take her children out of the state, Mr. Maroney was informed of the expected plans. And we have likewise demonstrated that while the plans may have changed, there was never any intent to deceive Mr. Maroney or to keep him from knowing the whereabouts of his children. We have, in fact, proven that the opposite is true." I raised the phone records again. "Ms. Maroney is innocent of this crime because there *is* no crime. Truth and reason leave you no choice but to find the defendant not guilty. Thank you for your service here today."

Whatever Perry Mason effect I hoped to create was ruined by the sound of my left hearing aid throwing feedback into the otherwise hushed courtroom. I must've brushed the stack of papers I was holding too close to my ear as I lowered them histrionically. One juror covered his own ears; another jumped in her seat, startled. I looked at the floor to conceal my red cheeks as I retreated to my seat at the defendant's table.

As was my habit, I attempted to get a furtive read of the jurors' faces as they filed out of the box and through the door to the deliberation room, hoping to get a sense of what they were thinking. Granted, for all my bluster during closing, this wasn't exactly the crime of the century, and my client would probably never face real prison time if found guilty. But this case bothered me more than most. I'd represented all kinds of clients back in New Hampshire—some innocent, many guilty—but none of them were being railroaded like Shannon Maroney.

One of the jurors stopped just before exiting and turned to look straight at me. He was pulling at his right earlobe. I wondered, did he also wear hearing aids? Or was he judging me, wondering why someone my age would have a hearing problem? It was only a matter of time before the good people of Bar Harbor learned the truth. Spencer Dunn got beat up by the son of one of his clients—an innocent man now sitting in a cell in Concord, New Hampshire, doing eight to fifteen. In retrospect, my ability to hear properly was a small price to pay for such bad lawyering. Would that get out too? Bar Harbor's newest transplant was a washed-up attorney on the run from his failures, his demons.

"What now?"

"Huh? Oh. We wait."

Shannon Maroney put her hand on my right forearm, pulling me out of my thought spiral. "Do you think they will really do it? Will they, could they, find me guilty?"

"They shouldn't. I meant what I said up there. This is one of the most ridiculous cases I've ever defended. Let's grab a coffee. The clerk will call me when the verdict is ready."

Forty-five minutes later, we were back in the courtroom watching the jurors enter and take their seats. This time, none of them looked at me or my client. That could be a bad sign. Then again, a short deliberation was usually good news for the defendant.

"Ladies and gentlemen of the jury, I understand you have reached a verdict."

"Yes, Your Honor," the forewoman replied, standing.

"And your decision is unanimous?"

"Yes, Your Honor."

Unanimous. My gut fluttered at the word. No matter how large or small the case, the impending verdict always evoked a nervous reaction. It's an experience shared by most trial attorneys. But I've often felt that the suspense hits me harder than most. Maybe I just take these things too personally.

"Excellent. Please hand the verdict to the clerk."

The clerk took the sheet and gave it to the judge, who scanned it quickly and snapped it back to the clerk without any hint of what it contained. I made a mental note never to play poker with Judge Dickenson.

"Please read the verdict, madam clerk."

"In the case of the State of Maine versus Shannon Jean Maroney, the court finds the defendant not guilty of the crime of Criminal Restraint by Parent, as defined by section three-zero-three of the Maine Family Code."

"Thank you, clerk, and thank you for your service, members of the jury. Please remain seated. This matter is not yet closed."

Not yet closed?

"I wish to offer my remarks on this matter, which we have all been a party to these last few days."

Judge Dickenson's tone was serious. This was the first case I'd argued before the man—hell, the first case I had in the whole state of Maine. But I could tell a lecture was coming.

"Ms. Greathouse, Mr. Carter, far be it for me to suggest frivolousness on the part of the Hancock County prosecutor's office. I like to believe the best of our public servants."

"I'm sorry, Your Honor?" The man at the prosecution table shot to his feet.

"Sit down, Mr. Carter. I'm not looking for a rebuttal. Now, since we have what I believe was the correct verdict in this matter... It was very obvious that Mr. Maroney—are you in the gallery, sir? Yes, you, Mr. Maroney. I'm talking about you. Mr. Maroney, as an aggrieved ex-husband, clearly embellished the circumstances of his children's supposed disappearance at the hands of his former wife. He made remarkably little effort to find them. One wonders if he was even trying to find his kids at all. I agree with defense counsel. This complaint smacks of retribution and a misuse of the law. I am also inclined to admonish the prosecution for bringing us to this point."

"Thank you, Your Honor," I said.

"Sit down, Mr. Dunn. As I was saying, Ms. Greathouse and Mr. Carter, I would be remiss if I did not take this opportunity to reacquaint you with our mediation process. This matter could have been adjudicated with much less fanfare and, I would add, less jeopardy to a mother who has demonstrated a willingness and desire to do the right thing for both her children and the law."

Get your copy of *Small Town Trial*
Available January 23, 2025
(Available for pre-order now)
www.peterkirklandauthor.com

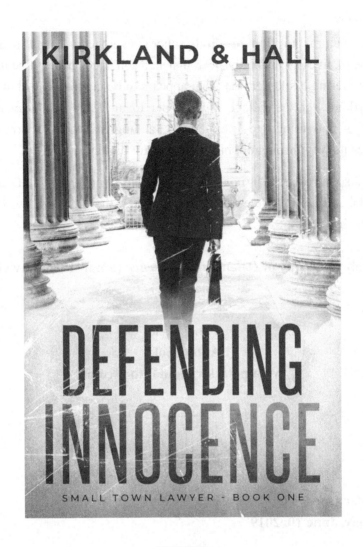

KIRKLAND & HALL

DEFENDING INNOCENCE

SMALL TOWN LAWYER · BOOK ONE

BLURB

An innocent client harbors dark secrets…

Defense attorney Leland Monroe lost it all: his big-city job, his reputation and, worst of all, his loving wife. Now he's back in his hometown to hit restart and repair the relationship with his troubled son. But the past is always present in a small town.

Leland returns to find his high school sweetheart hasn't had the easiest of lives—especially now that her son faces a death sentence for murdering his father. Yet what appears to be an open and shut case is anything but. As Leland digs deeper to uncover a truth even his client is determined to keep buried, a tangled web of corruption weaves its way throughout his once tranquil hometown.

Leland soon realizes it's not just his innocent young client's life that's at stake—powerful forces surface to threaten the precious few loved ones he has left.

Grab your copy of *Defending Innocence* (Small Town Lawyer Book One)
eBook
Paperback
Audiobook
www.peterkirklandauthor.com

———

EXCERPT

Chapter One:
Monday, June 10, 2019

The Ocean View Diner, where I was waiting for my fried shrimp basket, was a dump with a view of nothing but the courthouse parking lot. It was already shabby when I was in high school, living on fries and coffee while I brainstormed the college application essays that were my ticket out. Much to the surprise of folks in my hometown, I'd made it to law school and beyond. I owned more than a dozen suits. I had tan for summers in the office, navy for opening statements to the jury, charcoal for talking to the media on the Charleston court-house steps. My kid had admired me at an age when it was almost unnatural to think your dad was anything but a loser. I was a law-and-order guy trying to make the world safer. I'd thought I might run for office.

I nodded to the bailiff who walked through the door giving him a cordial "howdy", but he looked right through me, as he walked past. We'd certainly seen enough of each other in the courthouse, and I tried not to take offense at the slight but there's only so much a man can put up with when it comes to small town judgment.

They say pride goeth before a fall.

I'd seen enough, in my past life representing the great state of South Carolina, to know a man could have it a lot worse. The amount of depravity and human misery that had flowed across my desk made me know I ought to be grateful for what I still had left. My son, in other words, and my license to practice. I'd nearly lost both. The accident that took my wife had nearly killed him too, and even if he still hadn't entirely recovered from it, he'd come farther than anyone expected at the time, but Noah was incredibly angry all the time. Mostly at me but I tried not to let it get to me.

Like water off a duck's back, the little things ought not to have bothered me at all. It shouldn't have mattered that the locals at the next table had stopped talking when I walked in, apparently suspicious of anyone who wasn't a regular. Which I wasn't yet, since it'd been barely six months since I dragged my sorry ass back from the big city. Getting to be a regular took years.

A better man would not have been annoyed by the smell of rancid grease or the creak of ancient ceiling fans. It was even hotter in here than in the June glare outside, and a good man would've sympathized with my waitress, who was stuck here all day and probably never even got to sit down.

But I was not that man. I did say "Thank you kindly" when she dropped my order on the table and sloshed another dose of coffee in my cup, but I was irrationally annoyed that no one had ever fixed the menu sign on the wall between the cash register and the kitchen. The word "cheeseburger" was still missing its first R. When my friends and I were sixteen-year-old jackasses, we thought it was hilarious to order a "cheese booger." Now it was just pathetic that I was back. Especially since the reason I wasn't in the new '50s-style diner on the next corner—the popular lunch place for judges, local politicians, and successful attorneys—was that I couldn't afford it. Here, in exchange for tolerating the broken AC and worn-out furniture, I got decent shrimp at prices that were fifteen or twenty years behind the times.

The folks at the next table had gotten back to jawing, though at a lower volume on account of my being unfamiliar, I supposed. Between crunches of my dinner, I caught the gist: a body had washed ashore a little ways down the coast, where tourists rented beach houses. Maybe I shouldn't have eavesdropped. But although I wasn't a prosecutor anymore, I was probably never going to lose the habit of keeping a close eye on every local crime.

"Bunch of them Yankees was playing volleyball on the beach," the man said. "You know, girls in their bikinis, one of them thousand-dollar gas grills fired up on the deck." His voice held a mix of humor and scorn. "They were having themselves just a perfect vacation. And then this *corpse* washes up! This, I swear to you, decomposing *corpse* crashes the party!"

The table erupted with guffaws.

"So what'd they do?" a man said. "Hop in the Subarus and hightail it back to New York or wherever?"

"No, the thing is—and I heard this from my cousin, you know, the one working for the sheriff? The thing is, they thought a gator got him! Thought they had a gator in the water! And I'll be damned if they weren't pissing themselves like little girls, trying to get everybody back out of the water. Couple of them was so scared they started puking!"

They all lost it. One of them was so entertained he slammed a hand on the table, rattling the silverware. As the laughter started fading, one of them wondered aloud who the dead man might be.

"Aw, don't matter none," the storyteller said. "We ain't missing nobody."

I felt a sourness in my gut. I couldn't go a day here without being reminded why I'd left. In Basking Rock, compassion for your fellow man was strictly circumscribed. Tourists got none. The wrong kind of people, whatever that meant, got none. Your family and lifelong friends could do no wrong, and everybody else could go straight to hell.

I signaled the waitress and asked for a doggie bag. Might as well finish eating at home, away from present company. She scowled, probably thinking I was switching to takeout to avoid leaving a tip. I scrounged through my wallet, sure I'd had a few ones in there and grudgingly set down a five knowing I was leaving more than necessary. Making any kind of enemy was not my style. You never knew who might help you out one day, if you'd taken care not to get on their bad side. More to the point, I knew from friends who worked in health code enforcement that there were few things stupider than making enemies of the folks who make your food.

———

I'd parked my Chevy outside. It used to be the beater, until the nice car was totaled in the accident. When I fired it up, the engine light came on again. I kept right on ignoring it. I'd yet to find a local mechanic I could trust. The one I knew of had been a bully back in high school, and from what I'd heard, age had only refined his techniques. If he thought you'd gotten too big for your britches—which I certainly had, what with my law degree and my former big-city career—he took his rage out on your wallet.

The Chevy heroically made it home once again. I parked beside the clump of fan palms that were starting to block the driveway. I needed to get them pruned, and to fix the wobbly porch railing that would've been a lawsuit waiting to happen if we ever had visitors. I needed a haircut. My geriatric Yorkie, Squatter, who limped to the door to greet me, needed a trip to the vet. The to-do list never stopped growing, and checking anything off it required money I no longer had.

I tossed the mail on the table and scratched the dog on the head. He'd come with the house—the landlord said he'd been abandoned by the previous tenants, and I couldn't bring myself to dump him at the pound. As he wagged his tail, I called out to my son. "Noah?"

All I could hear was the breeze outside and Squatter's nails scrabbling on the tile. I was no scientist—my major, long ago when I thought I was smart, was US history—but I knew physics did not allow a house to be that quiet if it contained a teenage boy. It looked like I'd be eating another dinner alone. I'd texted Noah when I got to the diner, to see if he wanted anything, but he hadn't answered. I never knew where he was lately, unless he was at a doctor's appointment I'd driven him to myself.

After feeding Squatter I pulled up a chair, took a bite of now-cold shrimp, and flipped through the mail. The monthly health insurance bill—nearly thirteen hundred bucks just for the two of us—went into the small pile of things I couldn't get out of paying. Noah's physical therapy bills did too; as long as he still needed PT, I couldn't risk getting blacklisted there.

And he was going to need it for a good while yet, to have a shot at something like the life he'd been hoping for. We were both still hanging on to the thread of hope that he could get back into the shape that had earned him a baseball scholarship to USC in Columbia. The accident had cost him that, but he was determined to try again.

Or so he'd said at first. Lately he'd gotten depressed with how long it was taking, and how much fun he saw his high-school buddies having on Instagram. They'd gone to college and moved on with their lives. He'd started making new friends here, but to my dismay, they were not what you'd call college bound. College didn't seem to have occurred to them. One worked in a fast-food joint, and another didn't seem to work much at all.

I heard gravel crunching in the driveway. Even without the odd rhythm his limp gave him, I knew it had to be Noah; our little bungalow was an okay place to eat and sleep but too small to be much of a gathering place. I stuffed the bills into my battered briefcase. He didn't need to know we were struggling.

Squatter raced to the door to celebrate Noah's return and accompanied him back to the kitchen in a state of high canine excitement. Noah looked a little glum, or bored, as usual. Without bothering to say hi, he poured himself some tea from the fridge, sat down in the chair next to mine, and took one of my shrimp.

"I would've brought you some," I said. "I texted you from the diner."

He shrugged. "I didn't see it in time," he said, feeding the crispy tail to Squatter.

"That's a shame," I said. "What were you so busy doing?"

He glared at me. That look was a one-two punch every time. He had his mother's eyes, so it felt like the hostility was coming from both of them.

I knew I should back off, but I was never good at drawing the line in the right place. "Hanging out with Jackson again?"

He took another shrimp, got up, and went into the living room. At fourteen, Noah had perfected the art of sullen teenager. Now at nineteen, he'd turned it into a lost art as he immersed himself in the depression and apathy that comes with having your life turned completely upside down.

Grab your copy of *Defending Innocence* (Small Town Lawyer
Book One)
eBook
Paperback
Audiobook
www.peterkirklandauthor.com

Made in United States
Orlando, FL
29 October 2024

53229476R00186